The Fallen Angels
Book Club

The Fallen Angels Book Club

A HOLLIS MORGAN MYSTERY

R. FRANKLIN JAMES

CAMEL PRESS

Seattle, WA

Camel Press
PO Box 70515
Seattle, WA 98127

For more information go to: www.camelpress.com
www.rfranklinjames.com

Cover design by Sabrina Sun

The Fallen Angels Book Club
Copyright © 2013 by R. Franklin James

ISBN: 978-1-60381-917-6 (Trade Paper)
ISBN: 978-1-60381-918-3 (eBook)

Library of Congress Control Number: 2013933745

Printed in the United States of America

ACKNOWLEDGMENTS

FIRST AND FOREMOST, thanks to my dream critique group: Kathy Asay, Pat Foulk, Norma Lehr, Terri Judd and Cindy Sample.

Special thanks to Linda Townsdin, Michele Drier and Sean Watkins—my loyal readers of earlier rough versions.

Thanks to Kristen Weber, who helped me from the beginning with her heart, skill and know-how.

Huge thanks to Coffeetown/Camel Press publisher and editors Catherine Treadgold and Jennifer McCord, who worked their magic and transformed my manuscript into a published book.

To my agent, Dawn Dowdle, who brought my work to light.

And to my wonderful husband, Leonard James, the kindest man I know.

For Bobbi Franklin and Lillian Shannon,

who make me grateful,

For Sean and Stefan, who make me proud, and

For Leonard, who makes me happy

CHAPTER ONE

THAT NIGHT IT was my turn to arrive early and set up the space for our book club meeting. Our monthly gatherings were held in a small, windowless conference room adjacent to San Lucian Library's main reading room. The Fallen Angels Book Club has only two requirements. Members must be 1) book lovers and 2) white collar ex-felons.

I peeled off my gloves and rubbed my hands together. The March chill was typical for the San Francisco Bay Area and made my fingers feel like icicles. Thank goodness someone had remembered to turn on the heat. The door opened and a gush of wind blew in a cluster of leaves along with Gene Donovan, who tossed his hoodie and a small brown leather "man purse" onto one of the folding chairs.

"Hollis, let me help you with that." His tousled blond hair was more askew than usual. Placing his book on the floor, he came over to where I struggled to roll out the meeting table.

"Appreciate it." I straightened my back and allowed him to carry the bulk of the table's weight. Fortunately, when I was with Gene, we didn't have to speak. I caught a glance of his manicured nails and tucked mine into my palms. I liked Gene.

He wasn't afraid to show his feminine side.

We took special care not to drag the metal chair legs across the glowing veneer of the hardwood floor. Its pristine condition was the handiwork of the night cleaning crew, who waited for us to leave so they could begin their labor.

We had settled into our chairs when Rory Norris strode in, let the door slam and dumped his books on the table. His hazel green eyes did a sweep across the room, as if expecting an ambush. A few more pounds had crept onto his already thickening middle-aged frame.

Rory patted his buzz cut and laid his black leather jacket over the chair. "Hey, people, did you notice if they lock the gates to the parking lot? My Beemer just got detailed and I don't want some neighborhood juvenile mistaking it for a marker board."

"Nice touch, Norris, letting us know you got a new BMW," Richard Kleh said as he pulled off his knitted skullcap, revealing an emerging bald crown. He sucked on his front tooth and nodded toward the door. "Go check for yourself. Hey, Hollis, did you finish the read?"

"Of course. You're the one who never finishes a book."

"Well, I finished this one. It had me going until the end. The characters were realistic and … and—"

"Memorable?" I could tell from his frown he wasn't kidding.

My ability to catch people in lies started when I was about ten years old. My parents were alternately appalled and fascinated with their youngest daughter. As I grew older, I became somewhat of an expert, except when someone close to me lied. Over the years I realized the gift of my internal lie detector was turning into a curse. I caught myself lying just because it was convenient and I was good at it. After prison, I committed to becoming reacquainted with the truth, and now I'm on my way to being a reformed liar. However, the best liars, hands down, were my fellow book club members.

The door opened again and Abby Caldwell entered with

Miller Thornton a step behind her. Both pulled off coats and scarves.

I glanced down at my jeans and smoothed out a few wrinkles on my well-worn Berkeley Cal Bears sweatshirt. I looked up to see Gene gazing at me. He shrugged and flashed a smug smile.

If Gene made me feel self-conscious, Abby made me feel downright inferior. She was clothed like a high-powered executive. Her sky-blue eyes picked up the slightly darker blue in her silk blouse and her shiny, wavy black hair was pulled back in a low ponytail that rested over a black wool suit. Richard and Rory exchanged knowing—and male—looks. Once more I wondered where she worked. The rules of the club required we keep our current circumstances private, so I could only imagine.

Abby was oblivious to her effect on us. She smiled. "Hello, everyone, sounds like we have good comments already. I made a list of questions, but we probably won't need them. Why don't we get started with our meeting?"

Adding insult to injury, Abby was smart and kind. Last year she brought to our attention that the children's section in the library had more empty shelves than full and asked us to donate money for books and child-sized furniture. Then, on her own, she worked with the librarians to buy two research computers. She never told us about that purchase. I happened to see the acknowledgment card posted on the notice board in the entry.

"Madame President, aren't we going to wait for Rena?" Miller said in a mocking voice, taking his book out of his briefcase.

We didn't have officers, but with a little prodding, Abby had assumed the unofficial leadership role with ease. At first she resisted, especially after Rory suggested we call her "warden"—a joke no one thought funny. Still, she took her role seriously and without her sense of order, we'd never have gotten past our propensity to talk all at the same time. She was such a good leader we never needed to appoint another.

She took a quick look at her slim black Movado watch. While I don't wear a lot of jewelry, just a few choice pieces, I had a background in insurance appraisals. The diamonds encrusted around its face were real.

"Let's give her another couple of minutes. She has to come across the bridge."

Gene sighed. "It's not like Rena walks. She takes rapid transit." He picked at his eyebrows, a habit when he got agitated.

"I'm here. I'm here." Rena Gabriel rushed through the door. Tall, pretty and African American, she had glowing, honey-colored skin and brought an energy with her that never ceased to amaze me. It was as if we all slept until she turned on the light.

We straightened in our chairs.

She quickly removed her parka and hood. Her long, tightly curled black hair sprang free. "I apologize. My train was late. I don't see any open books so I can't be too tardy."

She beamed at me and Gene then turned her warm smile on the rest of the group.

I slowly shook my head. "Rena, I know this is only your second club meeting, but if you're late, you have to bring refreshments."

Her large brown eyes opened wider. "Really? I'm sorry. I didn't know. Each time I come here I learn more rules. Do I go back out and return with some goodies?"

"Hollis, give her a break." Richard sucked on a tooth. "Rena, there's no such rule. Unfortunately, our rules aren't written down, but you already know the important ones. Of course, if you feel you have to feed us, we won't protest."

I gave her a reassuring nod and tried to look contrite. She appeared relieved.

Miller lifted a pair of glasses to his eyes. He'd started to gray at the temples—a striking contrast with his youthful face. "Okay. We're all here. Let's get started. I, for one, liked *World at Midnight*. At first I had a hard time getting into it, but about thirty pages in, I couldn't put it down."

"Come on. It wasn't that good," I said.

"All right then." Gene nudged his elbow into my arm. "Hollis, why don't you tell us what you thought of the book?"

I paused for a moment. "Unlike Miller and Richard, I could put it down. Rosemarie had no redeeming qualities. She was one dimensional. No one can be evil all the time."

Abby broke in. "For me, she was believable. I know people just like her—without a conscience." Her voice rose half an octave. "Someone should lock her up and throw away the key."

There was a thick silence. I couldn't help giving the normally pacifist Abby a questioning look.

"Nobody here, of course," she added.

Miller and Richard gave a short laugh.

Rena raised her hand. "I agree with Hollis. The author could have shown us why Rosemarie was so angry. I liked the book because of the storyline, not so much the characters."

Gene snorted. "First, you don't have to raise your hand when you want to speak. Second, what are you saying, not so much the characters? A book *is* its characters. Just because you don't like them doesn't mean they weren't well developed. I think the book fell short. It was good but not great. Too much reliance on coincidences. What's the likelihood that a group of misfits would meet and form a society? It's not real."

"What about us?" I said. I couldn't believe he didn't see the connection. "We came together in a book club."

Gene nodded. "Good point. Some people would say we're misfits."

I could tell from the downward cast eyes of the others that he'd struck home.

Misfits.

My deepest fear was that I wouldn't be given another chance to fit in. It didn't matter to society that my crime was a white collar offense. It didn't matter that I was innocent. What mattered to me was having a chance to prove I wasn't a misfit.

With any luck at all, I would soon obtain my pardon and restart my life the way I'd always planned.

Rena wasn't to be deterred. "That's what touched me. It's the reason I thought it would be a good thing to join you guys. I like the idea of people like us coming together and building trust again. It's just that these characters wouldn't be the ones I would have chosen."

Rory started clicking his ballpoint pen. More than a little irritated by this habit, I looked at the ceiling and started counting down from ten. He didn't disappoint me; I didn't make it to six.

"Rena, how long did you spend inside?" Clickety-click.

Rena looked as if she was about to gag.

Abby jumped in, "Rory, that's none of your business. You know it's against the rules to ask about our prison terms and personal lives."

He gave his pen a couple of quick clicks and shrugged. "You're right. One of those rules. Forgive me, Rena."

Clickety-click.

Rena shifted uncomfortably in her seat. "Why did you ask about how long I was in prison?"

"Because you still seem hopeful." Rory took a deep breath. "People like us come with a label; we've been branded as non-redeemable. The longer you're inside, the more likely you are to forget who you are. Why do you think we're all here? Not to assure others we're just like anyone else, but to assure ourselves."

Miller was folding his usual tiny origami pelicans with thin colored sheets of paper. Ordinarily, I was transfixed by his artistry. Not tonight. He looked up. "I would have joined this group even if I hadn't been to prison. Books have always been a refuge for me. Admittedly, I feel accepted here."

I added, "I never thought about it much, but I guess I'm a Fallen Angel for the same reason as Miller. I just hate being eligible."

My internment in prison was the lowest point of my life. There I wasn't Hollis Morgan. I was a number. Five years later a smell, a sound, a name could take me back there.

My fellow members were silent, probably reliving moments from their own prison stays.

Rory cleared his throat. "Sorry. I didn't mean to get us off track. Anyway, Georg Oster wrote this book because he needed money. It was largely plagiarized from a little known nineteen-thirties playwright."

"How in the hell do you know all that?" I said.

The emotion that flashed across his face was gone before I could be sure I saw it.

"Ms. Morgan, you'd be surprised what all I know." He ran his hand over his hair. "Look, *The New Yorker* had a review a couple of months ago that pointed to this play from nineteen thirty. Sadly, for the author, the reviewer's mother was a cousin to the playwright. She recognized the story line."

Miller sat up. "Why didn't you tell us this when I brought the book list in for our selection?"

Rory shrugged. "I didn't know it until I Googled the book. Remember, I'm a research-aholic." He stopped clicking his pen. "Besides, since you can get books for free, who cares? It beats that wandering ode to egotism we read last month."

Miller mumbled something under his breath that sounded like "sandbag."

Richard sucked on his tooth and took out a page of notes. "Well, like I said, I found the book to be pretty good. Oster had a good grasp of the time and setting. It could have had a better ending, though."

"All right now," Abby said. "It's my turn. If I could talk without being interrupted." She lifted her book in the air. "I did some research, too. Oster came from an upper-class family in an upper-class neighborhood. His back cover said he wrote this novel as a thinly disguised memoir of his own coming of age."

Abby always wanted our full attention if she had the floor.

"I agree," Gene said. "I don't know anyone who'd consider *World at Midnight* to be a lightweight reading escape. It got me thinking."

Rory snorted. "Give me a break. He wrote it for the money. His last two books flopped. He had to get something out in the market."

"Not everyone has your money motive." Richard looked at Gene and they both rolled their eyes.

"What the hell does that mean?" Rory's cheeks turned deep pink.

Gene wasn't intimidated. He loved drama. "Well, maybe it means that unless we're reading a self-help book, your comments always center on getting, keeping or losing money."

I waved my hand. "Time out, guys. For Pete's sake, let's focus on the book. I think we all agree that the female protagonist is caught in a time warp of values. When the villain is finally killed, we don't feel a thing for him and not a lot of sympathy for her, either. The book was good. Not great, but good. So, I agree with Gene."

Miller, usually the peacemaker, cleared his throat. "Same here. I think this was a well-written book."

I snuck a peek at Rory, whose face and neck were turning rage red. A muscle spasm flickered in his jaw.

"Do us a favor," Richard said. "Just this one time admit you might be wrong. It would be so refreshing."

"Go to hell." Rory grabbed his jacket and snatched up his book. His chair screeched as he pushed it backward. When the door slammed behind him, the thin glass in the windows shivered.

I winced at the scar-like gash left behind in the once-flawless hardwood floor.

CHAPTER TWO

THE MORNING AFTER our meeting I was sitting in my kitchen. Daylight slicing through the wide window blinds made bars of shadows on the floor. It reminded me of the good old days in my cell. At times like these, in surroundings that seemed outwardly ordinary and serene, I would find myself musing over how I had come to this point in my life. And wonder what I would do to Bill when I saw him again.

I was relatively bright, young—well, thirty-two—and free as a bird. When I stopped to think about it, these qualities didn't sound like a big deal, but I couldn't say the same for myself five years ago. Back then I was coming off parole after serving half of a three-year sentence for insurance fraud. I was innocent, but my guilty ex-husband cut a deal with the prosecutor and left me behind for shark bait.

I poured myself another cup of tea. I found myself going through this thinking ritual every morning. I couldn't seem to let go.

It had taken me a while to make peace with the fact that Bill set me up. He knew I'd stopped loving him and it was only a matter of time before I left. For that, Bill hated me as much as he loved me—or maybe he hated himself *because* he loved me.

As I put my mug in the sink, my reflection in the stainless steel refrigerator caught my eye. Running my fingers through my auburn hair, I peered closer. The beginning of bags under my big brown eyes were a product of my sleepless study nights. I stretched the skin taut. It was time to find a better stainless steel cleaner.

The numerals on the wall clock rolled over. I still had time before I had to leave for my appointment. I reached for the thick hardback novel perched precariously on top of three other books and tried to relax. Unfortunately, this time reading didn't provide its usual escape. My brain kept going to the meeting with my attorney, Clay Boone. A meeting that would mark another step toward getting my life back.

One thing was in my favor. Certain ex-felons, like me, may petition the court for a Certificate of Rehabilitation and Pardon, as long as they could show they had stayed out of trouble for at least five years after parole. I qualified. Boone said it was never a no-brainer, but I was a good candidate. If granted, the certificate would clear my record of conviction, allow me to complete law school and take the bar exam to become a lawyer. I had to stop saying "if." There was nothing I wouldn't do to get that pardon. Nothing.

I put the cup to my lips and took a deep drink. The doorbell rang.

I never had visitors.

Peering through the peephole, I didn't recognize the pair of suits standing on my porch.

I glanced around, taking deep breaths to calm my nerves. Luckily, the living room was always the most together. Typically, things went downhill as one moved through my condo. Grabbing my purse, I put it behind the sofa. The doorbell rang again. I pulled up my sweats. At five-feet-three inches tall, I find it hard to buy pants that don't drag on the floor. I opened the door.

"Ms. Morgan? Detectives Faber and Lincoln with the San Lucian Police Department. May we come in?"

My hand shook. I was afraid to let go of the doorknob. It required an enormous effort to put on my best blank face, smile my sweetest smile and step aside to let them in. "Sure. What's this about?"

"Thank you. We shouldn't be long," the tall one, Faber, responded. He hadn't answered my question. Faber looked around the room without seeming to look around. I used the opportunity to observe him. His smooth, olive-toned skin belied his almond-shaped eyes and wavy brown hair. He reminded me of a Heinz 57 pooch. Not that he was a dog, but rather an interesting combination of ethnicities. Not a bad-looking guy.

I pointed to the overstuffed chairs next to the fireplace and sat down on the sofa arm.

"We understand you know a Rory Norris," Faber said.

I nodded.

"Last night Mr. Norris was murdered."

"Murdered?" I couldn't catch my breath. I slid down onto a sofa cushion. "What happened?"

Lincoln ignored my question. "We know you are in a book club together. One of the other members had their name and number in Norris' car. He gave us the club's contact list." He kept rubbing his collar. He was only a few inches taller than me with carrot-red hair and freckles. He looked about twelve. "We understand you were good friends with the deceased."

"Good friends? I wouldn't say we were good friends. I know next to nothing about him." I shifted in my seat, hoping they wouldn't hear the half-lie. "Sometimes we went out after a meeting for coffee to keep talking about a book. However, I wouldn't say we were good friends."

"Were you going to New Zealand with him?"

"New Zealand? No way. I don't know what you're talking about. I didn't even know he was going." I refrained from adding that the thought of going anywhere with Rory made me nauseous. I'd learned never to volunteer any information.

Lincoln kept his eyes on me. "We found a travel confirmation on him. Did he say anything about a trip?"

"Not to me."

"When was the last time you saw him?" Faber asked.

"At our meeting last night." A bead of sweat slipped down my back. My warning radar engaged.

"How did he seem to you?"

I took another deep breath and mentally debated the idea of telling the complete truth. There was no need to lie. "Rory was upset. He could be somewhat rigid. We read *World at Midnight*. Have you read it?" They both shook their heads. "Well, it's a deep book. He had his own views on the author's theme, and some of us disagreed with him."

"Some?" It was Faber again.

"Well, all of us, actually. None of us agreed with him."

This time Lincoln spoke. "What happens when you don't agree at a book club meeting?"

"Well, Detective, we kill the person."

Shut up. Nerves.

They both glared at me.

I wanted to kick myself. "Sorry." I hoped I looked remorseful. "This is still unbelievable to me. Rory was a good guy. He's been—I mean he was with the group for over a year. We met once a month and Rory rarely missed a meeting. He seemed fine last night. He even told a little joke."

"What time did he leave?"

I knew they must be checking our stories. "We all started to leave around nine o'clock. Rory left before that. Now, can you answer a question for me? What happened?"

Faber flipped through several sheets of paper in a small pad. I was paranoid enough to think he was buying time— trying to make me crazy with waiting. "A passerby discovered Mr. Norris' body in a parking lot about five miles from your meeting location. Where did you go after the meeting?"

"I came home." My mind flashed back to the last time the police asked me for an alibi. Now, I sat on my hands to hide the shaking. My resolve to turn over a new leaf by never lying was being fully tested.

"That it?" Faber persisted. "Were you alone?"

"Yes and yes."

He got up and peered through the glass doors of the étagère I inherited from my grandmother, which held her ceramic frog collection. It was my least favorite possession—the solid walnut piece weighed a ton and didn't fit the rest of my décor— but I didn't have the heart to give it away. My relationship with Gram made up for the lack of one I had with the rest of the family.

"It took us a while to ID him," Faber said. "He was beaten and then run over several times."

I stared at the back of his head. A knot of dread grew larger and larger in my stomach as my words tumbled out. "Beaten? With a baseball bat?"

"Yes."

"And his clothing … were all the labels cut out?"

Detective Lincoln's look snared me with laser accuracy. "What do you know about how Norris was murdered?"

I finally got air into my lungs. "I don't believe it." I stood and walked over to the windows then back toward the sofa.

"Ms. Morgan," Faber said, "I'm sorry, but we're going to need some better answers from you. So far there don't appear to be any witnesses, but you seem to know quite a bit. We're checking with all the book club members, and we didn't tell anyone details."

I waved my hand at them. "No, no. It's the similarity. It's—it's about the crime scene. It's the way he died."

"I don't understand." Lincoln frowned. "Enlighten me."

I could hardly get the words out. My voice sounded like a

whisper to my own ears. "The scene, it's the same as in the book we reviewed last night."

Faber sat up. "What do you mean?"

I sank into the sofa cushions. This wasn't going to be easy. "Well, we read *World at Midnight,* like I said. There's this murder. The vic is beaten with a baseball bat and then run over by the bad guy. He's a tailor. Anyway, he's run over back and forth. The murderer takes the ID and cuts the labels out of the vic's clothes to stall identification. It gives him time to cover his tracks and get away."

Faber nodded. "I see." He gave me an amused glance. "I notice your use of the term 'vic.' Is that something you read about, too?"

"What? Oh, yeah. I guess I get carried away," I murmured.

"Do you have a copy of this book we can borrow?" Lincoln asked.

I nodded and reached under the coffee table. The book wasn't there. "I must have left it in the office with my other lunchtime reading."

Faber shrugged. "That's not a problem. We'll get a copy. Ms. Morgan, you didn't answer our earlier question. What happened when Rory disagreed with the group about the book?"

Warning bells went off in my head. I licked my lips. I was uncomfortable with his tone. "There was a lot of loud talk. He got defensive and we all said things that weren't too cool."

My mind drifted. I couldn't believe it. Rory. He wasn't my favorite or anything, but he had a great way of deciphering a book's characters and often suggested alternative plots. Regrettably, that talent wasn't enough to offset his compulsive behavior and annoying tendency to let his cynicism get out of control. He was a man of contradictions. He could be aloof as well as charming or witty or depressing as hell.

We were different people, with different reasons for joining the same book club. We were avid readers who happened to be ex-felons. Three years and one recent addition later, we were going strong, except that we now appeared to be minus one member.

Lincoln coughed, breaking my reverie.

"I'm sorry. Could you repeat that? I was trying to remember."

"We're talkin' about a book, right? What could be so bad?" Detective Lincoln clearly didn't get it. He picked up our next month's selection, which rested on top of my coffee table, and weighed it in his hand as if its mass could lead to an answer.

"You're so right," I replied. "It was stupid to argue. We get carried away sometimes. We don't always agree with each other, but this time ..." I remembered Rory's red face and his finger pointing at each of us around the room.

"This time what?" Faber asked.

"Nothing. I was trying to think if there was anything else, but there isn't. I'm sorry. I just can't believe he's gone." I pasted on a spacey smile. "Can I offer you some tea?" I prayed they would say no.

"No, thank you." Lincoln reached into his wallet and handed me a couple of business cards. "Call us if you remember something about Mr. Norris."

I put the cards in my pocket. "Not a problem."

As soon as the detectives left, I dialed Abby's cellphone number. She'd be grateful to get a heads up or maybe we could share reactions to the police visits. No answer. I left a message for her to contact me.

As I picked up my book again, I remembered that the murderer in *World at Midnight* was a policeman.

I WAITED IN Clay Boone's law office lobby, trying to ignore the slight headache targeting my temples as I flipped mindlessly through the pages of a magazine. Rory's death was still slowly sinking in. My eyes fell on an ad for Hastings Law School, my old alma mater, and I felt a familiar pang. My goal to serve in the courts had been cut short by my felony conviction. So, as a distant second choice, I got my paralegal certification. Free from background checks and fingerprint databases, I was hired by a well-respected Oakland law firm, Dodson, Dodson & Doyle LLP, known by its employees as Triple D. At first I thought it strange that a firm would continue to have the names of dead partners on its masthead, but later I thought it made perfect sense. No one knew who really ran the place.

Rory had been murdered the same way as in our book club selection.

I got up and checked in for a second time with the receptionist, who was multitasking—acknowledging me with a nod while murmuring into the phone and typing energetically. Boone's building was only a few blocks from the one where I worked. Not as upscale as Triple D, his office was located in one of the downtown Victorians in a quiet setting without any real view. After a few moments, Clay came out, extending one beefy hand as he directed me down the hall to his office.

"Hollis, sorry to keep you waiting. Come on in. How are things going?" He pointed to one of two black leather chairs facing his desk.

"Things are going well. I've started on my pardon statement. I've identified all my references and I should be able to have everything to you by the end of May."

Boone epitomized self-assurance. Since I've known him, he's made me feel that if anything could be done, he not only could, but would, do it. I know a lot of attorneys. When I went looking for one to help me file and obtain a Certificate of Rehabilitation, his name was first on my list. It's too bad he didn't work at Triple D. Legal fees were costing me megabucks, but as far as I was concerned, my privacy was priceless. Research told me Boone had successfully represented many ex-felons. He knew what it took to get the desired court decision. I trusted him. Looking at him now, I could see something was wrong.

He pursed his thin lips and shook his head. "You're going to have to move a little faster. Judge Pine announced his retirement at the end of the summer. He's known to be a strong supporter of the rehabilitation program. However, he's being replaced by Judge Mathis who is … well, let's just say he's not soft on crime."

Great.

My heart beat a little faster. "When do I have to have it all done?"

"I need your paperwork by the first week in May."

"You've got to be kidding. That's only six weeks!"

"I know it's a little tight, but it's important we get the right judge."

"Believe me. No one knows that better than I do."

He held up his hand. "You can do this. How many references are you missing?"

"Well, I don't have any yet. I know who I have to ask, but I wanted to get the notice that I qualified first."

The most critical reference would come from my employer. After paralegal school, I didn't lie on my employment application about my conviction. My current boss, Avery Mitchell, knew my circumstances. He interviewed me through a temp agency. Unlike the several other law firms I interviewed with, he gave me the break I needed.

Clay sat up. "Well, now you've got the notice. It's time to get moving. We can't let this window close. If you wait, we have to assume it'll take one to two months for your petition to make its way through the system again. We don't want to be given a judge like Mathis midstream. You need to finish your statement as soon as possible. Judge Pine likes to have plenty of time to read a petitioner's request."

"I've got it outlined." I put the events of the last couple of days out of my mind and energized my voice to sound upbeat. "I just need to write it. I can be finished with a draft by the end of next week, along with securing my first reference."

"Good, good. Let me see the rough draft as soon as you finish." He glanced over at the clock. "Is there anything else?"

It briefly crossed my mind to mention Rory's murder. Instead, I lied and shook my head.

CHAPTER THREE

THE NEXT MORNING was Saturday and I was on a mission. I had a statement to write. Clearing the kitchen table, I opened my laptop and listed the points I needed to cover. I could only imagine what Boone would say about my application if he knew I might be on speaking terms with a murderer. I certainly had been friendly enough with the victim. I shoved all doubts to the back of my mind and started typing. Three hours and six pages later, my eyes started to glaze over.

Needing a break, I decided to pay a visit to my favorite bookstore, Do Over, on the other side of town. The day was clear but bone-chilling cold. I pulled my coat closer. Once again I thanked the gods for pointing me to San Lucian. Located next to the cities of San Leandro and San Lorenzo, San Lucian was a much-admired San Francisco East Bay Area community. Warm and welcoming, it was more of an oversized neighborhood than a city.

A yoga class was finishing up. Theo, the owner, nodded in recognition when I came in. He wouldn't engage me in conversation unless I gave him a high sign and this time I didn't.

Taking out my statement draft, I poured myself a cup of the orange cinnamon tea offered at the complimentary station and sat in one of the overstuffed chairs in the reading corner. I took my time sipping tea and looking at the few customers who appeared to be like me—trying to find a temporary refuge from whatever.

Murdered like the victim in our book club selection.

Why would a Fallen Angel kill Rory?

Any way I looked at it, Rory must have said or done something that had seriously aggravated a member, but who? No one ever took him seriously.

I glanced up at the door when the bell jingled and then turned my head away in disbelief as the tall lean frame of Detective John Faber appeared. Dressed in faded jeans and a maroon V-neck pullover, he wore an Oakland A's cap and a speculative look. Our eyes locked. Seemingly as surprised as I, he walked over.

"Good morning," he said. "This is my first time here. I didn't realize it would be on your list of bookstores." As if sensing my discomfort he stood a couple of feet away.

I mentally collected myself and came up with a half-smile. "It's one of my favorite getaways. I didn't know you were a book lover."

"Actually, I read quite a lot." Faber paused. "Well, considering the circumstances, I think it's best I leave and return another time."

I frowned. "Yes, I guess so. It was nice seeing you, Detective, outside of the 'circumstances,' I mean."

He gave me an appraising look. "Yeah, it was nice seeing you, too, Ms. Morgan."

Then he walked away.

It took some effort to shake off the encounter. Two cups of tea and four new sentences later I was calmer and ready to settle down and write.

CR

BACK AT HOME, the light on my answering machine blinked with two messages. It didn't matter. I didn't want any distractions. I moved to the dining room and glanced blankly at the stack of pages on the table.

"What the hell." I turned, went back to the kitchen, and pushed the message button.

"Hey, Rebecca, it's me." I stiffened and slid down the wall to sit on the floor. "I know you must be blown away with my calling. I had a hard time finding you. You changed your name, but I still had Rita's number. Boy, did I give my ex sister-in-law a shock when she heard my voice on the phone. Look, we need to talk. I know you must hate me, but this is serious. It's important to both of us. Give me a call. I'm at the Holiday Inn in San Francisco. I'm checking out tomorrow. Call me, please."

Anger welled up inside me even as I pushed the button to get the next message. I caught my breath. Anger was replaced by shock.

"Rebecca, Bill called. I gave him your number. I didn't tell him where you live or work. He tried hard to find out. He said it was urgent and he had to speak to you. He threatened to bother Mom next, and well … I had to give him your number. Give me a call if you want to talk. I'm sorry. There was nothing I could do."

I pushed erase.

Rita hadn't spoken to me in five years and just knowing Bill had my phone number made me feel defiled.

William Edwin Lynley was four years my senior. He swept me off my feet with his easy smile and bedroom eyes. He made me laugh. He taught me how to love. Then he taught me how to be stupid. I trusted him without question. We honeymooned in Carmel at the Marriott Hotel and then set up housekeeping in the little community of Montclair in the East Bay Area.

Our first year together was heaven. The second year was purgatory, the third, hell. His insurance practice made enough for me to go to law school without having to take a part-time job, and his periodic traveling gave me the solid blocks of time I needed to study. Bill said he didn't want me to worry about money.

I believed him when he said he just needed me to sign a few contracts he worked on because his fiduciary responsibility as a consultant might give him a conflict of interest. To my credit—I was attending law school after all—I pointed out that my involvement could be seen as a violation of client trust. I ignored all the signs that he was lying to me because more than anything I wanted to believe him. So, to my shame, I accepted his lame explanations and signed. When the California Insurance Commissioner caught up to him, Bill gave him me. He couldn't testify against me as my husband, but with my signatures on contracts, he didn't need to. He and the great lawyer he retained told me that if I pleaded no contest, I wouldn't have to do any time. That was before I had a change of judges. Five years ago, when my sentence came down, all my dreams came crashing around me. I looked past the bailiff to catch Bill's eyes. He shrugged and walked out the courtroom door.

That was the last time I saw Bill.

CHAPTER FOUR

I WENT UPSTAIRS, shoved yesterday's mail to the other side of my bed, and lifted up the comforter to uncover the edge of the frame. On my knees, I reached under, feeling rather than seeing, remembering rather than feeling.

I jerked my hand back with a small cry of pain. A splinter. It figured. I sucked my finger, then with both hands pulled out the small cherry wood chest. It had been months since I felt the need to go through its contents. It contained remnants from a life I'd walked away from years before. Pushing aside mementos and my parole papers, I removed a small brass key and returned the chest to its nesting place.

I looked up at my bed clock to check the time. If I hurried, I could make it to the bank. Otherwise, I'd have to wait until Monday.

With five minutes to closing, I strode past a visibly annoyed security guard and walked over to the cluster of desks on the right. There were at least eight other last-minute visitors winding their way along a red rope to the tellers.

"Excuse me," I said to the young blond who tried to ignore me as she tapped out commands on her computer.

"We're closed. Our system is down."

I sat anyway. "Not a problem. I just want access to my safe-deposit box—not your system."

At that, she looked me in the eye with a less than convincing show of regret and pointed to the clock. "Sorry, the safe-deposit center closes at two thirty on Saturdays—almost a half hour ago."

"Wait, I've been here after two thirty before, and as long as I was in before three, I got access."

"New rules." She shook her head with fake sympathy.

"New rules? Well, unless you want to be even later getting home, I suggest you signal the bank manager to come over here and give me access to my box. Never mind. I'll call him over myself."

She clicked out an extension on the phone. I couldn't help staring at her one-inch fire-red nails with delicate yellow roses painted on the tips. Once again I found myself tucking my own unadorned nails out of sight.

In prison, I mastered the art of ignoring glares. Certainly the twenty-something manager who strode up to the desk was not in my league. I disregarded his ill-concealed irritation.

"I'll only be a moment." I smiled sweetly.

Saying something under his breath about people wanting to go home to their families, he pointed toward the wrought-iron side gate that led to a secured area. I followed him and waited for the automatic door to buzz open and then close behind us as if air-locked. I went straight to the box at the end of the third row, a few inches from the floor. After I had signed the required card, he inserted his key into the lock and I did the same. Finally alone, I gingerly opened the container, grabbed a pile of Polaroids and flipped through them. They had started to fade a little. Next time I'd have to bring my digital camera to take shots of the photos. I skimmed through them one more time.

My smile hadn't changed over the years, but my eyes had.

In a crowd of revelers, the twenty-three-year-old who grinned back at me with her arm loosely thrown around the shoulders of her sister was long gone. The shot was taken BB—Before Bill, when I still had expectations of doing good in the world. Rita insisted on taking a picture with me holding my acceptance letter to Hastings Law School. It was the only picture I had of my sister. Bill destroyed all of our photographs in a futile effort to get rid of anything incriminating. Baby brother, Greg, had taken the photos with Mom's old camera. I didn't have any pictures of him. I could only imagine how he must look now. Blinking back tears, I knew this train of thought would take me to a past that had abandoned me, and I it.

Taking the pictures I came for, I neither thanked nor looked at the manager as he stiffly stood at attention holding the front door open.

I AM A so-so cook, but I make great salads. I find that the right ingredients can make the most stressful day come to a peaceful end with a simple toss of salad greens.

I hummed along to a CD of Diana Krall as I added chopped endive, sliced artichoke hearts and heirloom cherry tomatoes and topped it all with cannelloni beans, a few chunks of blue cheese and leftover pancetta. I pulled a bottle of my favorite pinot noir from the pantry shelf and took everything to the table.

At last.

The first sip of wine brought a satisfied smile to my face. As I reached for the honey-mustard vinaigrette, the doorbell sounded. Figures.

I looked through the peephole and froze.

"Who is it?" I said, hoping to buy myself a couple of seconds.

"Ms. Morgan? It's Detective Faber. I'm with Detective Lincoln. Can we speak to you for a few minutes?" His voice sounded loud and clear, even through the door.

Taking a deep breath, I let them in. "Why have you come back?"

They looked around with curiosity as if they'd never been here before. I guided them once more into the living room. I didn't sit because I didn't want them to. We all stood around the coffee table.

Faber took out that thin black notebook of his and flipped open a page. "Ms. Morgan, do you know a Rebecca Lynley?"

They had me. I knew my voice would have a tremble. "I think you already know the answer to that. Yes, I legally changed my name. Hollis is my middle name and Morgan is my maiden name."

Rebecca Hollis Morgan Lynley was my unlucky name. It was the name that brought shame to me, my family and my friends. It was the name I was known by when I served time in prison. It was the name I acquired when I married that jerk. Rebecca Hollis Morgan Lynley. It was a name I never wanted to hear again, but here it was, turning up like a bad penny. For one insane moment, I wondered what was behind that bad penny saying. I knew how that penny felt.

Lincoln said, "I see. Well, we talked to your former parole officer and he spoke highly of you. Does your employer know of your record?"

Ah, a man after my own way of thinking. Straight to the point of pain. My heart raced. "The ones who need to know do. Why? Is there a reason you're asking?"

Lincoln seemed to come to life. "I wondered if you checked the felon box on your job application." His expression told me that he expected I had lied.

So that was it; he liked pulling wings off butterflies. He wanted me to squirm.

"Detectives, is there a reason why you're here? I admitted I changed my name. I don't know any more about Rory's death now than I did when you were last here."

"Mrs. Lynley—"

"Morgan," I insisted.

Faber gave me a condescending smile. "Okay, Ms. Morgan, we followed up on that book tip you gave us, linking it to the mode of Norris' death. It was right on. Then we took things a little further, did a little research on the other members of the book club. You know what we discovered? A club of ex-felons."

At that I had to sit. They followed suit.

My thoughts raced. "I know there's a temptation to conclude that we're plotting the downfall of the Western world, but all that we have in common—well, not *all*, I guess—is that we love books."

"That so?" Faber's lips were pursed just shy of a smirk. "Yet I would imagine all of you must live in fear of having your prison backgrounds exposed. A blackmailer would think he hit the lotto."

Lincoln leaned over and picked a foil-wrapped chocolate out of the glass candy dish on the table. I tried to remember how long the candy had been there. One of the prison staff had given me a small box as a good luck gift. Could people die from eating candy three years past the "best by" date? He popped it in without noticing the thin whitish coating and grabbed for another.

I stared at the chocolates. "We don't pry into each others' pasts. That's one of our rules. We only get together to share our opinions about books."

Lincoln gave me a hard look. "We visited Mr. Norris' apartment. We found canceled checks and bank statements that raise the possibility he might have been a blackmailer." Lincoln chewed. "Was he blackmailing you?"

"Rory, a blackmailer?" I couldn't stop my voice from trembling. "No. No. I'm not being blackmailed."

"You didn't know Norris was a blackmailer?" Faber asked.

"No," I answered weakly. "I only knew him through the book club."

"Yeah, so you said." Faber flipped back a couple of pages in his notebook. "Mrs. Lynley—excuse me, Ms. Morgan—would you be surprised to know your husband's name was in an address book we found in Mr. Norris' apartment?"

The air fled my lungs as if I'd been punched. On top of that I thought my hearing must be impaired. "I'm sorry. Did you say *Bill's* name was in Rory's address book?"

"That's right. How did they know each other?" Faber asked.

"Bill and Rory knew each other?" The words left my lips but sounded far away.

Faber leaned over to my side of the table. "Do you know where your husband is?"

"*Ex*-husband. I haven't seen him since my trial."

Only a half-lie.

To my relief, Lincoln pushed the candy dish away. "You haven't had any contact with William Lynley since your conviction?"

I chose my words carefully. "We haven't spoken since I was sentenced."

Let's try to maintain some integrity here.

I couldn't tell if they believed me. They asked a few more questions about the club and then left with the promise to get back to me if they thought of anything else. Based on my last law enforcement encounter, I had a feeling their next step would be to obtain a search warrant.

I tossed the salad down the disposal and went out on the deck with my wine. I'd lost my appetite. The opposite of love isn't hatred, it's indifference. I was working on it, not every day, but as often as my sanity allowed. I was glad to feel *almost* nothing.

Nighttime was always the worst for me. Insomnia had become my companion. At night, I'd close my eyes, and the noises and smells from prison would assail me. A few months ago there was a special on TV about women in prison. I couldn't watch it. Even though my cell was behind a door and not bars, I heard my fellow inmates crying and praying. It went on for hours on end. I could neither cry nor pray now.

I had to get a pardon. I'd do whatever it took. Rory's unsolved murder could threaten my future dreams. I had to have another chance.

I had to.

CHAPTER FIVE

SATURDAY EVENING SLID into Sunday. To keep busy, I spent the day cleaning out my garage. Thinking about Bill and Rory would only take me back to how much I had at stake and the one prospect that froze my heart—returning to prison. By the weekend's end, I'd finished a rough draft of my statement but Abby still hadn't returned my call. I wasn't surprised not to hear from the other members. I didn't want my name to crop up on their caller ID, either.

It was difficult, but I was able to avoid even contemplating Bill's request to call him. If it seemed as if my thoughts might venture in that direction, I recalled the bad case of poison ivy I caught during my internment.

I was more than ready for Monday when it came. It might appear ironic to an outsider that I had found a job working in a law firm. After my tour in California's residence hotel at Chowchilla Prison, I was wary of the law enforcement profession, but I had an immense amount of respect for the law.

I passed my key card over the gray panel next to the ceiling-high wooden doors and listened for the sound of the opening click. I loved the firm's front entry. Plush maroon and deep purple Persian area rugs covered wide-planked hickory floors. Three sage green upholstered sofas encircled an oblong glass table covered with an assortment of art catalogs, stock market newsletters and regional magazines. Something for everyone. The cleaning crew rubbed lemon oil on the massive oak bookshelves holding antique Chinese curios and artifacts. The place not only looked rich, it smelled rich.

I headed along the wide hallway for my office, determined to let work keep my thoughts from returning to the vision of a murdered Rory. I stopped. Mark Haddan, a new young associate, came toward me with rolled up sleeves and a loosened tie.

"Thank goodness, Hollis. I'm so glad you came in early. Can you help me with the copy machine? I've got my first deposition at eight thirty and my opening questions are jammed inside this wretched piece of junk."

"Good morning to you, too, Mark. Why did you wait until this morning to prepare your questions?" I shook my head and followed him down the narrow corridor. As we rounded the corner leading to the staff offices, the luxury décor of the front reception area abruptly ended, and we trod on well-worn indoor-outdoor carpet.

"Spare me," Mark said. "If I admit I'm an idiot, will you fix the damn thing?"

"You'll owe me." Even as I said it, I knew I couldn't count on collecting. Attorneys never noticed the administrative staff until they needed something.

Ordinarily, on a Monday morning, the lineup of gray steel copy machines stood in welcome for the onslaught of us Type-A workaholics. During the week, the stacked files, scattered paperwork, discarded half-filled coffee cups, and open law books would incrementally take possession of the room, coming to a crescendo of chaos by week's end. I looked unbelievingly at the room. Mark had already wreaked enough havoc to make it look like Friday. I put my purse down near the door, in the only spot not covered in paper.

I decided to give him a break. Everyone knew the law partners weren't pleased with his progress in the firm, and I didn't want to contribute to his demise. "How did you create such a mess? I'll show you how to fix it, just in case no one is around next time."

Waving him around to the side panel, I showed him how to open the various drawers, doors and roller pins. Finally, I tugged free an accordion folded piece of paper jammed under a row of clamps. The printer churned to life.

"Thanks. You saved my day." A flushed Mark grabbed another sheet to place under the copier cover.

"Don't forget to put the client number on the log sheet." I picked up my purse and left him to clean up the mess.

In my office I went straight to work. Opening a green legal folder stretched to its limit with draft court documents, I entered the client number into the electronic billing system and sorted the pleadings by date. Unlike my home, my office was a bastion of order and organization. Reference books lined the shelves according to topic and my current case files were stacked neatly in deadline order on the credenza behind my chair. An hour later, I hefted several bulky files into my arms and stacked them in the outgoing file cart parked in the hallway.

I pulled out my petition application, tucked into a thin manila file folder in my bottom desk drawer. These few pages were my passport to a real life. I wasn't looking forward to asking for letters of recommendation. I thought of writing them myself, but I figured it wasn't worth the risk of getting caught. A lesson I learned the last time. I decided not to question my better judgment.

"Hey, good morning." Avery Mitchell, my supervising attorney, stood in the doorway.

My breath caught in my throat. I hoped he didn't notice the

folder I slid out of sight into a drawer. I wasn't ready to share my plans.

"Hey." I closed the drawer with my foot. Avoiding those sexy green eyes of his, I feigned avid interest in my desk pad. "I want to get the Clarkson filings over to the clerks for the court run. Are you going to be around for a bit?"

"I'll be around. As always, you're ahead of schedule. By the way, that Ninth District case you found saved the day." The sincere note of appreciation in his voice brought a lump to my throat. I looked up.

I struggled to sound breezy. "Thanks. I remembered *California v. Ellison Trust* from one of our conferences."

He looked a second too long into my eyes, gave me a thumbs-up and walked back down the hall. We were good at playing the game. A touch that lasted more than a moment, innuendos that only had one meaning. Thank god we hadn't become lovers. We had come real close, but both of us were afraid of fire. Maybe after I got my pardon there might be a chance, but right now the pardon was my highest priority.

I was gathering up my purse and coat to leave when one of our new female law school interns came in. "Excuse me," she said. "I thought I heard you tell Avery you had some filings ready to go to the courthouse. Can you get the clerks to file a settlement conference statement for me, before lunch?"

"No." I didn't break my stride.

Helping Mark was one thing. Interns were another. Besides, I had revisions to my statement to finish, fast.

ABBY FINALLY CALLED back, and we agreed to meet for lunch at Sam's Deli. She worked downtown, not far from Triple D. Abby was easy to get along with. I knew she was forty, because she left her driver's license on a store counter once, but she looked a lot younger. Over time we had developed a friendship. Not a close one—I don't have any of those anymore—but I cared about what she thought.

"I don't think it's a good idea," she said, looking directly into my eyes.

I knew I'd have a hard time convincing her. I wanted a special meeting of the Fallen Angels. I had to get my name off the suspect list and that meant finding Rory's murderer. We needed to compare stories. Shaking off her gaze, I took a bite of my chicken salad. I didn't understand why she didn't want the club to get together.

"Everyone will want to meet," I said. "We have to talk about Rory's death." I leaned in for emphasis. "He was killed the same way as the guy in the club's book."

"Hollis, you're not listening. I don't think it's a good idea." She repeated her words as if putting an objection on record. "Don't you think that with our backgrounds it'll look like we tried to cover things up?"

"I hear you." I decided to start over. "Clearly, you're not hearing me. Like you said, it's not like we're just some ordinary book club. We all have reasons for getting this thing resolved fast. We need to talk about what happened."

"I know. That's my point. I don't want it to look like some group conspiracy to come up with a story. That's how I got into trouble in the first place." Abby's face was flushed and her hand shook as she reached for her glass of water. I often wondered why she had served time, but she never offered to tell me and I was too polite to ask. I took our club's oath of "don't ask, don't tell" to heart.

I pretended not to see her reaction. My head didn't itch, but I scratched it anyway. "You just can't run away from the fact that Rory was killed like the villain in a book our club read. Doesn't that worry an ex-con like you?"

Her jaw tightened. "Yes, it does. Don't *you* get it? I'm sick and tired of worrying." Her voice rose. "I'm sick and tired of jumping every time I hear a door slam. Of sitting up every time I hear a bell ring."

"Abby—"

THE FALLEN ANGELS BOOK CLUB

"Honestly, I'm sorry about Rory." She was loud enough to attract the attention of the diners at the next table. "Yet I can't … I can't care about him."

I lowered my voice. "Listen to me. You need to care who might have killed him. We may all be in trouble."

Abby ran her ringed fingers through her hair. "Okay, okay. I'll call a meeting and set a date as soon as I hear back from the others."

Without another word, she wiped her mouth with a napkin, got up and left me there to finish my salad.

For once I didn't feel like dashing back to work. I ordered another cup of tea and pondered the Fallen Angels. The club had helped save my sanity. It was like my personal halfway house. I didn't have to hide who I was; we all shared a life-altering experience. I had a hard time thinking people who loved books were anything but basically good. Still, I had to face the real possibility that one of my book-reading kindred spirit club members might have killed Rory.

I'd grown comfortable with the group when it was just the original members, but a few weeks ago Richard had wanted to add one more—Rena.

I wasn't thrilled. "Not so fast. I'm not trying to be a spoiler, but we've lasted as a group these past three years because of the trust we've built up over time."

"I can't believe you're so resistant," Abby said. "You're the one who always complains about how limited our viewpoints are. Jeffry and Richard checked her out. Now we have an opportunity to reach out to someone else who's looking for a connection back to the real world, and you're up in arms, arguing 'no change.' "

She was right, of course. Jeffry Wallace was another thing we had in common. He had been the parole officer for all of us at one time or another. There were very few people in this world I trusted unconditionally. Actually, there was only one, Jeffry. The book club was his idea. A transition to new beginnings. Last month we brought in the new member, Rena, age twenty-nine. With Rena, our only African-American, our ranks swelled to seven—three women and four men.

However, now we were six.

CHAPTER SIX

AT HOME THE first thing I saw was the blinking red light on my answering machine. This time I didn't hesitate to push the button.

The first was Abby. "Okay, Hollis. I called a special meeting of the club for tomorrow evening. Sorry for the short notice, but it was the only night I could get the library space. I'm not sure who's going to show up, but Richard agreed we should all get together. There'll be at least three of us there. Since this was your idea, don't you dare tell me you can't come. Call me on my cell if you want to talk this evening. Otherwise, we can talk tomorrow or I'll see you there."

A smile crept across my face. Good. Now we could sort things out.

Next message.

"Hey, it's me again. We have to talk. You're in danger and I can help. Becky, I know you hate my guts, but I've never stopped loving you. You've got to talk to me. It has always been only you. We didn't break up because of another woman. Remember—"

I hit delete.

Danger, what kind of danger could I be in?

On the other hand, even though it had been five years since I saw him, I knew Bill always put himself first. He was likely the one in danger. What was his connection to Rory?

Despite protestations to the contrary, Bill was only interested in Bill. I knew, too, that I had to be prepared for him to show up on my doorstep. If he'd gotten this far, somehow he'd find me.

THE NEXT MORNING I tried not to think about Bill's message. I wrestled with calling and telling him I'd be blocking his calls. I didn't want him bothering my family. Still, if he'd gotten involved with Rory's mess, he would have to resolve it on his own. I didn't think Bill had it in him to kill, but he had to prove it to the police. I was determined not to get caught up in his drama.

Resolved to have a couple of hours without thoughts of Rory's murder or Bill, I checked out of the office. Once a week, or sometimes twice a week, I visited and assisted at the San Lucian Senior Residence & Community Center. For the past two years, I had helped the seniors complete Social Security forms, write complaint letters to recalcitrant merchants and draft wills. I even bought them special occasion cards to send to friends and family. It started when an eager coworker who wanted to "give back" during the Christmas season talked me into going with her. After she left to go to the East Coast with her new husband, I continued on. Now I had to admit I was hooked.

I made it a habit to precede my trip to the center with a stop at the bakery.

"Here's your order of gluten-free, dairy-free sweet rolls for the center." The bakery clerk passed three pink boxes over to me. "I added a couple of our new unhealthy cherry cake donuts."

I gave her a smile, gathered the boxes, and thanked her.

In order to keep the cost for resident care modest, the center did not invest in renovations, and the physical facilities had become faded, tired and outdated. Many seniors still feeling the cold opted to wear several layers of clothing, so they kept the thermostat turned up. As a result, the center was sweltering inside.

"Honey, put those pastries on the counter. We've all been waiting for you—'specially the older ones." Tiny Collins pointed me toward the large community room. Tiny was at least two hundred pounds and had to be in her late seventies. She once told me she and her husband had owned a restaurant in Oakland on Grand Avenue. Her fog-gray hair was secured in a waist-length ponytail. Horn-rimmed glasses rested on the top of her head. Another pair hung around her neck. She peered at me through a third bright red pair that sat up on her nose. Her son was an optometrist.

I knew better than to question her orders. "There are a couple of cake donuts in there, too," I told the slow-moving Tiny over my shoulder as I headed for the kitchen.

"Put those aside for me." Tiny wobbled behind me. "Lily's in the library. I helped her get all her papers together."

We'd fallen into a routine. Tiny was the self-appointed director of operations. As long as I'd helped the seniors get their legal affairs in order, I could count the number of times I'd encountered the center's paid director, Opal Murray, although she had given me a key. Nursing assistants always seemed to be elsewhere. The residents didn't appear to mind. They took care of their own.

I quickly laid out the baked goods on cafeteria trays and placed them in the dining area, trying to finish before the seniors got to the table. Over the months, I had suffered through endless comments about my weight—too fat or too thin, my poor skin, my bright eyes, my hair too long, my hair too short, my unmarried status and my preferences in men. One of the male residents slowly came through the door with his walker, followed by a few of his comrades. I rushed to finish putting out the napkins. The men were just a few feet away when I was finally able to escape down the hallway with a hearty wave.

The center's "library" was not a friendly place. It was a plain room with four six-foot-high, mismatched faux wood bookshelves. I brought the finished books from the Fallen Angels here. They fit right in with all the other well-worn discards. In one corner, two squeaky wooden chairs faced off on either side of a small battered desk. In the center of the room sat an oblong metal reading table and Lily Wilson.

"Good morning, Lily." I sat next to her. "How are you today?"

"I began to wonder if you'd forgotten me. What's wrong with your hair? You need to let it grow." Arthritic fingers grasped the handle of a coffee mug. Her other hand gripped her wheelchair armrest. "Here are my papers. I need you to read this letter from Social Security and tell me what it means. Please speak clearly. Don't mumble."

I was used to Lily's less than warm greetings and marked it up to "no good deed goes unpunished." I was the one who had asked the firm to adopt the senior center as our pro bono client.

"No problem. Remember, Avery Mitchell agreed to go over all your trust papers and real estate documents with you next Monday. I can be here with him, if you like."

"You're not listening. This letter is about my Social Security, not my will. Is that nice girl back from her vacation? She listened to me. She can come back with Mr. Mitchell."

Ignoring the slight, I pulled the letter out of the envelope. "Lily, remember Linda's not on vacation. She left the firm for a new job. I'm afraid you're stuck with me."

"Oh, that's right." She patted her thin hair. "Well, at least you try. Those Social Security people are changing my benefits. I earned that money. I worked thirty years as a teacher. So you're sure the nice girl isn't coming back?"

Inside the envelope was a piece of tablet paper folded in small squares. I spread it out and read it.

"Lily, this says Marla wants to see me, too."

"Oh, yes, yes. I wrote it to remind me. You're to see Marla in the kitchen. Or, was it the sunroom? Just help me first."

After about an hour of starts and stops, we finished. Wheeling her into the recreation room with the others, I placed her next to the windows.

She grabbed my hand. "You know, I have a beautiful stained glass window in my dining room. My daughter was an artist and made it for me. The windows here are ugly." She squeezed my fingers. Tears slipped down her pale cheek. "Now my daughter's gone. I miss her and I miss my window. Tell Mr. Mitchell to sell everything else. Not my window."

"I'll let him know. I won't let anything happen to your window. I'm going to your house in a few days to take an inventory. I'll make sure the window is excluded from the real estate listing papers."

I patted her hand and with a fragile smile, she waved me off like a servant.

Marla sat in the community room. "Hello, sweetie, it's so good to see you."

Bending over, I gave her a light kiss on her upturned cheek. "Good Morning. How are you?"

"Every day I wake up is a good day," she chuckled.

It was a ritual we went through. She walked around with two pairs of eyeglasses, evidence Tiny's son had made sales inroads at the center. Tall and thin, Marla wore pale blue jeans with an elastic waist and a bright yellow button-up sweater. Her almond-white hair was cut short and a little uneven, thanks to one of the seniors who used to be a barber before he got the shakes.

I took a cup and saucer from the counter. "You're looking well. Are you ready to fill out forms?"

She raised herself out of the chair and squinted at me. "Come closer, I don't want you to say anything, but there's something wrong with Lily."

I wanted to point out that there were likely a lot of things wrong with Lily, but instead, I took my cue from her loud whisper. "What's the matter?"

"I think she's getting the wrong medicine." She turned and looked over her shoulder.

There was no one there.

"Why do you say that?"

"I don't want to talk now. Can you come back on Friday? I know you don't usually come on that day, but Friday's when Joseph is gone."

Joseph was a nurse practitioner at the center. He looked to be in his forties, with a quarter-sized purple birthmark near the beginning of his hairline. He was cordial to me, and appeared to be professional and caring. I didn't see him that often and, when we passed each other in the halls, our brief exchanges centered on weather, sports and traffic conditions.

"Sure. I have some office things to get done, but I can be here in the late afternoon on Friday."

We agreed I should come at four.

That seemed to satisfy her. "Now, sweetie, what's up with you? You seem bothered today."

I had to laugh. At seventy-nine, Marla liked to think she kept up with the latest slang. "One of our book club members was killed a few days ago."

"They think you did it?"

I dropped my pen on the floor. A year ago Marla confided in me about her husband, who died full of bitterness trying to defend his name against a political opponent. In a moment of weakness, without going into a lot of detail, I shared my own loss of reputation. She promised to keep my confidence. Still, it threw me off balance when, from time to time, she made a reference to my past. I began to regret my possibly misplaced trust.

"I don't know—maybe." I retrieved my pen.

"Well, I don't think you could ever do something like that. When my Leland was alive, he worked for the DA's office. I can't tell you how many times he looked someone in the eye and could tell they were guilty. I look into your eyes, and I don't think you're guilty."

I squeezed her shoulder. "Thank you. Now, let's get to those forms."

While the police would give no credence to Marla's rather subjective litmus test, it made me feel a little better.

CHAPTER SEVEN

B Y THE TIME I got to our club meeting, the wall I'd built to contain my anxiety had started to crack. I mistakenly sent certified mail to myself and had to make three attempts before I remembered the main phone number to the office. Everyone was already in their seats. I gazed around the table and wondered if the book club would continue. I thought not.

"Let's get started." Abby put her glasses on and looked around the room. "You know why we're here."

Gene picked at his eyebrows. "I only came to clear the air about Rory."

Miller glanced at the ceiling, as if looking for divine intervention. "What's there to say? He's dead."

I ignored him. "I agree with Gene. Didn't anyone else take notice of the way he died?"

"Hell, yeah." Richard sat stiffly in his chair. "He died the same way Antonio did in our last book."

"I caught it, too." Rena's large brown eyes opened wide. "I mean, well, it's like—well, I'm just going to say what everyone's thinking. Maybe it could have been done by a club member. The police think it was one of us."

It was out. Silence screamed throughout the room.

Abby groaned and sank down in her chair.

Gene got up and leaned over the table. "Maybe a friend of his read the book and copied the killing."

"Some friend," Miller mumbled and reached for an origami sheet from his pocket.

"Wait a minute, folks." While I usually liked to sit back, letting other people speak before I committed myself, this wasn't what I had in mind. "Before we start climbing into our caves, let's pause a moment. What do we know about the killing, other than that it mimics a book we read?"

No one jumped in to answer.

"For that matter, what do we really know about Rory? Like each of us, he has a questionable past. We don't know anything about him outside of this group."

Richard peered over his rimless glasses and sucked a tooth. "Not true, Hollis. I was out about two weeks ago with … with a friend, and I saw Rory with a real nice-looking young lady. I figured he'd want me to walk past, but he stopped, said hello and introduced her."

"Well, dude, who was she?" Miller urged.

"Now, in retrospect, it seems kind of strange. He said she was his fiancée, but she looked totally bored with him." Richard paused. "There was something else about the way he reacted, like he was anxious for me to think she was hot, but I could tell he was nervous about me, too."

Gene said, "You think? He probably didn't know if you'd blow his cover."

Richard shook his head. "Nah, it was something else."

My impatience was growing. "Yeah, yeah. Cute girl aside, does anyone else know anything about his past?"

"I know what he went up for." Miller completed a tiny origami bird and passed it to me.

"What?" Rena said.

"Big league extortion."

"How do you know?" For the first time Abby showed interest in the conversation.

Miller apparently hadn't counted on being the center of attention. He hesitated, as though weighing what to say—or how much.

"I came across his background by accident. I just never said anything 'cause, well, you know, our pledge and everything." Blinking rapidly, he rubbed his hands back and forth on his pant legs.

Beads of sweat formed on his forehead. I didn't believe he had come across Rory's background by accident. The other members squirmed in their chairs. Did Miller have access to our histories, too?

Rena looked around at each of us. "Do you think he was extorting again?"

Miller cleared his throat. "The police think he might have been killed because he was a blackmailer."

We were all silent.

I had to think we probably all knew we were more or less fodder for an astute blackmailer. I, for one, to make it more difficult, changed my name shortly after coming off parole. I wouldn't be surprised to learn I didn't know the true identities of my fellow members. Jeffrey Wallace brought us all together. His insight and caring was rare in a parole officer. When the club first met, we speculated about why he chose us, and why a book club. He had given the same recruitment speech to each of us: book lovers were kindred spirits, and we were all in need of a path back to society. That sounded a bit like a crock to me, but it worked like therapy. Now I would miss the group if something came between us.

Abby stood. "I'm leaving. This is leading nowhere. I didn't want this meeting to begin with. My past is my own business."

"Sit tight, Abby. You're not going anywhere." Richard leaned forward. "None of us can risk leaving here without having a clear understanding of what kind of loyalty we can count on from each other."

I had hoped the meeting would give me a clue as to Bill's connection to Rory. Possibilities raced around in my head, but so far there just seemed to be a lot of rattled cages. "If Rory was… say, blackmailing one of us," I went on, "there's nothing we can do now. It's over."

"Over my ass," Miller said. "There's a killer in the room."

Richard coughed.

"Wait a second," Rena jumped in. "It's doesn't have to be one of us. Maybe somebody out there had it in for Rory and knew he read this book, and … and then copied the murder."

"We're still going in circles," Abby said.

Gene checked his watch. "I don't know about you guys, but I'm done. I have no intention of going back to prison. I'm going to tell the truth." He picked up his jacket. "Hollis, the police haven't confirmed the blackmail. He wasn't blackmailing me. No need for anyone to share their story. I'm not going to ask, so you don't have to tell me."

"Gene, no one is sharing their story. Miller, I don't think the killer is necessarily in this room. I want to know if anyone had any clue about him, something he might have said, or—"

"I'd hate to think one of you guys might have done it," Rena said.

I formed a *T* with my hands for time out. "Look, Rena, we'd hate to think that you did it, too." She opened her mouth to protest. "What I'm saying is that we all might have been set up. Maybe Rory told someone about the club, and we became easy suspects."

"So where is this going?" Abby asked.

"Maybe there's something one of us knows that the rest don't know we know. We could try to figure out—"

Miller spoke slowly. "This isn't television. We can't afford to play detective."

I caught myself glaring at the stress cracks in the ceiling.

Could Bill have set this up?

"Okay then, let's just let the police do their job," Abby said. "I think we should all agree to stick to our rules: we don't know anything about anybody."

Gene nodded. "Yeah, I'm with Abby."

The others nodded. Richard was the only one who looked over at me. I shrugged.

Abby picked up her purse. "I think we should suspend our meetings until further notice. In time I'll … I'll contact everyone to come up with a date for our next meeting."

Everybody got up as if a bell had rung. I helped put the table and chairs in the storage area. I was taking a last look around the room when I felt a tap on my shoulder. I jumped.

"Want to go to Starbucks?" Richard asked.

I gave him a small smile. "I drink tea."

"They have tea, too." He placed the last chair on the stack and guided me by my elbow toward the door. "There's something I want to tell you."

Richard was over a foot taller than me. I struggled to keep up with his relaxed stride. Looking at his neatly pressed shirt and Dockers, I wondered if he was married. The band of pale skin on the ring finger of his left hand and the gold band on his right raised more questions. His blond Dennis the Menace looks didn't hold an attraction for me.

The line at Starbucks was fairly short. I grabbed a small café table in the corner. Richard came over with his Venti Caramel Macchiato and passed me my green tea. I wrapped my hands around the cup.

"Okay, talk."

"I want to help you." Richard peered at me over the lip of the safety lid.

"Help me?"

"Don't be cute, Hollis. You and I both know you're not going to let this go. I know I can't." He set the cup down and scanned the room.

Something in his voice caught my attention. "Why's that?"

He took off his glasses and rubbed his eyes. "You may think you know me, but there's little you know that's minimally real."

"To tell you the truth," I said, "I don't think about you one way or the other. If you expect me to be surprised, I'm not. I have my own problems."

Richard nodded offhandedly and took another sip. "The pieces had finally started to come together. I recently found out Rory was blackmailing me. I think maybe he was blackmailing you, too."

Every once in a while—actually more often than I like to admit—I am at a loss for words.

I mentally scrambled to get back my balance. For once, Richard skipped sucking his teeth and patiently waited for me take a sip of tea.

"What do you mean you *just* found out he was blackmailing you? You didn't know?"

"I didn't know for sure. I got written instructions to leave an envelope at a particular location. In retrospect, I should have realized it was Rory." He took a slow sip of coffee. "It was stupid, of course, but I didn't know what else to do but pay."

"How long have you been paying?"

Richard looked around the café. "I made two payments."

"So the police told you he might be a blackmailer? How could he have found out where you live?"

"I don't know. Only a few people know about my past, but there's no one to make the connection to the life I live now."

I thought a moment. If Rory had discovered Richard's situation, he could have found out about all of us. "Since Rory was the blackmailer, you have nothing to worry about. He's dead."

"Yeah, except for one thing. I wonder if he kept records. You know how obsessive he was. If what he had on me gets out before they find the murderer, I'm toast."

"I see your point."

"Now, if we could quickly figure out who from the club was bold enough to kill him, there'd be no need to reveal our backgrounds."

I had to nip his "we" thinking in the bud. I had only a few weeks to prepare for a hearing that would hopefully launch my new life. Still, Richard was right about one thing: if I could put an end to this murder investigation by finding out who killed Rory, I'd do it. Having my name show up on a murder suspect list wasn't in my best interests.

"I'm not convinced it's someone from the club." The thought made me hopeful and depressed at the same time.

"It's got to be." He ran his hands through his hair. "Look, I have a new life and a new wife. Cristina's prominent in the finance industry. She can't afford any scandals, and I can't be seen running around trying to find out who killed Rory."

"So, together we would …" I paused. "Ah, the 'we' is me."

"Are you married? Do you have a family?" He looked at me pointedly.

I didn't answer.

"I didn't think so."

Fortunately, he was saved a sharp retort when he jumped slightly. He pulled out a smartphone. It must have vibrated. He motioned that he needed to take the call and walked outside.

I took a final sip of tea.

Returning, he slipped his phone into its case and sat.

"Richard—"

"My real name is Ryan—"

"Ryan." *Okay.* "If you don't mind, I'll just keep calling you Richard. Why tell me any of this? I didn't think you even liked me. You act as if I annoy you."

"Yes, sometimes, but I like the way you reason things out in the club. I trust your instincts. If anyone in our group can figure this out, it's you."

"I—"

"Just let me talk. I'm taking this chance with you because

I'm desperate. If the blackmailer was Rory, he was slime. He betrayed us all. He squeezed me just enough to keep me from howling. I didn't kill him and I don't think you did, either." He leaned in across the table. "I've got a new career. I can't let my life go down the toilet again. Tell me about you."

"Me?"

"Yeah, you. What did he have on you? Was he going to 'out' you? We have to find out who killed him because whoever did probably took the files Rory had on us."

"What files?"

"Earth to Hollis. How do you think he kept the goods on everyone? Rory had to have files or a book, or maybe a laptop that contained information on all his victims. Remember how he never let any of us touch his laptop? Maybe the files are on a computer thumb drive. The killer must have gotten tired of paying."

"Rory's killer's a member? It makes no sense. Why would he or she pick a plot from a book we selected to read? There has to be more to it. We are all too smart to do something so stupid."

"I know it's nuts. Except that the killer is likely a blackmail victim who wants the goods as much as we do." He hit the top of the table with his fists. "You realize we may have exchanged one blackmailer for another. So, I'll ask again. What about you?"

"Richard, calm down. This is catching me by surprise." I rubbed my forehead and took a deep breath. "Like you, when I got out, I changed my name. Jeffrey turned me on to the club so I wouldn't become a recluse. That's all there is. You can bet the police have found out about our prison records anyway."

Richard's eyes darted back and forth as if watching a tennis match. "Wait a minute. Are you trying to tell me Rory wasn't blackmailing you?"

I looked him in the eye. "Richard, I'm telling you Rory wasn't blackmailing me."

He clenched his jaw. "What are you trying to prove? You're

better than me?" He pounded the table. "You got me to spill my guts."

We were attracting a few glances. In a soft voice, I said, "I'm sorry, but no one is blackmailing me. What made you so sure?"

"He told me he had you over a barrel and you were helping him out of a mess."

It was my turn to call out. "What? He referred to me by name?"

"Didn't have to. He pointed at you. It was at the meeting before this last one."

I could only shake my head in denial.

Richard stood. "If you don't want to work together, fine. I've got to locate his ledger. I'm out of here."

"Wait. I want to identify his killer, too. I can't stay on a suspect list. I'll see what I can come up with."

He gave me a nod and a small smile. Then he left, along with his fake glasses and fake persona.

What the hell was going on? I could have told Richard why I wanted to find out who killed Rory. However, unlike him, I never would have trusted me, or anyone, enough to be so open about my past conviction, or my present situation. Did he realize he had given me his motive for killing Rory?

One thing was for sure, having a murder victim as an acquaintance was a little too close for comfort.

CHAPTER EIGHT

IN THE MORNING I decided to put aside all wishful
thinking that things would work out on their own. The more
I tried not to think about Bill's message or Rory's death, the
more I obsessed about it. I'm not a big believer in coincidences,
so the fact Bill knew Rory made me think the worst. It didn't
take a big leap to conclude Rory's death and Bill's warnings
were linked. On the other hand, while I still didn't believe
Bill had what it takes to kill, I thought it more likely he risked
exposure on some deal he and Rory had concocted.

I tapped numbers into my phone. "Abby, Hollis. I need to get
out. Do you have you any plans after work?"

"No, let's get together. I could use the distraction."

We agreed to meet at the Pause Wine Bar on Market Street in
San Francisco. It had a small, healthy menu, well-matched with
the best eco-friendly wine selection in Northern California.

Even on a weeknight the bar was relatively busy, and I parked
a block away. Abby had already arrived. She waved at me from
a far corner table near a window.

"I hope you're paying," Abby said with a grin. "I'm on a strict
budget. I'm saving up for a new car and it doesn't allow for

midweek dinners." She opened the menu.

"In that case," I said, smiling back, "you can order anything you want as long as it's a salad."

In fact, the salads looked tasty and we each ordered one, along with glasses of Sauvignon Blanc.

She took a sip of water. "Hollis, I want to apologize for giving you such a hard time. You were right to get the club together. I was wrong. We did need closure."

"I'm not sure a lot got accomplished." I caught the eye of our waiter, who motioned that we were next.

She shrugged. "We got it out of our systems. That was important."

"Abby, what do you really think about Rory's killer? It has to be one of us, right? On the other hand, how stupid would one of the members have to be to commit murder in the same way as a book we just read? It would point the finger at him—or her—as well."

"Yeah, I know." Her forehead creased.

"Who do you think Rory was blackmailing?"

Abby reached for her purse as if to get up, then paused and reached inside. Pulling out hand sanitizer, she offered it to me before rubbing it on.

I shook my head, pretending not to notice her trembling hand.

"I don't know. It could be anyone. I mean …"

Our salads and drinks came at that moment, and I took the opportunity to rein in my impatience. I hadn't spoken about my past life to anyone except—in a sketchy version—Marla. My family kept their distance. Other than perfunctory Christmas and birthday calls, we never talked about the time I served. Still, I needed Abby to trust me, so I'd have to trust her. Anyway, all of our pasts were likely to be revealed all too soon.

"The police found my ex-husband's name in Rory's address book," I said.

She looked up. "I didn't know you were ever married. How

long have you been divorced?"

"My marriage was relatively short. I divorced him while I was in prison."

Abby was silent. I waited for her to comment.

"Could you pass the … what is this, crostini at an Asian restaurant?"

I ignored the remark and passed the basket to her. "Rory was blackmailing Richard."

Abby frowned and seemed to be deliberately avoiding my eyes.

"Richard thought Rory was blackmailing me," I continued, "because Rory appeared to point to me at our last meeting. He wasn't pointing at me; I was standing and talking to you. Rory was pointing at you, wasn't he, Abby?"

She picked up a napkin and slowly dabbed at her mouth. Finally, she nodded. "I didn't know he was my blackmailer until the police told me. They say they have some kind of proof. Remember our meeting in January? When I went to my car? There was a letter under my wiper blade. The writer—now I know it was Rory—claimed to know about my prison record."

"How did he—"

"I don't know. He didn't say. Worse, he somehow knew about my life now."

"Why did you spend time in prison?"

Silence.

I picked at my salad until she was ready to talk.

She waited a moment more. "I used to be married, too. I still am. We never got a divorce. Even now, though we live apart, we're trying to make it work. I was the one who dragged him down. He was doing okay until he met me." Tears began to glisten in her eyes. "I worked as an executive for a large pharmaceutical supply company. The charge in Sacramento Superior Court was 'Misstatement of Services Rendered or Goods Provided.' "

I must have looked confused.

"I went up for fraud," she explained.

She went back into her purse. If I hadn't known her better, I would have sworn she was looking for cigarettes. I wanted one, and I didn't even smoke.

"I take it your current employer wouldn't look kindly upon a felony record?"

Abby's shoulders sagged. "When I got out, I wanted nothing to do with my past. I learned my lesson inside. Wallace got me a job as a museum assistant. That was okay for a while, but it paid peanuts. I was bored. I began going to school at night to get certified as a hospital administrator. It was ... it was a career I knew something about and it was challenging. Early on, I worked in various positions in small local hospitals. I eventually caught the eye of a hospital board member in the East Bay and they offered me a fantastic position. I was off parole and, with the help of a friend who worked in personnel, I got around the background check, so ..."

I smiled to give her reassurance as I said, "Hey, I may have left a line or two off my résumé, too."

"Yes well, it was a little more than a line or two, but you get the idea." She rested her forehead on her hands. "Every day I wonder how I could have allowed myself to get into this mess. I come from a straight-laced American family. My parents were loving people who taught their children to do the right thing. I married my college sweetheart."

Our waiter came by to check on us and Abby stopped speaking. I was afraid she would change the subject.

She took a few bites of salad. "I guess it started to go bad when Paul, my husband, said he wanted children. Suddenly it was all he talked about. It was as if he had the ticking biological clock instead of me. I couldn't stand the thought of having someone dependent on me. I didn't want to share my time or money. Paul made a good salary, but not good enough to support my spending habit. To make a long story short, I ran through my money and his. Soon I crossed a line and started dreaming up ways to take other people's money."

I hoped my mouth wasn't hanging open. I never would have guessed that selfless Abby, who did so much for our club, could have ever been a thief.

"How do you think Rory found out where you work?"

"I don't know. Remember, up until a couple of days ago, I honestly didn't know it was Rory. I never heard his voice. I still find it hard to believe. I'd changed my name to protect myself, as well as Paul." She frowned. "I bet I know what you're thinking, but Paul would never put me at risk."

She was wrong. I wasn't thinking of Paul, only that Rory's behavior was starting to make sense.

"He may have tried to get something on each of us." I spoke more to myself than to Abby. "Still, Wallace is the only person who has our histories. He could have revealed everything a long time ago. I refuse to believe he's involved in blackmail."

"Hollis, there's more. If it was Rory at the money drop the night he was killed, he stayed in the dark. A note left on my windshield told me to put the money in a certain can in an alley. When I got there, a typed note was taped to the top saying this was my last payment. I didn't have to worry about meeting him again."

"Well, that was polite of him. Of course it was Rory. Didn't you think it was someone you knew when he didn't allow you to hear his voice?"

Abby shook her head. "Well, now I would assume that, but I just thought he wanted to make sure I couldn't identify him. Anyway, when I got in my car, this other car pulled in the lot. I didn't hang around. I just got out of there."

"You saw the killer?"

"I saw a silver car. It looked like a Mercedes, but it could have been a BMW. I don't know who was in it. I didn't get a good look. It could have nothing to do with the murder."

"Get real. I hope you told the police. Even if it wasn't the killer, that person might know something. You have to go to the police."

"No."

"What do you mean 'no'? If they find out you withheld information, you'll be in even more trouble. They could decide you did it."

"I know. I know." She twisted her glass on its coaster.

I leaned back in the seat and gazed out the window. People moved busily down the sidewalk. It never ceased to amaze me how normal things looked when all hell was breaking loose in my life.

"Why'd you decide to tell me all this?"

She hesitated for a moment. "I want you to tell the police."

I gave her what I hoped was an incredulous look. "Me? Just what good do you think that will do?"

She leaned into the table. "I don't want *you* to tell the police what *I* saw. I want you to tell them *you* saw it."

I almost fell off my chair. "You have got to be kidding."

Abby gasped. A shadow came over our table and I looked up.

Avery Mitchell stood tall and handsome at my side. "Good evening, ladies. Hollis, I saw you from across the room and just wanted to say hello."

Abby gave me a questioning look.

"Abby, this is Avery Mitchell, one of the senior attorneys at the law firm where I work. Avery—Abby Caldwell."

Avery nodded and shook Abby's offered hand. "You've discovered one of my favorite hangouts. You seem engrossed. I'll be on my way."

Abby gave him a tentative smile. "Maybe we could use a break."

Avery and I exchanged looks. He straightened up.

"No. Maybe another time. I'm meeting my brother. He's running a little late." He looked over his shoulder. "I'd better get back to my table. Ladies, have a pleasant dinner." At that he turned and moved smoothly through the twisted path of tables.

Abby squinted at his back. "Attorneys make me nervous. You work at a law firm?"

"I'm a paralegal." I smiled.

She didn't smile back. "Don't brag. I never want to see another lawyer again. Although, it is interesting."

"What?"

"Our table isn't in his line of sight. Maybe he was looking for you. Is he your boyfriend? Is this one of your regular haunts?"

I shook my head. "Enough with the interrogation. He has a better pool of candidates. Let's get back to the subject at hand. You can't really be asking me to speak to the police for you."

"You're right. Just forget it." She dabbed her lips with her napkin and pulled out her wallet. "What's the check?"

"I'll treat. I said I would." I took out a credit card. "Don't be upset with me. Let's come up with some other plan."

"I spoke to you in confidence. I hope I didn't make a mistake. Like I said, just forget it. Won't be the first bad idea I've had." She rose. "I'll tell the police. I agree with you. It's the right thing to do."

She didn't fool me. I knew she had absolutely no intention of talking to the police.

CHAPTER NINE

EVERY ONCE IN a while I missed having a best friend. Dinner with Abby reminded me of how I'd isolated myself since getting out. I didn't know what else to do. I couldn't let anyone in. There was no room. I was too full of shame.

At work the next morning, I decided to do something I never thought I'd do. I'd run all the club members through PeopleSearch. At Triple D, we used PeopleSearch to verify client backgrounds and track down missing heirs. We weren't supposed to use it for personal reasons, but I had to know who I was dealing with. I could only check under the names that club members used now. I started with Gene—the guy with the meticulously groomed eyebrows—who apparently hadn't changed his name. Even so, his profile was limited. Now thirty-seven, Gene had served his time for libel and bribing a federal official. I read the pages quickly. There didn't appear to be any gaping holes.

Putting aside my guilt, I finished gathering information on all the remaining members. Nothing incriminating popped up.

I checked the newspaper. A small article reported Rory's murder and one of his aliases. I took a slow breath when nothing showed up about the club.

"Hi." Avery stood in my doorway. "Something interesting in today's paper?"

"No, just taking a break at my desk." Heart pounding, I put the paper aside and clicked my screen to dark. "What can I help you with?"

I saw him glance over the stacks of my files.

"A new probate assignment. Pretty straightforward. Not a big estate." He dropped the paperwork on top of the files closest to the edge. "Finish your break and then come see me."

"No, it's …" I started to protest but realized I needed the time to reset my state of mind.

The new probate assignment would help distract me from obsessing over Rory's murder for a brief while; I was in danger of driving myself crazy. I sought the reassuring smell of law books sitting solidly on library shelves to center me. Researching appeal cases to defend inheritance claims was my specialty. I placed yellow Post-its to mark the applicable case citations, which would save time when it came to drafting the lengthy points and authorities. I put aside a stack of books on a nearby library table. Mark, in the opposite aisle going through the federal directory, smiled at me.

"Mark, how would you track down someone who may or may not have had a name changed by the court?"

"You got a social?"

"No."

"Did you run him through PeopleSearch?"

"That was the first thing I did."

"Okay. There's this new software called Inquiry First. I've been beta-testing it for the other associates, and it seems reliable. You can use my computer with the network password. The icon is on the start-up screen. All you need is the name he's using now, the state of residence and his birth date. His known aliases should show up. Remember, even though it's a beta site and we're not being billed, you still need a case code to charge it to."

"Thanks. I'm trying to anticipate what Avery needs for this real picky client we're trying to sign." I told myself to shut up. Any ex-con knows explanations are dead giveaways that you're lying.

"Sure. Well, it should get you what you want." He turned back to the shelves.

I was glad I had helped Mark the other morning. Now we were even.

How would I get birth dates? The club talked about celebrating birthdays, but it made too many of us nervous to give up personal information about ourselves. I was a terrible judge of age and I'd have to guess. Then I'd have to be careful not to get locked out of the software application with multiple guessing of dates. I had no intention of raising a red flag in Accounting from having to keep logging in each time I got kicked out.

Fortunately, the attorneys were out of the office at a half-day management meeting. The day went by quickly. The other paralegals apparently picked up on my pensive mood and left me alone. I tried to reach Abby several times without success. I wanted to know if she had gone to the police.

Eventually, I got some time to work on my petition. I was on my third draft. Having to detail the state of mind that led to my crime and the new thinking that filled me now wasn't easy. I didn't want it to sound like a confession or a denial. Still, I knew I grappled with too much anger and blame. I would have to get it out of my system before I could move on.

I glanced at the picture of me holding my Hastings acceptance letter and finally the words came. Slowly at first and then nonstop, as if they had just been waiting for me to get out of the way.

I finished.

Emily, the office receptionist, knocked gently on the open door and told me to make sure to turn off the lights in our hallway when I left.

"Avery, Phil and Simon are still behind closed doors. I think Grace is with a client in the conference room. You're the last one on this side of the floor."

"Thanks. Good night." I waved her on. She was used to leaving me to turn off the lights. It wasn't unusual for paralegals to spend time after hours on a case. The firm didn't encourage it, but they didn't discourage it, either.

I went into Mark's office, shut the door and keyed up Inquiry First on the computer. I still lacked birthdates, but I had to give it a try. It loaded in seconds. I quickly read down the small print to see what search and sort options they offered. Mark was right, it could do skip tracing and alias tracking. I did a quick test using Rory's name, but after I had tried three different birth dates, Inquiry First kicked me out. I hit the keyboard with my fist. I wouldn't get far without Rory's real name or birth date.

Taking in a deep breath and blowing it out slowly, I decided to use my own name to see if my information was accurate. A chill went up my arms as my life, captured in a few sheets of paper, spilled out for the entire world to see. I scanned the pages then logged off, feeling strangely as if I'd violated my own privacy. I'd try again later with the others, but for now I'd had enough and wanted to go home.

THE NEXT DAY I left work a little early for my appointment with Jeffrey Wallace. As I approached his office, I took deep breaths to calm myself. I hadn't realized how much I had counted on this meeting. When I had been on parole, Wallace had believed me when I said I was innocent. He was the only one who had. My former parole officer's support meant everything to me.

Being in the familiar hallway gave me an odd sense of

comfort. Wallace was on the phone. "Yeah, well, I don't want to hear it," he was saying. "You've played me for the last time."

He looked up. I was in the doorway. He put his hand over the receiver and said, "You're early. I'm glad." Pushing aside a stack of papers, he signaled for me to sit. "Bear with me. I need to finish this call."

"I'll wait outside." I started to rise.

"No. Stay," he mouthed.

From the conversation, I could tell it was a parolee, not a friend or acquaintance. I realized I didn't know anything about Jeffrey Wallace's family. I slowly looked around the room for pictures or awards—nothing. Bare walls, except for a calendar and the inevitable poster with a cat hanging on a bar with the saying, "Hang in there."

True to his word, he finished the call and smiled at me. "You look good, Rebecca. Sorry—Hollis."

"Old habits die hard." I sat back in the chair.

"Okay, let's cut to the chase. Why the visit? It's been years since the last time I saw you. Then you said, and I quote, 'No, offense, I'm never coming back here again.' "

I nodded. "What can I say? That's why you should never burn any bridges." I went over to his bookshelf. "Jeffrey, do you have a family? I mean—"

"I'm a loner. Don't avoid my question."

I gave him a look to let him know I didn't believe him. I wouldn't want ex-felons to know anything about my personal life, either. I placed my manila folder on the only cleared space on his desk. "I spoke without thinking back then. Now I need your help."

A crease formed between his eyebrows. "Does this have to do with Norris' death?" The tone of his voice had changed.

"Why would you think that?"

"The police were here yesterday. They requested club members' background records. They asked a lot of questions about the initial formation of the club and how members were selected."

My heart took off in my chest. *Breathe. Breathe.* "They've already talked to me. I'm not here about the club."

"You okay?" He offered me a cup of water.

I shook my head.

"I'm kind of bummed out about the whole thing," he said. "I thought the club was one of my success stories."

"Don't write us off so fast." I took another breath. "I'm hoping you'll recommend me for a Certificate of Rehabilitation."

He raised an eyebrow but let me go on with my speech.

"About two years ago, I assisted one of Triple D's criminal attorneys who had a very rich client with an errant son. I learned California has a restoration of rights law. I prepared court documents to get his record cleared. Our client worked hard to write a statement and obtain the signatures and references that eventually led to his son's pardon. I want a pardon, too. Under the penal code, the law permits someone convicted of a crime to petition the court to re-open the case, set aside the plea and dismiss the matter. I've done my research and I know I qualify. I completed parole and I've kept my record clean for five years."

Jeffrey nodded in acknowledgment.

"I know expungement won't erase my criminal record, but my finding of guilt would be dismissed. I could then honestly and legally answer a question about my criminal history and say that I hadn't been convicted of a crime. Eventually, I'd submit a request to the court to have it converted to a full pardon."

I took another deep breath.

He gave me a long look. Finally he got up, took a book off a nearby shelf and started flipping through pages. I knew what he was searching for. A Rehabilitation Pardon is usually granted to persons who demonstrate exemplary behavior following a felony conviction. A useful, productive and law-abiding life wouldn't be enough. The life I'd led had to be stellar.

Jeffrey wasn't a large man, but he always looked huge to me. Kind of like a puffin I saw on the National Geographic channel. The bird is relatively small, but to help it survive in a big bird world, Mother Nature gave it guts and the ability to blow up its chest. These talents made it appear just as large and formidable as its peers. That was Jeffrey.

He set the open book in front of me. "I'm familiar with the petition. They aren't easy to come by." His index finger tapped a long paragraph and then, without saying another word, he sat down at his desk.

I knew it by heart—the checklist of qualifying requirements. "I'm determined. I know what it takes but I think I can make my case. I want to finish law school and take the California Bar."

"I see." He fiddled with the pens on his desk. "It's going to take some paperwork and you're going to need a lawyer."

"Jeffrey, I work for a law firm. I know a few lawyers." I grinned at him, but he didn't grin back. "Okay, I retained an attorney from another firm. To save money, I'm assisting by coming up with all the section codes and citations. All my attorney has to do is review my brief and declaration."

"First of all, it goes without saying that you have my strongest recommendation." His forehead creased again.

"Second?" I paused. "What is it? There's something you're not saying."

"You know I'm one of your biggest supporters."

I waited for the "but."

"But until this Rory thing gets settled, all club members will come under a lot of scrutiny. I know you don't want to hear this, but all the club members are prime suspects."

I slumped in my chair. "Okay. What do you think I should do?"

"Tell the truth. Tell the others to do the same. I know each of you and I don't think any of you did it. Misjudgments happen in my line of work. I misjudged Rory and—"

"Wallace, there's something else." My mouth went dry and I licked my lips. "The way Rory died. It mimicked the story line in the book the club discussed right before his murder."

"What?" He slammed the book on his desk.

My words rushed out. "I know. Who else could it be, but one of us? I can't believe it. Except for Rena, who barely knew Rory, we've been together almost three years. It just doesn't make sense. We're a pretty smart bunch; we would know that a murder mimicking the book would point to one of us. On the other hand, the fact is, Rory blackmailed Richard and Abby, maybe others. I guess the club wasn't the lifesaver you thought it might be."

"Do the police know about the plot from the book?"

"About how he died? Yes. I'm the one who told them."

Jeffrey drummed his fingers on the desk. "The police are convinced Rory was indeed a blackmailer."

I nodded. "I had this conversation with Abby. She thinks she might have seen the car of Rory's killer. I believe I talked her into going to the police, but she's not wild about the idea. She's scared. None of us wants any more contact with the cops than necessary. Until I find Rory's killer, the chances of me getting a pardon are …"

I couldn't finish.

He nodded. "It complicates things, but withholding information in a murder investigation is an offense. Be smart. If Abby doesn't tell them, you have to. I can give her a call if you don't feel comfortable talking to her."

"No, don't. She told me all this in confidence." Abby wouldn't be happy if she knew I'd revealed her secret. "I'll find out if she's gone to see the police. If not … okay, I'll do it."

Jeffrey looked worried. "Do it today, okay?"

THE AFTERNOON WAS mild but the sun shone warm upon my shoulders like a comforting sweater. I sat on the patio going through my Blackberry emails waiting for Marla to appear. She'd seen me arrive, but because she was on the phone in the community room, she'd motioned for me to wait for her here.

"I'm sorry, sweetie, but at the last minute I got a call about the results of my tests and I had a couple of questions."

I peered at her. "Everything's okay, isn't it?"

"Oh my, yes. Don't worry. I'm in tip-top shape." She brushed a gray curl off her forehead. "I don't want to waste time talking about me. I want to tell you about Lily."

I waited.

Marla leaned in. "You know Lily has a bad ticker along with her poor hearing and bouncing ball memory. Up until a few months ago, she slept and ate pretty well. She worked in the garden with me and we played Scrabble together."

"What happened a few months ago?"

"Joseph was hired. The center is actually down two nurses, but they're having a hard time finding people who want to work for low pay. Anyway, he replaced Marjorie. You remember her, the really tall nurse? Anyway, at first he seemed okay. Must have been on probation. Gradually, he's become curt and even snarly."

"A personality defect doesn't mean he isn't doing his job."

"I know that." Marla was clearly irritated. "Lily is supposed to receive pills three times a day. Marjorie made it a game at meal times. She had to take at least five of them. I know because I get my cholesterol pill at the same time."

She grabbed my wrist. "Now they don't give her as many, and she only gets them twice a day."

I gently pulled my arm back and put it around her shoulders. "Her doctor probably just ordered a change in her prescription. It doesn't mean anything."

Marla jerked back. "No, sweetie, Lily's not the same. She's changed. Besides, she hasn't seen her doctor since before Joseph came."

It was clear I wasn't responding the way Marla wanted. On

the other hand, while Joseph might not win any congeniality awards, he didn't strike me as incompetent.

"Is it the handling of the medication that has you concerned?"

"Yes, but there's more." Her face flushed and her voice trembled. Marla took my hand in hers. "I need to tell you the most important thing. Rosemary Hebert passed away about a week after Joseph started. She died in her sleep."

"Yes?" I squeezed Marla's hand.

"She used to take those little yellow pills for her cataracts. I think Joseph is giving Lily Rosemary's prescription."

"Why would he do that? What does he have to gain?"

She leaned in even farther. "Her white pills cost a lot more than the yellow ones. I think he's selling Lily's medication."

"Have you spoken to the director?"

"Yes. Other than looking at me as if I were senile, she said she'd look into it, but nothing has changed. Sweetie, Lily is getting worse."

If it had been anyone else, I would have tried to rationalize the situation as a simple medication change. I knew Marla wasn't one to raise an unwarranted alarm. I glanced at the garden clock.

"Marla, give me a couple of days. Let me see what I can find out. The privacy rules regarding medical file information are strict. I doubt I'll be able to learn much." I stood to leave. "However, I have to say that Lily seems about the same to me. Maybe a little grumpier, but about the same."

Marla heard what she wanted. Her face cleared and she gave a small nod of acceptance. "I know you have a lot on your plate right now. I wouldn't ask for your help if I didn't think this was important."

I took both her hands in mine and said goodbye.

I lectured myself all the way home for getting involved. But how could I ignore Marla's plea?

CHAPTER TEN

THE HANDS ON the clock hardly seemed to move as our morning staff meeting dragged on. Ed got into his billable hours speech and I predicted we had at least another twenty minutes to go. My mind went back to my meeting with Jeffrey and my dinner conversation with Abby. Maybe I was the one who needed to be more open and trusting.

Ed droned on, "I've decided to mix up our teams. Some of you struggle with bringing in new clients, and others have seen a marked reduction in billable hours." An outstanding civil litigator, Ed was a trial court legend. He often memorized closing arguments that ran for an hour or more. Today, however, he noticeably refused to glance up from his page of bulleted notes.

I didn't want to look at Mark, but I couldn't stop myself. A red flush had made its way up from his starched shirt collar. I wondered which non-performing category he was in.

I sneaked another peek at the clock. I wanted to print out the Inquiry First response for Gene. I had gotten his birth date from PeopleSearch. A stack of pages was waiting for me.

"The Management Committee met and we reassigned some

of you to new teams. I'll be posting the new support groups after this meeting."

Lisa, one of the more senior associates, asked, "Why all the drama? We're a small firm. Just tell us the new teams."

Ed shot her a look. "In the interest of saving time, which is the whole point I tried to make in my message, we must increase our billable hours and reduce overhead by charging our work to a client matter. Therefore, I'm not taking the time to go into administrative details."

"And face tough questions," one of the other associates murmured under his breath. He got a few chuckles. I stifled mine.

"Any questions, tough or otherwise, contact the senior attorney on your team." With a quick look at his watch and a final glance around the room, Ed walked out the door.

No one rushed to look at the paper taped to the whiteboard in the lunchroom. Clearly we were all too cool for that. After a minute of pretending not to look, we formed a short line in front of the board. I ended up near the end. Mark grinned after he read the list, and I quickly learned the reason. He was joining me on Avery's support team.

He caught up to me in the hallway.

"I knew Ed was referring to me. If there's a silver lining, I think I have a fair chance at getting my stride back by working with you and Avery."

I wasn't as enthusiastic. "It'll be interesting. Have you done any trust or probate work?"

"Some in law school and a little bit since, but anything has to be better than taxation and partnership agreements." Mark followed me back to my office.

Back at my desk, I pulled a Post-it note off my computer monitor: team meeting at three o'clock. "Our esteemed leader is calling us together." I showed the note to Mark. "I need to wrap up a couple of files. It's not likely we'll be taken off the open cases we've been working."

Mark took the hint. "Oh, yeah, you're right. I better get back to my office, too. I hoped to get out of having to assist in the Hayman corporate matter, but knowing Ed, he's going to make sure he doesn't get stuck with it."

I not-so-subtly motioned my head toward the clock. He finally got the message and hurriedly strode down the hallway.

Not long after, it was time for a break. Munching on carrot sticks and an energy bar, I made my way through the stack of file folders on the corner of my desk. I worked through lunch. In a couple of hours, all my files were up to date. Remembering the battered looking banana I'd taken from my fruit bowl, I dug into my purse, feeling for the softening flesh. A little tired potassium beat none.

I wanted time to just sit and think over what I knew about Rory's murder. He was a blackmailer who had somehow obtained current information on club members. I grabbed a notepad and pen and made a list under the headings: What I Know, What I Don't Know, and What I Need to Know. The Need to Know entries were a half page longer than the two other columns. I slammed my pen down, balled the paper up and tossed the wad into the trash. This exercise would get me nowhere fast.

When I arrived at the team meeting, Avery was sitting behind his desk looking official. Eager-beaver Mark had beaten me there and taken the front chair—my usual seat. I nodded to both of them and took the remaining chair between two file cabinets.

"Well, team," Avery said, "got any questions for me?"

I knew Avery's management style well enough not to respond, but Mark jumped right in. "What kind of matters are currently on your desk? Will you need me to go to court?"

Avery looked at him with what could only be described as amusement. "I'm glad to see your enthusiasm."

For the next half hour, Avery took us through his client list, which wasn't lengthy. He was considered one of the more successful attorneys in the firm. Though he only had a few clients, his retainers were substantial. From time to time, he took on civil litigation cases, but his cash cow was administering probate estate settlements.

"Most of my clients are wealthy seniors or seasoned entrepreneurs," he said. "It makes for a varied workload. The seniors are always amending their trusts and the entrepreneurs are always trying to protect their wealth." He leaned over his desk and gave us what I knew to be the practiced barrister gaze he reserved for a jury. "I want us to be a real team. No one takes on anything or makes decisions without notifying the rest of us."

"Got it," Mark said.

I nodded. Avery hated surprises.

From a leather portfolio, he took out a yellow pad of paper and a Montblanc pen. Despite his pretense of being down-to-earth, the man did have his toys.

"Okay, there's about an hour left until I have to leave. Let's go over the cases with pending court actions. I have one contested—"

Ed's sudden appearance in the doorway cut him off.

"Sorry, Avery," Ed said. "I need to speak with Hollis right away."

Avery looked at me, puzzled. I looked puzzled back.

Ed opened the door wide for me to pass. Out in the hallway, he steered me by the elbow toward his office.

"The police are here to see you." He'd dropped his usual paternal tone of voice. "You can use my private conference room. Come and find me before you leave today." His forehead wrinkled and his lips formed a thin pale line. He wasn't happy.

I nodded.

I was even less happy when I walked into the room and saw Detectives Lincoln and Faber standing around the conference table. The sight of Detective Lincoln's stern face made my heart sink.

"Ms. Morgan," Lincoln said, "do you know an Abigail Caldwell, also known as Abigail Tolman?"

I sat. "Yes."

"When was the last time you saw her?"

"We had dinner a couple of nights ago."

Faber leaned over the table. "When was the last time you spoke with her?"

I didn't feel good about this. "At our dinner. I haven't spoken with her since then. I tried calling her yesterday and this morning, but I didn't get her. Why are you asking questions about Abby?"

"She's dead," Detective Faber said. "Your name and phone number were on her desk pad and we know she's a member of your little book club."

I was struck mute with disbelief. In my heart I wanted to cry, but the pain and surprise left me dry-eyed. I must have started to glisten up because Detective Lincoln reached for the box of tissues sitting on the credenza and pushed them toward me.

"How did she die?" I choked out.

Lincoln sat down next to me and took his notebook out of his jacket. "We're not sure yet. It might have been a suicide." He kept clenching and unclenching his hands. "Is there anything she said at dinner that would lead you to believe she was despondent?"

"No, Abby was fine. She was ... she had a lot on her mind, but nothing that would make me think she would ... I never would have left her if—"

"It could have been murder. We'll know more after the autopsy." Detective Lincoln's eyes bored into mine.

"Murder," I whispered.

"Two murders in the same book club. That's not an everyday occurrence, would you say, Ms. Morgan?" Detective Faber said. "Can you think of any reason why anyone would want to kill Mrs. Caldwell?"

"No, I ..." I couldn't catch my breath.

"Would it surprise you that some of the club members think that you had a motive to kill Michael Rollins? You knew him as Rory Norris." Detective Lincoln played with a cup of pens on the edge of the table.

Yes, I'd be surprised.

"I don't know about *some* of the club members, but maybe one, Richard Kleh, might have said something along those lines."

"What makes you think it was him?" Faber asked.

I hesitated. I had to make a decision. I took the path of half-truths. "He thought Rory was blackmailing me. I told him I wasn't being blackmailed. I don't think he believed me."

"We already know Abigail Caldwell and Richard Kleh were blackmailed by Norris. Why not you?" Lincoln asked.

A question I'd asked myself for days.

"I don't know. Maybe because I didn't have as much to lose."

The detectives exchanged glances.

Detective Faber asked, "What do you mean?"

"I'm just a paralegal. I don't have a lot of money. The blackmailer … Rory … wouldn't gain a lot from blackmailing me." I hoped my deep swallow would be attributed to sorrow and not the fact I had everything to lose if the police found out how vulnerable my pending pardon would make me to blackmail.

"Were Gene Donovan and Miller Thornton being blackmailed?" Detective Faber asked.

The worry in my heart sat like a weight on my chest. I shrugged. "I don't know. You need to ask them."

Detective Lincoln moved over until our shoulders almost touched. "All of a sudden, you don't seem to know very much. Can you tell us again about your last conversation with Abigail Caldwell? We want to move on to our other suspects."

He's lying. He can't even look me in the face "We had dinner. We talked about the investigation. The night Rory Norris died she made a payoff. He told her it would be her last payment.

As she drove out of the parking lot, she saw a car she didn't recognize. She was planning to tell you this, or so she said. That's everything. That's all of it."

Detective Lincoln said, "She didn't come talk to us."

"No, I guess she didn't."

"You were the only one who knew that she had decided to talk to the police," Lincoln said.

My survival antenna sent warning signals to my brain. "I … I don't know that."

Detective Faber said, "Did you try to talk her out of talking to us? Maybe avoid getting involved."

Breathe. Just breathe. "No, I'd never do that. She was nervous about being an ex-con and connected to … to a crime."

"That's what she told you?" Detective Lincoln asked.

"Yes."

Detective Faber walked around the room. "The question is, Ms. Morgan, what can you tell us about Ms. Caldwell's state of mind? Was she depressed?"

I looked him in the eye. "I told you, no. She wanted to keep her life simple and stay out of trouble. She worried about her family and having to deal with the threat of blackmail."

"What was she trying to hide?" Lincoln asked.

I hesitated, but realized it no longer mattered. "She lied to her employer … on her application. She didn't list her conviction."

The detectives looked at each other and simultaneously set pens to paper.

Lincoln said, "She must have been distraught and desperate. Maybe desperate enough to kill Norris." He tapped his pad with the tip of his pen.

"No, Abby couldn't kill," I shot back.

"Could she kill herself?"

I kept shaking my head. "No. You had to know Abby. Ask any of the other members."

Detective Faber persisted. "So you would say she was *not* suicidal?"

"No, Detective Faber, Abby was *not* suicidal. Stressed maybe, but not suicidal."

Now Detective Lincoln tapped the table with his pen. "Good. Then you agree with us. We don't think so, either. Like I said, we'll know more with the autopsy results. This morning her body was found on the street below where she worked. It appears she jumped, or was pushed, from a fifteenth floor window; however, marks on her body and other evidence raise a lot of questions about what really took place. Her office was fairly warm, but there were a couple of strange things. She was found wearing a winter scarf—"

"A heavy red wool scarf?" I asked.

"Yeah." Detective Lincoln's eyes narrowed. "You've seen it?"

"No. I read about it in *Storm Crossing*. It was our club selection earlier this year."

The detectives again exchanged looks.

"Another plot from one of your books?" Detective Faber asked.

My mind raced. This didn't make any sense. Why were Fallen Angels being murdered? Who from the club would be crazy enough to use plots from our book list?

"Ms. Morgan, are you still with us?" Detective Faber asked.

I could only nod.

He pressed, "Where were you around nine thirty this morning?"

"Is that when … she died? Here. I was here at work."

Lincoln nodded. "If those autopsy results come back today, we may want to question you and your fellow members at the station this evening, so stay close to your phone. One way or the other we're going to get answers."

Detective Faber moved to the door. "Oh, yeah, and bring me the book."

After they left, I sat for a few minutes, numb. It was as if someone had shot a cannonball clear through my gut and left a giant hole. When I entered the lobby, I wasn't surprised to see

Ed lurking in the hallway. He waved me into his office.

"You want to tell me what's going on?"

I put my shaking hand into my pocket. "A friend, a member of my book club, died in her office this morning. They're not sure if it's suicide or not. The police wanted to know what I knew." I couldn't bring myself to say "murder" out loud.

He was silent for a moment. "I see. I'm sorry about your friend. You have an alibi. You were here all morning. I saw you myself."

"They're checking with all book club members. I'm sure I'm not a suspect." I hoped I sounded more confident than I felt.

"Hollis, I've worked in the DA's office. There has to be a good reason why San Lucian's finest shows up at our workplace. They don't need two of their four homicide detectives to verify an alibi." Ed was a thin, wiry man; his once-blond hair was now fringed with white. He had a deceptively warm smile that usually distracted from his cold eyes. He was smiling now, and the chilly stare from those eyes was unrelenting. He wasn't pleased.

Before I could think of a plausible response—the truth not necessarily an option—there was a light knock on the door and Avery popped his head in. "My turn to interrupt. Is everything okay?"

Ed cocked his head toward me. "There's no problem, but you may want to stay, since Hollis reports to you. I just asked her why the police were here to see her."

Avery perched on the edge of the low bookcase that lined the length of the wall.

I had a couple of options. Only one made sense. "Ed, you know I'm an ex-felon. My fellow book club members are also ex-felons, as was the woman who ... who died this morning." To stop my hands from shaking, I tightly interlaced my fingers. "Last week another member was murdered. They think there's a connection. I—they thought I might have some information."

"Good grief. I don't mean to be callous. You were hired

based on Avery's recommendation. We've been pleased with your work, but the firm can't handle bad publicity."

"There won't be any bad publicity. I didn't do it."

Avery crossed his arms. "Hollis, can I assume the police were following up, since all the members are ex-felons?"

"Yes." I wasn't about to go into the manner of the deaths. "It was Abby Caldwell, my book club friend you met at the restaurant, who died."

"I'm sorry to hear that."

Ed dropped all pretense of commiseration. "You realize, of course, that we have an obligation to protect our staff and clients."

"Yes. I'm not going on a killing rampage, Ed." I turned to Avery. "You trusted me once. I promise you, I'm not involved."

Ed spoke to Avery as though he hadn't heard me. "Perhaps we should allow Hollis to go on paid leave until this is all settled."

Avery stood. "Now wait, Ed. I think we should talk this over with the personnel committee before we go down any particular path."

I didn't know how telepathy worked, but I looked at him with all the hope I could communicate.

Ed continued to regard me as if I were a hostile witness. "All right. That makes sense. After all, that's why we have a process for handling these things. Hollis, go ahead and go home." He looked up at Avery. "Call an emergency meeting of the personnel committee for tomorrow morning."

"It's just you, Lisa and me," Avery said. "Lisa's still here. Why don't I see if she can meet this evening? Tomorrow morning's bad for me. I've got to make a court appearance."

I gave him a grateful look.

Ed nodded. "Okay, that works. I have to be gone by seven. I promised to take my wife to the theater in San Francisco."

Avery opened the office door for me. "Oh, I don't think this will take long."

Saying nothing, I moved past him. I just wanted out of there.

AT HOME, I hurriedly changed clothes before heading to the police station with *Storm Crossing*.

"I'm here to see Detective Faber or Detective Lincoln," I said to the uniformed receptionist.

"They're out in the field. Were they expecting you?" She assessed me with curiosity.

"Yes … well, no, it wasn't decided for sure. I told them I'd bring this book." I handed over the copy of *Storm Crossing*.

"I'll make sure they get it."

Back in the sunlight, I didn't mind missing another opportunity to bond with the detectives. The autopsy results must have been delayed. There was little more I could do but wait for another verdict about my future.

CHAPTER ELEVEN

SITTING IN MY living room, I replayed my conversation with Ed and came up with a multitude of more effective responses that had escaped me at the time. I was a wreck. Each passing minute I waited for the phone to ring seemed like an hour. I knew I needed to finalize my court statement, but I couldn't focus. My life was back on hold until I heard from Avery. I couldn't do anything even if I had wanted to. Why bother with the statement? I needed to be employed to qualify for the pardon.

My stomach growled and I remembered my skimpy lunch. There was a frozen dinner in the freezer, but after reading what was in it, I put it back. My appetite just wasn't cooperating. My emotions always affected my belly.

I was debating making a PB & J sandwich when the phone rang, flashing Avery's office number on caller ID. I made an effort to adjust my breathing to an even pace before I answered.

"Hey, you okay?" Avery asked.

"You tell me."

"You're okay." I heard his smile. "Ed brought the personnel policy handbook and quoted chapter and verse on the ability of the firm to suspend or place you on unpaid leave for cause. I didn't even have to speak up for you. Lisa jumped in and said your work spoke for your character. She also reminded Ed that there's this legal premise about being innocent until proven guilty."

"I can see why she's a defense attorney."

"Anyway, we both convinced him that, as a law firm, we owed you the benefit of the doubt to stand by you. Just try to keep our name out of the media, okay?"

Hearing his last words, I let out the breath I'd been holding. My eyes welled up and I started to cough.

"Hollis, are you okay? Do you want me to come over?"

If I did, it wouldn't be under these circumstances.

"No, no. I'm going to be all right." It took me a moment to gain control. "I was afraid that if Triple D knew I was a possible murder suspect, I wouldn't have anyone in my corner. I really appreciate what you and Lisa said on my behalf."

"You could have told me. You didn't have to spend these past days looking over your shoulder."

"Maybe not, but thank you for making it right for me now." I meant it more than he knew.

"You sure you don't need me to come over?"

A red warning sign started blinking inside my head. My resistance was too low. "No, I need time by myself. I'll see you tomorrow after court."

I jumped up and down and danced around my living room without missing a beat. Energy depleted, I poured a glass of wine and put a steak in the microwave to defrost. I tried to compartmentalize the day's events. Abby was gone. The thought slowed me down. Poor Abby; I hated to imagine her dying that way. I didn't care what she'd said about being greedy and selfish; she was kind and warm to me. Besides, I liked Abby and, but for the hand of fate, we might have been good friends.

I was okay … for now, but for how long? Unless I figured out who murdered Rory and Abby and revealed which of my club members was an undercover psychopath, I could be *not* okay very soon. I poured myself another glass of wine, sat down and looked at the Inquiry First printout on Gene. He had been convicted as a co-conspirator under a bribery penal code when he went in. There was a cross-reference to another case number. It wouldn't take long to run a locator search.

AT WORK THE next day I waited until lunchtime, when it was less likely I'd be interrupted. "Hello, my name is Hollis Morgan. Is Patrick Brennan there?"

The male voice on the other end took a long time to reply. "What do you want with him?"

The voice had a bit of a southern twang and suspicion came through the line loud and clear.

I pushed ahead. "I'd like to talk to him about Gene Donovan. We're in the same book club together."

"Book club. What has that got to do with me?"

Got him.

"Mr. Brennan, I know you and he spent some time together in prison. I just want to know if—"

"Look, lady, I don't know you, and I haven't spoken to Gene in over a year. We didn't end on the best of terms." He sniffed. "Besides, I heard that if you want to talk about Gene, you should talk to the Reverend Campbell."

"Where can I find—"

The click in my ear was my answer.

I felt stupid for not having a better story ready, but it wasn't a complete loss. I could follow up on the name he gave me. Still, I needed another pitch.

I punched Gene's number into my cellphone.

"Hi, Hollis."

"I hope I didn't catch you at a bad time, but I'd like to get together and go over the events of the past few days." I paused. "Maybe we could brainstorm about the Fallen Angels and who might have killed Rory and Abby."

"Uh-huh. What are you up to?"

Good question. I was glad he couldn't see that my bravado was faked. "For my own reasons, I need to get these murders solved as quickly as possible. If I ... if we could find the killer, then we'd both be left alone."

"What's your reason?"

"My reason? How about dealing with Abby's death and just plain survival. I'm trying to figure this out before anyone else gets killed—me, for instance. You seem to have a line on everybody. It looks like all of us, well, except for one, are targets for a killer. There have been two murders based on our book selections. We could be next."

He took an extra moment to answer. "Right. Okay, I'm game. Are you available this evening? I'll come over to your house so we can talk."

I didn't like telling people where I lived, but I knew Gene was testing me.

"Sure, that'd be fine, but wouldn't you rather meet at a restaurant? I could eat a little something. How about you?"

Gene snorted a small laugh. "I'm not that hungry. We can meet at Barnes and Noble. They're open until eleven. They don't rush you and there's a small sandwich and beverage bar. Meet me at seven. It's not too far from you."

How did Gene know that?

For the rest of the day, I focused on clearing my desk. I left a little before five to beat the traffic. At home I dressed hurriedly so that I could arrive before Gene. When he pulled up, I wanted to be able to jot down his license plate. I didn't have to wait long. He drove up in his dark green Honda. I took down his plate number and followed him into the store. Intuition told me I could probably take Gene off my suspect list, but I had to make sure before I asked him for help.

We settled in at the table farthest from the front door. Except for a couple other tables, we had almost the entire lounge area to ourselves.

"Understand me," I said. "I didn't kill Rory or Abby. Assuming we give you the benefit of doubt, too, that leaves Richard, Rena and Miller."

"Thanks for the insta-trial acquittal." He shook his head. "So, now what?"

I leaned forward. "I think we should look at each member one at a time. Go through their backgrounds and find out who has the most on the line."

He looked skeptical. "It's doable, I guess. I have my doubts about our ability to uncover any secrets."

"We have to start somewhere."

He shook his head and smiled again. "Okay. I'll show good faith and share first. I have nothing to lose. I'm a columnist for the *Herald*. I worked there before I went in. My brother is one of the owners, so I didn't have to lie about my past."

I was mildly impressed. I was a *Herald* subscriber, but I never paid attention to bylines. "They always say hiding in plain sight is the best disguise."

Gene suddenly sat straight up. "I am not in disguise. I have never changed my name or tried to hide my conviction. *You* might be, but I'm certainly not material for a blackmailer. I got caught up in a … in a bribery sting. I was stupid, but I learned."

"Okay, okay." My curiosity took over. "So, what do you think you know about me?"

He put two fingers against his forehead. "Let's see. Rebecca Hollis Morgan Lynley, born in Alameda, California. Married William Lynley. No children. Divorced after three years. It coincided with a prison term for insurance fraud. Current residence is Montclair."

I clenched my teeth in anger. "How dare you violate my privacy."

Gene raised his eyebrows. "It's not private information. It's all public. I didn't say I knew where you shopped for clothes. Although, you should consider going a little more upscale."

I looked at him in disbelief. After a moment, a smile creased my face. "I'm not a clothes hound like you. How do you know these things?"

He relaxed. "The stitching on your clothes is a real giveaway—"

"Not my clothes. How do you know about my background?"

"I never join anything without knowing who the members are."

A wise idea.

I took my notepad from my purse.

"Hey, what's with the paper and pen?"

No more answers. I had a few questions of my own. "How do you know where I live?"

He smiled down at the bottle of water he'd brought with him. "Don't worry, I haven't been to your house. I only know your address. Why don't you tell me what you're up to and maybe I can help you."

"Maybe."

Gene stood. "I think we better get something to munch on. This may take a while."

I didn't have an appetite, so I ordered an iced tea. Gene bought a turkey sandwich, four cookies and a bag of chips.

Unwrapping the sandwich, he said, "Miller's real name is Marshall Sloane. I found out he served four years in Corona for embezzling bonds from his clients' stock portfolios. Appears our boy had a brother with quite a cocaine habit. Which I would venture to say was why he didn't get more time. He tried to save his brother. I couldn't find out anything more on his family, but he used to live in Marin County … in Cliffside Shores."

"Interesting. It's not a lot, but having a real name gives me a little more to go on. Miller's quiet and can be defensive. Maybe he couldn't take Rory's pressure anymore."

"He had to have a better reason than that."

"Maybe we could follow—"

"Hollis, I'll try to help you, but I don't want to join you in the crusade."

"Okay, because—"

"No, wait. I'll help you because if you pull this off before the police do, I want your story for the *Herald*."

"You've got it." My promise to Ed to avoid the media came back to me, but surely once this was over, if I found the killer, our firm would be even more sought after.

"Cliffside Shores is expensive real estate. Miller always gets us free books. Do you think he manages a bookstore?"

He shrugged. "More likely he owns a bookstore. All I know is he tried to get us to think he worked for a newspaper. I checked. He doesn't. For obvious reasons, I'd know if he did."

"He says the books are from a distribution house."

"Maybe. I don't know."

"Tell me about Rena."

A smile crept to his lips. "Ah, the lady in black."

"Yeah, what's with that?"

Gene cut his eyes to look at the ceiling. "Hollis, I can't believe you sometimes. Haven't you noticed Rena is always in DKNY? She hasn't worn the same thing twice, and she knows what looks good on her. It's her style. Black is her color. She always wears it."

"Do you write a fashion column for the paper? Could we move past her wardrobe for a moment? What did she go up for?"

"Don't paralegals read the newspaper? Do you remember the story involving a budding local fashion designer paying her bills with bad checks and writing other bad checks to cover them?"

"That was Rena?"

"It was Marilyn Shana Reynolds. Her picture was in the *Herald*, but I didn't recognize her until later. It was lousy photography. She only spent one year inside. She got out because she had to take care of her mother. She was under house arrest for another year. She has a little boy from her marriage to a political consultant. He left when she went in. Sound familiar? I think she must work as a fashion buyer. That's how she gets her clothes. I bet she has a great employee discount. I wonder if she could get me a pair of—"

"Please try and focus. Where does she live now?"

"The last address I could find was in Berkeley."

I scrambled to take down the information. There was only one other person I wanted information on. "Now, tell me about Rory."

He nodded, digging into his bag of chips. "Well, after the murder, I did a little investigating of my own. Once I had his alias from the police, and Miller told us about his extortion conviction, I had enough to look him up in our archives. He'd been arrested twice before but had only one conviction. If he was ever married, it must have been over long ago."

He took a long swallow of his water.

"Anything else? What brand of jeans did he wear?"

"Don't be cute. The guy did have expensive habits. He owned a loft in San Francisco with a three-hundred-sixty-degree view. His job—and I use that term loosely—was real estate broker. He specialized in the very rich. I don't think his specialty was selling houses as much as it was gleaning information from them. Trust me. You'd never want him to have an open house to show your home."

Why would a guy like that want to be in our little book club? I wanted to get back home and go over everything to see if I could connect the dots. I was tired, but I had to pull a couple of loose strings to see what might unravel.

I cleared my throat. "Gene, who is Reverend Campbell?"

Gene's eyes became slits. Thank goodness looks couldn't kill. "Who in the hell have you been talking to?"

His anger flicked at me like a high flame. I cringed.

"I … I did some research, and I—"

"He's none of your business." His face turned red. "Very

smart. You pumped me for information before you attacked. You're in over your head, Hollis. Be a good little girl and—"

That did it. I lowered my voice. "Look, you drone, don't speak to me like I'm an imbecile. I've got a lot to lose here and I'm not going to stop looking for the killer, so you be—"

"Excuse me." One of the servers appeared at our side.

"What?" we said in unison.

He shifted on his feet. "Look, could you keep it down? Or you're going to have to leave. It's not fair to everyone else here."

I looked into the curious, but clearly annoyed, stares of the couple at the next table and an elderly man sitting at the table beyond them.

"I'm sorry. I didn't realize."

"Yeah, we were rude." Gene turned to the couple and mouthed, "Sorry." Then he turned back to me and said in a low voice, "Where did you hear about David?"

I wasn't ready to reveal my source, but I needed to know more.

"I told you, I did some research. Is he important to you?"

He started to pull at his eyebrows. "Yeah, he's important. I'm going to get more coffee."

He didn't ask if I wanted anything.

When he returned, we sat in silence for a few moments.

"Gene, I'm not trying to out you or get you in trouble. I'm not going back to prison. While I find it hard to believe you could kill anyone, if someone had told me you had a flash temper, I would have found that hard to believe, too, until just now."

He took a long sip of coffee. "It's doesn't just involve me. David's a minister. His church would frown on our ... our relationship. I'll do anything to protect him."

"I'm sorry." I chose my next words carefully. "Was Rory blackmailing you?"

"No." Gene caught his protest when the server looked over at us. "No. I wasn't being blackmailed."

"You can see you'd have an excellent motive. I mean ... I

mean if Rory found out about the two of you."

Gene glared at me. "That's it. I'm out of here."

I returned to my lukewarm tea.

Methinks he doth protest too much.

CHAPTER TWELVE

A T FIVE A.M., the office was as silent as a sleeping child, except for the faraway hum of a vacuum on the floor above. The cleaning crew would be leaving soon. In Mark's office I booted up his computer, called up Inquiry First and keyed in his password. I would make sure that Mark never knew I was here. I glanced at the new files Avery had placed in his inbox. A few simple probate cases; nothing I couldn't handle in a few hours.

I tried Rena's name first—or Marilyn, as I now knew her. I entered all the information Gene had given me. After a few seconds, I hit confirm to verify my request and download the report. My screen scrolled with lines of text, but it took fifteen minutes for the report to download and be sent to my printer. I looked up at the clock. At this rate, it would take me an hour to get printouts for Miller and Rory. By then I could be at risk of running into Ed, who usually came in early. I decided to use the central printer in the workroom at the same time.

Rena done, I submitted Miller's data and waited for the computer to respond. I looked over my notes from Gene. If I had only one shot at this, I wanted Abby's information as well. There might be some connection to Rory. From talking with Abby, it was clear, at first, that she didn't know who blackmailed her or who killed Rory. It was also clear Rory's murderer thought she did. That was enough to get her killed.

Thirty minutes.

I downloaded Rory's information. Then I ran down the hallway to get Miller's from the high speed central printer. Back in Mark's office, I was tempted to read the screen. Downloading was taking too much time. Likely another Inquiry First beta version flaw. I glanced up at the clock. It was already going on six thirty. I quickly entered Abby's name for a download and sent her data to the central printer. I had time for one last name: Richard.

I gathered up the sizable stack of printouts and stuffed it all into a huge manila envelope I shoved under my desk. I had maybe ten minutes before Ed showed up and I didn't want the printouts out in the open where he might see them. The software output clock showed twelve minutes to complete Richard's download. I'd send his printout to my desk.

Making another dash to the central printer, I grabbed Abby's printout and crossed into the lobby, where I turned on the main office lights. I was just heading back to my office when I heard the lock click on the entry door.

"Hollis, what are you doing here so early?" Avery asked.

I forgot he had a hearing in Los Angeles. "I couldn't sleep. I knew you'd have some work for me. So I followed my hunch and came in early."

We walked back toward my office. I made the printout into what I hoped looked like an innocent roll of paper.

He eyed me with curiosity. "How long have you been here?"

"Not long." *Relatively speaking.*

He paused in my doorway. Richard's download had completed. The bright orange ready flash on the computer screen shone like a beacon. I slipped past Avery to stand in front of my computer and grabbed the top file folder from my inbox.

If he noticed any strangeness in my moves, or the flashing light, he said nothing.

"My goodness, this is impressive." Ed came to the door. "I couldn't believe it when I saw the lights. Both of you here … Avery, I thought you'd be on your way to the airport."

"I'm headed there now. I just stopped by to pick up some additional worksheets Mark and Hollis prepared." Avery moved back out into the hallway to give Ed a friendly pat on the back.

"That's right. You've got the Landry matter. I'm glad I caught you before you left. I need to speak to you about Mrs. Ignacio's trust. It will only take a couple of minutes. Let me put my briefcase down and I'll come see you." Ed turned to look at me. "Good morning, Hollis."

"Good morning, Ed."

After their voices faded down the hallway, I hit the print key.

By the time the rest of the office had arrived, I was well into my first assignment. I was grateful that the morning passed without surprise. The protruding envelope at my feet made me anxious. At lunchtime, I moved it to my car. After having my prison cell tossed by a fellow inmate, I learned to consider paranoia a friend.

With Avery out of the office, I had few interruptions. Only Mark popped in a couple of times with questions and simple requests. By the afternoon, I was counting down the hours to the end of the day. Finishing up with a few client calls, I left a half hour early. After all, I had come in early.

AT HOME, I put on a pot of hot water and sat down at the kitchen table to work. I tackled the thinnest run: Rena. It only took me a few minutes to figure out how Inquiry First sorted information with the oldest records first. Gene was right. It was amazing how much of our lives were captured under "public information." Rena was born in southern California to Barbara and Lloyd Clarkson. She attended Cal State University Los Angeles and received a degree in fashion design. There was a notation she was one of the youngest people to receive an award nomination from the Council of American Fashion Designers for women's wear. At twenty-two, she married Devon Reynolds. Seven months later, a son, Christopher, was born. Her credit report covered the next three pages. At least Inquiry First didn't give out her social security number.

I chuckled. Why was I always so worried about identity theft? The joke would be on the person who thought they wanted to be me.

I flipped through her financials. She had a lot of credit cards for someone so young. Judging from the notations, she struggled under the load, and many of her debts ended up with collection agencies. She filed for bankruptcy. I returned to the narrative section of the report. Despite the bankruptcy, she petitioned and received permission from the court to be the trustee of her mother's estate. Except for a police action three-and-a-half years ago for fraudulent check writing, her record was clean. It surprised me to see how fast the court had acted to take her off the street. Rena must have pleaded "No Contest." If so, that would give us something in common— we'd both had bad advice. I went back to look at the personal section. Her husband filed for divorce three days after her arrest. *Great guy.* Custody of Christopher was given to Rena's mother. Rena served her time at the California Institution for Women. Released from parole a little over a year ago, she lived with her mother in El Cerrito, California.

I took a sip of pinot noir. She had chosen to do her five hundred hours of community service at a library. No wonder Richard and Jeffrey thought she might fit in. Other than her current employer being Neiman Marcus, a store I could only afford to walk past, I found little else out of the ordinary.

I picked up the next printout: Miller Thornton, aka Marshall Sloane.

Miller was from Illinois. He joined the Marines out of high school and served in the National Guard. My interest was piqued when I read he received a medal for rescuing his squad leader. *Miller*? I wondered if they had that backwards. He went on to get a degree in education and was briefly employed as a high school teacher. He later returned for a master's degree in finance. Odd combination, but if Illinois' teachers' salaries were on par with those of California's, I could understand his thinking. I skimmed through the file. He got his stock exchange license when he was thirty and married Gloria Mori around the same time. She must have taught him origami. They lived in Marin County—Sausalito—and then moved to Cliffside Shores. His wife must have the money. Miller had been sentenced to three years for bond embezzlement, followed by three years on parole. There was no mention of the brother with a cocaine habit and no indication of what secret Rory might have had on him.

The file on Rory was twice the size of Miller's. Born Michael Rollins in Hayward, California, Rory attended Cal State University there. No degree was listed. Maybe he never earned one. He was forty-one when he died, the day before his forty-second birthday. His first arrest had been fifteen years earlier, for computer hacking, but he was released without a conviction. Three years later he was arrested a second time, for extortion. Once again, no conviction. He received a real estate broker's license about ten years ago. Not too long after, he was finally convicted of computer fraud and extortion. He went to Kern Prison and served his full sentence. I found that a bit odd. Knowing our crowded jail system, he should have been out a lot earlier. Under California's early release program, they let out bank robbers sooner than that. I went to his personal data section. Divorced. His little girl lived with her mother.

The thickness of Rory's file had little to do with actual information. There were at least eight pages of address changes. A blackmailer probably had to stay on the move. His

last address was here in Oakland. The file hadn't been updated
with his death notice.

I needed a break. Closing my eyes, I leaned back in my chair.
It was only days since Abby had been killed and almost a week
since Rory's death. Abby was the closest I'd had to a friend. I
wanted to find her killer for her sake and mine. One thing I
was willing to bet on: whoever killed Abby also killed Rory.

I CALLED AND made an appointment with Lily's doctor,
Wade Walker. At first the receptionist was reluctant to give me
a time slot, but when I dropped the name of the law firm, she
graciously put me down for fifteen minutes the next day. I was
glad I'd have time to think of what to say.

"Dr. Walker will be fitting you in, so please don't be late."

Unfortunately, when I slipped away from work and arrived
the next day, it was Dr. Walker who was late. He rushed in the
waiting room with his arm outstretched. We shook hands.

"Miss Morgan, how can I help you?" He led me to a large
office with a wall of windows facing the bay, where we sat in
comfortable overstuffed chairs around a small coffee table.

"I'm actually here about one of your patients and our client,
Lily Wilson."

Dr. Walker's face flashed an emotion I initially read as
annoyance; then he quickly shifted to seeming indifference.

"Lily Wilson, yes, of course. She's a wonderful woman. In
relatively good health, considering her age."

"Uh, can you tell me if she has cataracts?"

"I'm sorry. You're an attorney for Mrs. Wilson?"

I was afraid of this. "No, I work for the law firm that
represents Mrs. Wilson's estate."

"I see. Then you know I can't reveal any medical information."

I was treading on thin ice, but all I could think of was the
worry on Marla's face.

"Doctor, we have reason to believe Lily Wilson may be
receiving the wrong medication. Before I go any further down

this trail, it would be very helpful if you could verify she's receiving the proper medicine."

"Are you making an accusation against me?"

I sat up in the chair. "Oh, no. Not at all. It's just some of the residents have seen a recent change for the worse in her behavior and maybe health. There's some question as to whether her medication has been adjusted."

"Has anyone spoken with the director?"

"I can't answer that. I don't know."

He went over to his desk and tapped on his keyboard. He evidently found what he was looking for and read the screen.

After a moment he turned to me. "As I said, there's nothing I can say to you about Mrs. Wilson. However, I'm scheduled to give her a regular examination in a few days. I'll review her chart and dosage."

On my way home, I remembered my mother once told me, "If you were a dog, you'd be a rottweiler." Once I got something in my head, I wouldn't let go. At first I thought she meant this as a put-down, but now I considered it a compliment. Until I hit a wall I couldn't see my way around, I'd go forward with finding Abby's killer. I wouldn't let that person get away with Abby's death or kill my chance for a pardon. There was this thing with Lily, too. I really hoped Marla was overreacting.

It was ten p.m., and I realized I hadn't gone through my mail. On top of the stack was a tan envelope from the Department of Corrections & Rehabilitation. I opened it with growing trepidation. There was just one sheet of paper. I could hardly bear to read it. The words were few. The notice indicated the date, location and time of my hearing.

I consulted my watch and did the calculations—six weeks, eight days, ten hours and forty-seven minutes to freedom. If nothing screwed it up.

CHAPTER THIRTEEN

THE NEXT MORNING I went to Mark's office to put several date holds on his calendar. We needed to prep our cases together. Avery would be back late in the afternoon and it was a chance for Mark, with me pushing him, to shine. He wasn't there so I left him a note. I caught myself. Except for the seniors, I hadn't helped anyone in a long time. I'd almost forgotten how it felt to help someone.

It was a slow workday, so I used the rest of the morning to lay out potential killer interview questions on a legal pad. I went through my Inquiry First pages. It was clear the only way I'd get tough questions answered would be with direct confrontation.

"What are you concentrating so hard on?"

My head snapped up. Mark stood in my doorway eating an apple.

I rolled my chair to the left of my desk, hoping to block any view he might have of my monitor. "I'm working on getting the Landry matter ready for Avery. Did you get my note?"

"That's why I'm here. Avery indicated Mrs. Landry left no heirs and no will, but I remembered something in the paper about her having a strong participation in her church. Mrs. Landry wasn't stupid. She worked hard for her money. I checked with the pastor at the church where she was buried and, sure enough, she had a will, or what we'd call a poor excuse for a will."

"Bravo, Mark. Good work. So, let me guess, the will was handwritten on the back of an envelope?"

"Just about. It was on the back of a paper church fan, but it still had two witnessed signatures."

"Why hadn't the pastor come forward?"

"He was going to. He didn't think things would move so quickly and he had several church issues that were taking up his time."

"Well, I guess that means I can move on to getting the estate documents ready for probate. Did you get the fan?"

"I'm on my way to pick it up now." Mark stood tall. His tone was confident.

"Great. We can have everything set up by the time Avery gets back." I smiled. I had to hand it to him. Mark deserved full credit on this one. "We won't get as many billable hours, but it will give us a little breathing room to work on new clients."

He grinned and gave me a mock salute.

I smiled. I needed breathing room all right, but not to work on new clients—to finish obtaining references.

THE OFFICE OF the center's director, Opal Murray, was the farthest from the front door. In the years I'd been coming to visit the seniors, I'd never been inside. It was furnished modestly in neutral tones and had three small windows covered with drapes and sheers. With its carpeted floors and small colorful area rugs, it exuded warmth, which was negated by the cold looks cast by the woman sitting at the large desk.

"You have a very nice office."

"Thank you," Opal responded primly. "I've never taken the time to formally tell you, but I want to thank you and your firm for all you're doing to assist the seniors. It's a tremendous help to us and I know the seniors are happy as well."

I smiled graciously. "We feel pretty good about our participation."

She smiled back and paused. She was obviously waiting for me to get to the point.

"Ms. Murray ... Opal, this is a little awkward, but I'm going to just jump in. I've noticed Lily Wilson doesn't seem to be herself. She's become more absentminded and frail, almost overnight."

She tapped her left forefinger to her lips. "I see. Do you think she needs special care? Is she a danger to herself, or others?"

I shook my head. "No, she told me she was taking this new medicine and I thought it might be having a detrimental effect on her."

Opal frowned. "I'm not aware of any new medication for her. She's a long-time resident and her treatment regimen hasn't varied for the last two years. Maybe you misunderstood."

I was now out on the proverbial limb with a saw in hand. "Well, she didn't actually tell me, I just happened to notice she's taking a pill of another color. She has been dealing with a heart condition and—"

"Hold on a moment. I can't discuss her condition with you." She opened a folder. "Her physician is due to see her later on this week. I'll alert him to your concerns."

My frustration gauge was starting to climb. If I was having this much difficulty trying to communicate, how much harder must it be for the seniors?

"I've spoken with the doctor. He couldn't tell me anything, either." I sighed. "I just want to make sure she's getting the proper medication."

A knowing smile came to Opal's face. "I understand and appreciate your efforts. We'll take it from here."

I got up. "Thank you."

"Oh, and you can tell Marla Jacobs she can stop pulling the fire alarm."

CLAY HANDED BACK my manila envelope.

"It's a good statement. Heartfelt but not a soap opera. I like the fact that you made a point of accepting responsibility. That will go over well with Pine."

I nodded. I had no problem writing complicated legal briefs for Avery's clients, but this simple statement had taken a lot out of me.

"Thanks, Clay. I'll get the changes back to you before the end of the week." I put the envelope in my backpack. "I know my reference letters have to be in at least two weeks prior to my hearing date."

He came from around his desk. "*At least* two weeks prior. I'd like to file them three weeks in advance."

"I don't know if—"

"I'm going to push you on this. Get them in as soon as possible. Is that going to be a problem?"

I didn't try to hide my deep sigh. "No. I'll make it happen."

I made sure he couldn't hear me mumble that it would be at the same time I was trying to get off the murder suspect radar screen.

I CHECKED THE time. Gene had called and asked if I wanted to attend Abby's memorial with him.

He had apparently decided to forgive me after our last conversation. "I would have asked the same questions, if the shoe had been on the other foot."

I was glad to be in his company.

The service was small and low key. Abby would have liked it. At the front of the chapel was a picture of a younger, smiling Abby. Her husband appeared to be in a fog. My heart went out to him. Gene and I sat in the last row, next to the door. No one else from the club was there.

"Had any luck?" Gene whispered.

"Ssh … wait until this is over. I came to say goodbye to Abby."

"Sure, sorry." He leaned in. "Since when did you become so situation appropriate?"

I focused on the service. Gratefully, it was over in less than an hour. Not wanting to explain how we knew Abby, Gene and I didn't think it wise to pay our respects to the family. We walked silently back to the car.

"So, are you having any luck?" He buckled himself in and drove the car out of the church lot.

"No." I was ready to take him off my list of possible suspects but couldn't totally let go of considering his strong motive. "I talked with Richard and he seemed unduly agitated. I've got a lot of little pieces, but nothing sticks together."

"I know a lot of people in San Francisco real estate. I could check around and see if any of them knew Rory."

I nodded absently in agreement. I was ready to move on to my next suspect.

"I COULDN'T BELIEVE it when I saw your name show up on caller ID," Richard said.

"Thank you for taking my call."

"Believe me, it crossed my mind not to. What do you want?"

Best to cut to the chase. "I'm taking you up on your offer to help figure out who killed Abby and Rory. I mean, I know now that Rory pointed at Abby, not me. I didn't lie to you." I took a deep breath. "So who from our club would want her and Rory dead? The only person we … well, the one I don't know anything about is Rena."

"Since I brought her into the club, you think I introduced a murderer to the group?"

When he put it that way, I understood his wary tone of voice. "Believe me, I'm as unhappy as you are. You were right about me wanting to solve the murders. I have a reason I want to see them solved."

"Apology accepted."

He agreed to meet me after work.

Considering that the small downtown Oakland Plaza was off the beaten path and backed one of the older storefronts along Telegraph Avenue, it had quite a few patrons. We sat on stone blocks that circled a raised flower bed.

"Let me share what I've been thinking." I looked straight at Richard. "Rena is our biggest unknown. The killings didn't start until after she joined our group."

Richard nodded. "That's true enough, but what's her motive?"

"That's where my theory breaks apart. Maybe she's a sociopath?"

He rolled his eyes.

"All right. You tell me why I should eliminate her from my list."

"What list? You've been watching too much TV or reading too many books." Rubbing his buzz cut, he sounded more than a little agitated. "I knew this would happen if I got involved. Get real, Hollis. We could be the next ones to be killed."

"I know, and no, I don't want to be the next victim. A few days ago you asked for my help."

"Yeah, well, I've moved on. It was a good book club." He paused. "Am I still on your suspect list?"

I thought for a minute. "To be honest, I don't know." I held his gaze. "Why did Rory blackmail you?"

He started to say something then changed his mind. "I told you my wife is a corporate executive. She can't afford to have it known her husband was a felon."

He was lying. I wondered if that was how I looked to others.

I backed off and took another tack. "All right. I'm sorry. So tell me what you know about Rena."

Richard took a sip from his coffee. "I met her through my wife's business. She was just getting off parole. Rena applied for a business loan and was turned down. Rachel, my wife, came home and told me how this young woman was trying to get back on her feet, but it wasn't going to happen, even though she tried to do all the right things. She'd moved away from her old friends, got a college degree and a decent job. Granted, it was a low-paying clerical position, but Rena took it."

"It was nice of you to reach out."

"While on parole, I promised myself that if I ever got out of this mess, I'd help others trying to go straight."

"Seems a bit risky, with a wife who has a high profile job."

His eyes flickered away from mine. "I needed to do it." Richard took a deep breath. "Anyway, Jeffrey Wallace got Rena's file and said he'd approach her about joining our group."

"No, I mean for your wife. Having a husband who is an ex-felon helping his ex-felon friends."

He turned pale. "Rachel—"

"The last time we talked, you said your wife's name was Cristina."

He had that deer-in-the-headlights stare. "What are you saying?"

"Does your wife know you're an ex-felon?"

He put his head in his hands, but it seemed like an act.

"Did Rory want more money? Did you kill Rory?"

Richard got up and walked around the circle. A young woman with a stroller and a dog on a leash sat across from us. The dog started to bark when Richard passed by. I didn't move.

He sat back down. "I'm not going to lie to you; I wanted to kill him. I didn't know that 'him' was Rory until after the police told me." He put his hand on my shoulder. "I need you to believe me."

I gave him my best half smile and shrugged out of his hand.

"I want to believe you."

I wasn't sure I did. He was a liar, and a bad one.

"YOU DID WHAT?" I blurted.

Marla patted my hand and looked around the community

room. Tiny looked up momentarily from the television but immediately turned back to her game show. We sat in the window alcove away from the others, but I knew our privacy could be aborted at any time.

"You need to watch yourself. You're under a lot of stress right now. You don't need to be getting all excited."

She shook her head.

"Marla, you can't be looking in other resident files. First of all, it's against the law and second, even if they don't have you arrested, they can kick you out of here. Remember what happened to Mr. Boyd?"

Mr. Boyd had been asked to leave after it was discovered he took pictures of the female residents for his enjoyment. Back then I had only been coming to the center for a couple of weeks, but the look of despair on his face at the prospect of being homeless haunted me for months.

"I don't care." She crossed her arms over her chest. "I tell you, Lily's getting worse. When you see her today, talk to her. You'll see what I'm talking about."

"All right, tell me what you found out."

Marla looked over her shoulder. "Well, for one thing, doctor whatever-his-name-is never mentioned anything about your visit or checking into Lily's medications. He said Lily seemed agitated and may require a tranquilizer. He authorized the center's nursing staff to administer it, if they felt it necessary."

"Interesting." I flashed back to prison, where certain inmates considered to be "agitated" were medicated into near zombieism in order to keep them under control. I didn't think it would be a good idea to share this information with Marla.

"That's not the important thing. Her chart didn't list any changes to her medication type or dosage. No changes since the year before last."

"Interesting."

GLAD TO BE home, I took off my shoes and fixed a pot of hot

tea, assuming the activities of normalcy. I needed to put my questions about Lily on hold. I could only effectively handle one issue at a time. I knew the police would be going over Rory's life with a magnifying glass. Like Richard said, Rory was a nitpicker. At club meetings he kept notes on who said what and even who brought refreshments.

He used a ledger.

I was betting they hadn't found Rory's blackmail ledger, at least not the one that mattered. The one with the list of his victims. It would likely point to one of the Fallen Angels, who would then be hauled off to jail.

I Googled Rory's last address. A Linda Rollins was shown as one of the occupants. Alongside her name was a phone number. My heart beat rapidly as I waited for someone to answer.

I responded to a weak greeting. "I'm trying to reach Linda Rollins. Is she available?"

"Are you a reporter?"

"No, no, not at all. I was a friend of Ror … Michael's and I wanted to talk to Ms. Rollins."

There was silence.

More silence.

"Hello. Are you still there?"

"Are you one of his girlfriends?"

"No, I'm just a friend. Really. He and I were in the same book club."

The laughter that followed caught me off guard. It went on almost as long as the silence had. "I'm sorry, darlin'. I can't quite picture Michael in a book club."

"Ror … I mean Michael, was a member in good standing of our club. I just had a couple of questions for Linda, if she can just spare the time."

"I'm Linda. What kind of questions?"

"Well, for one, I wanted to find out if this is where he lived. Our club wanted to send flowers. Are you his … his sister?"

"I'm his mother. Don't bother with any flowers. I'm allergic."

"Oh, I'm sorry, Mrs. Rollins. Did he live with you?"

"Why?"

"It's just that he borrowed a library book from me and I wondered if you'd noticed any books he might have had lying around?"

"No, I don't go through his stuff. He only slept here when he didn't want to drive back to San Francisco. There's no point looking in either place because the police already took everything."

"Okay. Well, I won't bother you any longer. I'm sorry for your loss."

After hanging up, I thought of one other question to ask her. Maybe she'd tell me if she knew any of Rory's friends. I dialed again.

"Hello." This time a man answered. It was my turn to be silent. My brain went into overdrive.

How could it be?

I slammed the phone down. It was Bill.

CHAPTER FOURTEEN

THE WHISTLE ON the teakettle blew. I poured the boiling water over the leaves and a gentle jasmine fragrance floated throughout the kitchen. I waited to feel the tension leave my shoulders as I poured the steaming water into my mug, but this time it didn't happen. I couldn't fathom Bill picking up Rory's mom's phone. By now the police probably knew the connection between Bill and Rory, and tomorrow I'd tell them where they could find him.

It would be nine p.m. in Colorado. I ignored the growing pit in my stomach. Rita would be fixing tomorrow's lunches for the girls. Kirk would be finishing cleaning the kitchen and half-listening to the news. I hadn't seen any of them for years, but I knew their routine because I knew my sister. I could think of a number of reasons I could put off calling her, but waiting wouldn't make it any easier.

Rita was older than me by five years, but it felt more like ten. We were completely different. I was like our dad, Rita like our mother. She was drop dead gorgeous, witty and charming and had a good sense of humor. Unfortunately, she was also manipulative, rigid, judgmental and had a harsh tongue. Dad and I often commiserated. We felt as if we were being run over by two sixteen-wheelers.

I set my shoulders and picked up the phone.

"Rita, it's Rebecca. How are you?" I wouldn't even try to get her to call me Hollis.

"You got my message about Bill." No greeting. Just the statement, not a question. No acknowledgment we hadn't spoken since my trial.

"I didn't talk to him. He left a message and told me what he wanted." My voice was small.

"So, why are you calling?"

Even though I'd steeled myself for my sister's accusatory tone, I could never be ready enough. She was a force I'd never learned to reckon with. "I need a favor."

"You've got to be kidding. Are you in trouble again?"

"Rita, you make it sound like I'm some sort of repeat offender. I only got into trouble once."

"Wasn't once enough? I referred my closest friends to you and Bill, and you defrauded them." She paused. "You must be desperate if you're contacting me."

I took a deep breath. She was right; I was desperate and I needed her. "There's a chance I can have my conviction erased and be given a pardon. Well, not a full pardon, but a legal acknowledgment I am 'rehabilitated,' and I wouldn't have a conviction on my record."

"And?"

I swallowed. "I need a family reference."

She laughed with harshness. "I can see why you didn't go to Mom or Dad. They think what you did was a terrible thing and that you got the punishment you deserved. Frankly, so do I."

I often wondered where the prototypes for functional families existed. My family was about as close as strangers who happened to get stranded in a bus station together. As children, my mother dressed Rita and me alike. We attended school events, went to church and visited the less fortunate.

We pretended. We wanted to be like everybody else, to fit in. My family didn't have a clue how to function. That was why we never went on vacation. I'm sure the thought of being alone together trying to seek enjoyment with only one another to rely on terrified my parents.

Even after hearing that Bill had set me up, that I was only guilty of putting my trust in the wrong person, my family judged me and found me wanting.

"Rita, I won't justify my actions or make excuses. I served my time with good behavior and now I'm trying to get on with my life. I want to pick up where I left off. I've been working in a law firm for five years. I want to go back and finish law school." She was listening; that was a good sign. "In order to do that, I need to get my record cleared. I need a family reference for that. Will you help me?"

"I honestly don't know, Becca."

I was encouraged to hear her use my nickname. "What do you want from me? What can I do?"

"You never called until now. I need to think. To be truthful, I'm glad you stayed away. Kirk was so embarrassed to have a sister-in-law in prison."

This was the excuse they used for not visiting in prison, although I knew that she was really the embarrassed one. Kirk was too easygoing to care.

"I need it within the next ten days. I'll send you the form. You have to send it back to my attorney certified mail. I'll pay the postage."

She was quiet.

"Rita?"

"Kirk has cancer." Her voice was toneless.

"Oh, Ri, I'm so sorry." I really was sorry for Kirk, for the family. I couldn't imagine my sister having to deal with someone else's feelings. "Is he going to be all right?"

"They don't know. He started treatment two days ago. It's his prostate. He waited a long time to have it checked out." Her voice caught. "I haven't told Mom or Dad, or anyone else. The girls don't even know."

The girls were fourteen and sixteen. They should be able to handle the news about their father. I wasn't so sure about our parents. They wouldn't know how to respond. At the very least, they might see it as an imposition and a disruption in their lives.

"Is there anything I can do?"

"You? No, no, there's nothing." Her voice returned to full strength. "We'll deal with this. Go ahead and send your form. I don't have time to write a treatise, but I'll try to get something to your attorney by next week. Can you email the form?"

She had caught me off guard. I couldn't disguise my surprise. My sister was technology-phobic. "You know how to work email?"

"Don't be so patronizing. I'm not the idiot you think I am."

"Ri, I didn't mean—"

"Yes, you did, but it's okay. If you can change, so can I. I've been taking classes at the community college. Gina's class is almost completely computerized and I wanted to be able to help her with her homework."

Whether it was due to the influence of my nieces or her own ambitions, Rita had changed.

"Okay then, give me your email address. I'll also overnight you a postage-paid envelope." I took a moment. "Rita, thank you very much. I'm sorry to hear about Kirk. I know you may not be able to think of anything now, but … but if there's anything I can do to help out, please let me know."

"Thanks, Becca, I appreciate your offer. I will."

Nicely said, but we both knew she wouldn't.

IN THE OFFICE the next day, I tried to keep my mind on my work, but it was only half there; the other half was with the Fallen Angels. By day's end, I'd tossed the last of my work on a stack of files that teetered precariously on top of my lateral file cabinet. Technically, it was work off of my desk and ready for the main file room. My last venture into the file room was more than six months ago. Usually I convinced one of the clerks to help me in exchange for doing court runs. I steered clear of the file room because of my hatred of filing, but the result was that I couldn't take long vacations; no one would be able to find a case without me.

I scrambled to get ready for our weekly meeting. Avery's team meetings were the key to his success. Not only did we review cases, we also discussed them in detail to ensure we weren't working at cross purposes. Avery was a stickler for the nuts and bolts. Mark would have to catch on.

Avery's office was located in a prime location in one of the four oversized corner suites. In addition to his large desk, he had a sitting area and a small conference table. That table was clear now except for a thin folder and a couple of California law books.

Avery sat between us at the head of the table. "Mark, I have to admit you did good work on the Landry matter. You saved the firm and the estate quite a bit of time and money."

Mark made a futile attempt to suppress his broad smile.

Avery opened up the next folder. "I anticipate this next matter will take four to six months if we have to go to trial. A lot less if we can settle with the family."

"What are the odds of getting the family to settle?" Mark asked.

Avery didn't look up. "Good, as a matter of fact. Imelda Riddick was last of her line of Phoenix Riddicks. No children, just several nieces and nephews once removed. She leaves an estate of close to two million dollars, not including a five-thousand-square-foot house down on the coast."

"I take it she died without a will," I said.

Avery turned to me. "No, she had a will. However, it was very old. She made it out before she got married, when she was in her twenties. She died a week ago at age eighty-nine."

Mark took notes on his legal pad. "Did she marry money, or is it her family's?"

"A little of both. George Riddick died twenty years ago. In this instance, money attracted more money." Avery pulled out a single sheet of paper from the folder. "One of Triple D's founding partners drew up the will in nineteen forty-seven. Riddick named us the attorney of record and the executor. Mark, I need you to draw up the declarations for the nieces and nephews. Seven of them are still living. Find them and get their signatures. Hollis can help you draft the declarations.

"Hollis, I want you to find the case law that supports our contention that the original will document still stands. However, approach it from the family's point of view and find any holes that could be used to punch through the will, argue in the alternative. I may be over-cautious, but I don't want to be caught off guard."

I nodded, taking notes. Work like this always got my adrenaline going. My eyes connected with Mark's, and I gave him a reassuring smile.

I asked, "Avery, how do you want us to bill our hours?"

He closed the folder and pushed it toward me. "You can charge a little overtime, but I don't think you'll need much. We'll keep meeting weekly for updates. If something comes up, or you hit a wall, see me immediately." He leaned back in the chair. "Mark, it might not be easy getting the signatures. I want you to also gather information about the lifestyles of the nieces and nephews, just in case I have to negotiate a settlement."

Mark nodded. "I'll get the job done."

Avery looked skeptical. "Use Hollis to help you and don't piss them off. If you can't get someone to sign, just back off and let me know."

Under California law, the legal work a paralegal can do is limited and unlimited at the same time. Paralegals can pretty much do anything a lawyer can as long as they do it under the supervision and name of a licensed attorney. One thing paralegals cannot do, however, is appear before the court.

At times such as these, it really hit home that if I hadn't made one mistake, one big mistake, I'd be sitting in Mark's office. I resolved to finish gathering all my references by the end of the week.

Avery spent the remaining time going through the open cases.

I motioned to a file in front of me. "Avery, I saw Lily yesterday. She wanted to know when her trust documents would be ready. Did you have a chance to look them over?"

"Darn it. Sorry, Hollis. I put them on the back burner. I'll get them back to you this afternoon." Avery wrote himself a note. "Pro bono cases are okay, but no more for a while."

"Is it okay if I order the appraisal? I don't think she has a sharp enough memory of her personal and household items to be able to suggest a value."

Avery nodded. "Her residence is *that* large?"

"I've only been by there once, but it was pretty impressive."

"Then tell me why we treat her as pro bono? She can afford to pay us out of the sale of her assets."

I knew the day would come when I'd have to explain why we helped Lily for free.

I took a deep breath and explained how I hadn't discovered Lily's healthy financial position until after I had promised Triple D would assist her. She was convinced the government was stealing her money and about to take her home. It wasn't until I met with the county worker that I discovered the government had no intention of taking her home and wanted only to pay her for the use of an easement. By then it was too late.

"I see," Avery said. "Well, let's put an end to this. I don't want you to order an appraisal. It's just more money that won't be reimbursed. I want you to take an inventory of all the belongings. I'll turn your list over to an evaluator who owes me a favor."

His answer was an implied slap on the wrist. "I'll do it next week."

After the meeting, I followed Mark to his office. "I have no problem drafting those declarations." I couldn't control the eagerness in my voice. "They're pretty straightforward. Then you can focus on securing signatures."

"Okay, Hollis, what's going on? What do you really want?"

I put on a show of being insulted. Using a self-righteous tone, I said, "How can you question my motives? We're a team. I want to pitch in. Actually, I could help you locate the beneficiaries, or ... or maybe even assist in getting them to sign."

Mark shook his head. "Oh, *that's* it. Sure, you can take an active role."

I took a mission-accomplished breath.

We spent the next few minutes splitting up the names. He gave me the cousins living in the Bay Area. He would handle those in Southern California.

"Not a problem. I'll get their signatures." I put the list in a file folder. "I'll still have all the court docs ready to go before our next meeting."

He nodded. "You know, you don't always have to be an overachiever."

"I don't know any other way."

I wasn't kidding.

WHEN I GOT home, I changed clothes and pulled out the club's phone list. Then I called Rena.

"Hollis, what's the matter?" Her voice sounded tentative and unsure.

I'd forgotten she was still in her twenties. "I want to talk about what's been going on. Can we meet?"

Silence. I could almost hear her brain whirring.

"Rena, I—"

"Okay. Where do you live?"

"Live? I thought we could meet over dinner in a restaurant."

"I see. I didn't think you'd want me to know where you live. Dinner? I think not. You don't want me in your business and I don't want you in mine. I've been straight ever since I got off parole. I don't want to chitchat and I don't want to get involved in any cover-up or—"

I had to stop her. "No, no cover-up. I'm just trying to figure out—"

"You're trying to figure things out? Who the hell are you? Look, Hollis, you seem to be an okay person, but I'm not okay with talking about murder with someone I barely know."

She had me there.

We exchanged polite goodbyes.

It wasn't like I'd been having a great day to begin with, so I was frustrated but not surprised when three San Lucian police officers appeared a half hour later with a warrant to search my condo, car and garage. If that was what it took to eliminate me as a suspect, then the sooner the better. I started out the door. I couldn't stand to watch. The last time I was subjected to a search, an arrest had come the next day.

A young officer blocked my exit. "I'm sorry, Ms. Morgan. You have to stay."

I turned around to take a seat in my living room. The sounds of drawers opening, doors closing and furniture being moved around assaulted my nerves. I felt like a stranger in my own house because it would never be home again. After about thirty minutes, the two officers came down the hall; one held my beloved memories chest in a plastic bag.

The irony of timing.

A young woman who avoided my eyes held out a paper on a clipboard. "We're going to check this out. Please sign for the contents."

My neighbors were likely having a field day trying to figure out what was going on with the marked police cars parked outside. Outreach was never my forte; I'd never gotten to know any of them. I thought briefly about calling Rena just to talk to a fellow club member, but more than likely her place was being searched as well. The police left as quickly as they had come.

I still wanted to leave.

Picking up my mail, I fled to the peaceful atmosphere of the law office. The office was my refuge during times of high stress and low self-esteem. Through the expanse of windows, the lobby glowed diamond blue from the reflected city lights. The rising crest of the water in the bay and the glistening colors of the San Francisco skyline might have graced a tourist postcard. The view always reminded me how truly great freedom is. I used to look out my cell window and realize the moon I looked at was the same one people who weren't incarcerated looked at. I envied but did not begrudge them that privilege.

I SAT AT my desk and sorted through mail. The bills went next to a stack of solicitations from various charities that sent me unwanted mailing labels. The pile seemed to mock me. Distracted, I pulled out my cellphone.

The thought of dealing with Bill again ignited a jumble of feelings in my chest, but sooner or later, I had to close this chapter, again.

I didn't realize I was holding my breath until I breathed a sigh of relief when he didn't pick up. "Bill, this is Hollis. I'm ready to talk. Call me." The moment of relief was fleeting. My phone rang seconds later.

"Becky, I can't believe I'm finally talking to you."

I closed my eyes. It was his voice that first attracted me, deep and promise-filled. However, right now it only sent up warning flares.

"Hello, what's so important?"

"God, it's good to hear your voice. You took a while to call back. I—"

"You said I'm in danger. How?"

"This isn't something I can talk about over the phone. I know you don't want me at your place. How about we meet downtown for dinner after you get off work tomorrow?"

His assumption irritated me, more than anything. "Ah, the old bait and switch. What happened to 'just call me'?"

"I need to talk to you in person. You pick the place. You'll agree it's the right thing." Bill pumped up the pleading in his voice.

"Tell me now. I'm not falling for your lying and con jobs anymore." I didn't even try to hide my anger. "Tell me now, or stop calling."

"I'll tell you part now and part over dinner. Or if no dinner, I just need to tell you to your face. Then I'll never call you again."

He hadn't changed. He was always cutting deals.

"We aren't negotiating. Tell me now, or I'm hanging up."

He sighed. "Okay. I'll tell you. I hope you're sitting down."

"Talk."

"All right. About four years ago I met Michael Rollins—you know him as Rory Norris—at a party in San Francisco. He and I had a mutual friend." He paused. "After … after your trial I did my time in county, then I went to Oregon and found a great therapist. She helped me get my head together and deal with all my missing pieces and—"

"You know, I'm sorry. I was wrong. I can't take this ball of crap. I take that back. I'm not sorry. Are you saying that while I was sitting in prison, prison, Bill … are you telling me you were piecing your psyche together?"

"If you'll let me explain, I—"

"No. I've had it with you. I'd had it a long time ago. You know, the police are looking for you. I'm going to give you to them."

There was silence on the other end, then, "I understand the police think you killed Rory."

I hadn't realized how much I still wanted to know he cared about me, and how much he didn't. His unspoken threat cut me like a knife. I knew it would be only a matter of time before his true colors came out. It hadn't taken long but this time I was ready for him.

"That's only because I haven't shown them the photos yet."

"Photos of what?"

"Remember the photos we took of all the property on the last two claims before we were arrested—I mean, before I got caught and you turned evidence? Well, I came across a few of them when I claimed my stuff from storage after I got out."

"What's on them?"

I knew he was running through his mental Rolodex, trying to remember what was in the pictures.

"Ask the police to show you copies."

"You know, Becky, we used to be good together. Because of the way things turned out, I wanted to give you something you could give to the police to get them off your back. Except your attitude is too much for me. You need to learn to get past your anger." He paused.

In the silence, it was all I could do to keep a few choice profanities from rolling off my tongue.

Bill, on the other hand, launched into his next pitch. "I know what I did was beyond forgiveness. That's why I'm trying to help you. There's big money involved in this. Rory was running his own game inside a much larger one. His greed complicated the works and they killed him."

"Who are 'they'? I know Rory's game was blackmail. What's the larger game?"

"Rory ran it like a business. I met him through a guy who was working for him as his private detective."

"What exactly do you do for a living? How did you and Rory know each other?"

I could almost hear the debate going on in his head: to tell the truth, or not? "I work as a fraud consultant for an insurance firm."

I couldn't stifle my laugh, but I could tell from the tone of his voice that he was telling the truth.

"I know, I know. I met Rory's guy in the line of business. He needed my help to do some—some, uh, research and he hooked Rory and me up to work on a couple of deals."

"Go on. You didn't answer my question. What was the larger game?"

"All I know is it involved a lot of rich people. Rory named his biggest client 'Jackpot.' He never let me get close to him. My job was to validate the insurance claim information to an appraiser."

"Insurance information. Who are these people?"

"I don't know that, either."

Bill's ego didn't allow him to admit easily to not knowing, so a part of me believed his answer.

"What are you doing with Rory's mother?"

"Rory wasn't a bad guy. I met his mom a couple of years ago when he invited me over to try her lasagna." He paused. "I needed to make sure there wasn't any information lying around her house about me—and, of course, I assisted her at the same time."

"Of course."

"Anyway, I've been helping her clear out the rest of his things."

"So, how am I in danger?"

I could swear I heard Bill taking a swallow from a drink. If memory served me right, he drank Wild Turkey on the rocks.

"You have sixty seconds," I added.

"Right, I know you. You'll want to get involved, and that's not healthy. Don't be pokin' your nose around. Let the police do their job. I'm trying to protect you, but I can't be around forever."

That did it. He'd pushed my last button. "You're trying to *protect* me? Buddy, I'm in bad shape if I have to count on you for protection. Right now, the police think I'm the murderer, so I'm really not anxious for them to move forward with doing their job."

"Becky—"

"No, *you* stop. Is this all you wanted to tell me?" My voice was getting louder. I took a calming breath.

"No, there's more I want to tell you. I want you to know that I'm so sorry."

"Don't bother. What are you going to do now?"

Bill couldn't talk without lying. I knew he'd fed me a few. I just had to figure out which ones were the lies. I didn't trust myself to be objective. But I patted myself on the back for my restraint.

"Now? I'm going to go … home. Becky—"

"Your time's up. My name is Hollis." I clicked off the phone.

I RETURNED TO the condo. The police had left the rooms relatively unscathed. I liked to imagine Faber told them not to trash the place. They must have gone through all my books. They were on the shelves but the fiction and nonfiction were mixed-up. Everything was slightly not where I left it. Upstairs in my bedroom, I tried not to notice the scuffs on the floor from moved furniture and the clear signs of closet dishevelment. I crawled into bed and pulled the blanket over my head. Eventually, I fell into a restless sleep.

CHAPTER FIFTEEN

FIRST THING IN the morning, I dropped off my finished statement at Clay Boone's office. It was the best I could do. I just hoped Judge Pine would think so, too.

I felt mentally drained and just plain tired. I'd stalled long enough. With both Mark and Avery out of the office on travel, it was easy to be away for a couple of hours without being missed. All I wanted to do was get my home back in order from the police search. Before long, my kitchen was back to normal and, with a determined focus to triumph over procrastination, I finished putting the bathrooms back together.

I had hoped for a feeling of accomplishment, but none came.

I checked the time. I'd waited to question Rena again. I wouldn't let her put me off so easily. Rory had upset someone. He'd started to blackmail Abby and Richard. Why just those two? Had he stopped there? Maybe he hadn't. Was Rena too new? Did Rory know about Gene's affair? Maybe he had started on Miller, and Miller didn't want to pay.

Killing Rory would be cheaper.

AFTER A LITTLE cajoling, Rena finally agreed to meet me

the next day after work at the Berkeley Marina. I got there first, and it felt good to just sit and stare out over the bay.

"Okay, I'm here. I had to get a babysitter." She leaned back on the bench and crossed her arms. "So, what have you found out?"

"After a lot of false starts, not much, but I'm willing to bet the reason why you said you'd see me is because you want to know what I found out about you. Am I right?"

Rena shoved her hands deep into the pockets of her cashmere sweater. She took a dramatic deep breath.

She stared at me a moment. "I talked with Gene. He said I could trust you."

If she'd hit me with a stick, I couldn't have been more surprised. Gene knew Rena? I hadn't realized they were that close.

"He's right."

She went on, but her voice trembled. "What he couldn't, or didn't tell me, is why you're taking it on yourself to find the killer."

I knew I only had this chance to prove myself to her. "The police still have me on their suspect list. Mine is a long story, but I can't completely prove my innocence, either. More than finding out who murdered Rory, I want to identify Abby's killer." There was tension in my voice.

"Abby was a good person. I get that. Why you? You're not qualified."

"Granted, I'm taking this on myself. Not only do I have a vested interest, but I think I can get into places and ask questions the police, who have to follow procedures, can't. The thought of going back to prison—well, I'm sure you can relate. It's not an option."

Rena got up and walked away a few feet then turned back and sat. She seemed to be deciding whether to trust me. She took a sip from a water bottle she'd brought with her.

"After the last Fallen Angels' meeting, I went to my car."

She hesitated. "There was this piece of paper stuck under my windshield wiper. I didn't know what it meant … except now … except now, after what happened to Rory and Abby, I think it means I'm next to be killed."

She reached into her purse and produced a folded piece of paper. I reached for it but she held on tight.

"Do you think the murderer is one of the members?" I asked. She nodded.

"I know you don't want to accuse someone without solid proof. We know what it's like to be accused of something you didn't do."

She spoke slowly. "Yes. I hated prison. I can't say I was entirely innocent, but I'd never give testimony about anyone when I didn't know for sure … for sure that they … I have a son. I can't leave him again. I … here." She handed it to me.

The plain paper had only three words written on it: *The Long Pause*. Rena leaned forward. "*The Long Pause* … that's our next book, isn't it?"

"Yes, it is. You have no idea who could have left this for you?"

"The only thing I can think of is that I had to park away from everyone else because I was late again and couldn't get a space. Miller left the meeting first. I left after he did. When I came out, his car was gone."

Finally, a break. "So, if nothing else, he had the opportunity to place the note?"

"Yes, but—"

"You've got to go to the police." I wasn't going to see someone else killed because they didn't tell the authorities what they knew.

Rena didn't seem to hear. "You know Rory was killed like in our January book and Abby—well, I heard Abby was killed like the victim in *Storm Crossing*. Do you think …?"

Her voice was strained. She seemed scared. I didn't blame her.

"We can't sit here and speculate. We've got to turn over this information."

Rena refolded the paper and tucked it back inside her purse. She continued to say nothing, but her wide brown eyes sought mine.

"My son Christopher is five." Her voice cracked. "I can't get caught up again. When Rory was killed, I was visiting my mom, who watches my son. When Abby was killed, I was at a buyers' conference."

"You told all this to the police?"

"Yes."

I held her shoulder. "Rena, you have nothing to worry about, but you can't ignore the note. You could be in danger. I work for a law firm, and I'm going to ask for some help from a friend."

Her expression became alarmed. "A lawyer ... I don't know about that. I can't afford to have anyone make trouble. I can't—"

"No, he's a friend who just happens to be a lawyer. I need his help to do some background checking." I paused. "I'll introduce you first and you can judge him for yourself. Look, if I were you I'd be wary of exposing my life to a stranger, but we can't deal with this by ourselves. We need help."

Rena hesitated. I thought she was going to say something else, but then she only nodded slowly.

"Do you know the Snow Museum? At Lake Merritt?"

She nodded again.

"Meet us there Saturday morning. In the afternoon a lot of families are out, but early in the morning, only runners are around. We'll be waiting for you on the bench behind the museum on the lake side."

"Who's your friend?"

"His name is Mark Haddan. He's a good guy. You can trust him."

"That's just great, but how do I know I can trust you?"

I WANTED TO check Lily out for myself. I stopped by the center on my way home.

"Why do you keep looking at me like that?" Lily's voice trembled and her hand shook. "I'm cold; tell them to bring me my shawl."

I nodded and walked over to the nurse, who was trying to put a videotape in the VCR. She said she'd get her shawl as soon as she finished.

"Lily, we're just about done. Avery Mitchell asked that I continue to work with you to save money." I spoke directly into her good ear. "I took down everything you said. I think we're through here. Is there anything else?"

She frowned and then a look of fear crossed her face. "Stop it, I said. Stop looking at me." She tried to rise out of her wheelchair.

I held onto her wrist but she scratched me with her nails from her other hand.

"Ouch."

"Go away. Where's Portia?"

"Who's Portia?"

The nurse finally heard the ruckus and started toward us. Before she could get midway across the floor, Marla entered the room, walked quickly over and held Lily's head to her chest. The nurse paused, saw things were under control and went back to the VCR.

"Lily dear, what's the matter?" Marla brushed Lily's thin hair with the palm of her hand.

Lily's voice was muffled but still distinct. "Why, nothing. Hollis and I are working on my trust. I hope we're almost finished. Are we?"

I inclined my head. If I hadn't witnessed Lily's Dr. Jekyll and Mrs. Hyde transformation, I would probably have thought Marla was exaggerating.

Marla looked at me and I nodded.

After leaving Lily, all I wanted to do was go home and have a glass of wine. Make that two glasses.

CHAPTER SIXTEEN

THE NEXT MORNING I beat the receptionist into the office and turned on all the lights. I saved the previous day's newspaper to read the follow-up article about Abby's murder; at least the police now concluded it was a murder. The article below the fold recounted Abby's death with fair accuracy. There were quotes from Faber and an understandably sorrowful one from her husband. I held my breath, looking for references to the book club, but there were none.

Mark was late, as usual. I prepared notes from my contacts with two local Riddick heirs and started to write the client letter that would go with the release statements.

"Hey."

I looked up at the sound of Avery's voice. "You're back early. How was Chicago?"

"Fast-paced, but worth it. We got the new client and a sixty-five thousand dollar retainer." He sat down and stretched his long legs out in front of him.

I smiled. "That's great. The Management Committee will be pleased."

He smiled, but the musing look that went with it silenced me.

"Anyway, how are things here? Are you and Mark making headway? I didn't get any emails on my Blackberry."

"We work well together. We divided up the cousins. He's clearing the ones who live in Southern California. I expect him back today." I looked down at my notes. "I secured two signatures and have one to go. We should have something good to report at our staff meeting."

"That's good news." He sat up. "God, I'm tired. I'll probably only be here a few hours to brief Ed. Then I'm going home. How's that other situation?"

The abrupt change in subject threw me. "What?"

"Your situation ... how's it going?"

My face warmed. "It's been quiet for the past couple of days. The police talked to another club member who was threatened."

"Are you a suspect in that, too?"

"Thanks for your faith in me."

"I didn't mean it like that." He looked uncharacteristically contrite. "How are you doing?"

"Sometimes I can put it out of my mind for a whole hour." My throat tightened. I took a breath. "I'm getting by."

He nodded. "If there's anything I can do, let me know."

"Actually, there is."

I explained the rehabilitation certificate requirement. "It would help ... I mean, would you give me a letter of recommendation?"

"Of course." He leaned forward in his chair. "I'm a little hurt you didn't come to me to handle your case."

I looked down, unable to meet his eyes. "You don't practice criminal law."

"I would have learned for you."

Visibly, his words surprised him as much as they did me.

"Thank you," I said in a rush. "Go, get some rest. I'll have the information and forms for you tomorrow."

He stood and resumed his business composure, his face a mask. "Good. Well, I'm going to talk to Ed. See you tomorrow."

Mark appeared at the door. "Avery, what are you doing back so soon?"

"I just told Hollis I had a successful trip that ended early." His voice turned cool.

"We've been busy, too." Mark rubbed his hands together. "I think we'll have some good news for you."

"So I've been hearing. Well, I'm about to drop." Avery moved away. "I'll check in with you two tomorrow."

I nodded.

Mark came in and sat. "He must be tired. He didn't even seem curious about what we're up to."

"He's hooked bigger fish—new clients." I pretended interest in a case file. "How was L.A.?"

"Not bad. I met with all three—Lisa, Cory and Neville. They're all middle-class, down-to-earth types. Evidently, Lisa and Cory are close, so I met with them together. Neville is in the service. I met with him on base. He wanted to have his wife there. Don't ask me why."

"Why?"

"I don't know. That's why I said don't ask."

My frustration thermometer was starting to register. "Very funny. So, what happened?"

He slapped a thick envelope on top of my desk. "Three signatures is what happened!"

I must have looked amazed. "You got them all to sign?"

"Yep, and their spouses. They all thought the mother lode had come in. Only Cory remembered Mrs. Riddick and that was because her father was Riddick's brother's favorite nephew." He picked imaginary lint off his suit.

"You got their spouses to sign, too?"

"Right. I had this thought that if Avery was concerned someone might contest a will, it's usually the spouse who wants to interfere. We don't know the status of their marriages.

Anyway, I noticed you put some blank forms in my briefcase, so I got their signatures, too."

Smug satisfaction came over me. While I didn't know if Mark would be offended if I presumed to tell him how to practice law, I didn't care. In two of the cases I had researched, the spouses had taken little time to file for divorce after an estate settlement and lay claim to the proceeds. I put the spousal forms in Mark's briefcase but hadn't had the chance to explain the need.

"Good, Mark. I've got agreement from two of the three cousins to sign. Laura Riddick moved to Oregon. I plan on contacting Allen Riddick today. He's still local."

He nodded. "He's the last one. I've got to unload my briefcase, so I'll catch up to you later. How about we get together this afternoon at around three thirty?"

"Sounds good, I'll see you then. I also need to ask a favor."

"Wait, tell me now. You've never asked me for a favor before."

"It's something personal." I knew I had his attention. "Is it still a good time to talk?"

He sat down and closed my office door. "I'm listening."

"Do you know my background?"

"That you didn't get into law school so you became a paralegal? By the way, I think you're an excellent paralegal."

"Thanks, but I'm still not going to do your client letters. I did get into law school. I went to Hastings." I knew I sounded defensive, so I changed the tone in my voice. "And ... well, there's more."

He looked at me expectantly, and I told my story.

The marriage, the insurance fraud, the prison term—unpracticed at sharing my life history, I filled him in surprisingly quickly. He patiently listened, and when I finished, the look of understanding on his face was exactly what I hoped to see. A load lifted from my shoulders.

Mark smiled. "You're a top-notch employee and you're not letting your past define who you are now. If the firm knows your background, then go for your dream."

"Yeah, well, there's a little more to it than that."

"I thought so. What's the favor?"

For the next few minutes I explained about The Fallen Angels Book Club. "We've had two murders from our reading list, and now another of our members has received a threat. It's a nightmare that won't stop."

Mark waited.

"I'd like you to speak with Rena Gabriel. She's the member who got the threat. You're the only one I could think of. The only one I trust."

"Okay. You can count on me. What about my client letters?"

I STOPPED BY the senior home to see Marla before going to get the final Riddick signature. It was foggy and cold, as only a spring day in the Bay Area could be. After placing donuts in the kitchen, Marla was in the day room with a stack of catalogs in front of her. She looked tired, even as she tried to straighten in her seat. She was paler than usual and her eyes had circles under them.

"Hello there. Planning on making a purchase?"

"You're here late." She smiled warmly. "No, I'm not buying anything. One of the residents was looking for a memory card reader for his great-grandson's camera. His eyesight's not too good and I said I'd help him. Besides, I don't think he knows what a card reader is."

"I'm with him. I don't know what one is, either." I pulled up a folding chair and sat down next to her. "How do you know about all this stuff?"

"You're too young to not keep up to date with technology." She looked at me and shook her head. "I read newspapers and catalogs. You can learn a lot from catalogs. In just a few short words, they describe a product and its uses. Listen, 'a USB 2.0 memory card reader is a camera accessory that helps to store photos until you can transfer them to your computer.'" She pushed her glasses up on her nose. "If I still don't understand, I make a call."

"A call? Who do you call?"

"Customer service, of course—the eight hundred number is free. I've got time on my hands and they get paid to answer questions. When I talk to a real helpful one, I even write a letter to their supervisor." She took off her glasses and let them swing down on the cord draped loosely around her neck.

"Okay." I made a mental note to come and keep Marla company more often. "Marla, you don't look well. Are you all right?"

She sighed. "I'm just worried about Lily."

"She mentioned the name Portia. Who's Portia?"

Marla closed her eyes and shook her head. "Portia was her daughter; she was six when she died. Lily's getting worse, I tell you. Something has to be done."

"I could go to the police, but if I do, they'll have to take things to their lawful conclusion. It could mean the end of the center."

"If you don't, it could mean the end of Lily." Marla wet her lips. "You're right. Maybe you could just let management know you know what they're up to and they'd stop."

I touched her hand. "I'd still have to identify you. I'm not here when the medications are given. How else would I know these things? Murray already suspects you're the whistle blower. Besides, I'm not absolutely convinced she's in on it."

I was pulling Marla's sweater around her. Joseph stood in the doorway looking at us. He didn't back down from my stare. I didn't say anything to Marla. It would only make her as paranoid as I was.

"Do you know Joseph's shift hours?"

"Saturday through Wednesday, seven to three. What are you thinking?"

I didn't answer because I didn't really know what I was thinking. It seemed I'd have to catch Joseph in the act in order to prove to the authorities that Marla—and now I—wasn't crazy.

"Can you show me where the medications are kept?"

"It's down the hall next to the director's office, but you don't need to go there. Staff pops in there all the time." Marla looked around again. "Joseph has a large office. I think that's where he tampers with the medications. Off of his office there's a small closet."

I doubted he'd keep any incriminating evidence out in the open, or even in his office space. On the other hand, he wouldn't be able to go far with bottles of pills.

"Marla, how do you know about the layout of Joseph's office? Never mind. Don't tell me. You need to stay clear of Joseph for the next few days. You don't want him suspecting you." *Especially if he has access to your medication.*

"All right. What are you going to do? I don't want you to get into trouble."

Me, neither.

"It's best you don't know. I promise I'll do what I can."

"Enough of Lily, I'm thinking you came here for another reason. What's wrong?"

Except for two senior ladies watching an *Oprah* rerun, we were alone in the sunroom. I leaned in closer. "Marla, I'm trying to get a pardon from the court to have my conviction cleared. It's called a Certificate of Rehabilitation."

Her eyes grew large, but she said nothing.

"Anyway, I need references from four different people. I've got most of them covered but I need one from a third-party who knows me but is not a relation or an employer. Would you feel comfortable giving me a letter of recommendation?"

"Why, of course." She rubbed her hands together. "You can count on me. You know, this is like an episode of *Law and Order*. How many words do you need?"

"There isn't a specific word count."

Her eagerness to take on her assignment warmed me. I

pulled out the manila envelope and form she'd need. "Here's the instruction sheet, the form and a self-addressed stamped envelope so you can mail it to my attorney."

"Fine, fine. Just leave it up to me. I'll get started today. I know exactly what I'll say." She took the materials from me. "When do you need it?"

"If you could possibly have it mailed by the end of next week, that would be great." I paused. "Now, Marla, it doesn't have to be a big deal. You can keep it simple."

"Not a problem. Your attorney will have it this week." She patted my hand. "Now get that worried look off your face and give me a smile. It's going to be all right."

Somehow I dug deep and came up with a smile.

At home, I leaned back on my bed, closed my eyes and let down my guard. Talk about a week on an emotional roller coaster. Avery. What was that all about? Then there was the conversation with Rita the other day. Had I shut my family out instead of the other way around? Now another member threatened. I tried to push it all away. I had a hearing to show up for and only three weeks to get my act together.

It was clear my attempt to read myself to sleep wasn't working. There was one thing I needed to get out of the way. I picked up the phone and then put it back in the handset. I picked it up again. Even as I punched in the number it irked me that I had memorized it. Good, I got voicemail.

"Bill … Bill I … just give me a call. I want to clear something up. My num—"

The phone clicked.

"Wait, Becky, er … Hollis, wait, I'm here." I could hear papers rustling. "What a surprise. A pleasant surprise, but a surprise."

"I bet." I took a deep breath. "Look, I called because I don't want you contacting my family again. What happened is between you and me. If you can't reach me, then you can't reach me. Don't call Rita, or Mom, or Dad, or Greg, just leave my family out of it."

There was silence.

"Bill?"

He sighed. "I'm here." He took a swallow. "Will you please put our past behind us and let me take you to dinner? Or, if that's too congenial for you, how about meeting for tea?"

I was glad he couldn't see me glancing around for an answer. He'd remembered I liked tea.

I stammered, "No … I don't think—"

"Let me come over." His voice deepened with promise.

I blinked, and pushed the phone at arm's length as I said a quick thank you to the patron saint of ice water.

"Are you kidding me? No, you can't come over." My voice gained strength. "And stay away from my family. Do you hear me?"

"Hollis, I—"

"Do you hear me?" I enunciated each word slowly.

"Yes, I hear you."

I hit end on the phone, and turned off the light.

I WAITED UNTIL Thursday after the last meals were served and the seniors were hopefully resting in their rooms. It was also the time I knew the staff had dinner in the dining room. The front door was locked, but I'd been given a key to the rear door when I first started to visit. I'd never used it, and I held my breath until I heard the lock click open. The key still worked. The locks hadn't been changed.

The door opened onto a hallway that I knew led to the administrative offices. The residence rooms were on the other side of the building, separated by the community room and lobby. Fortunately the lighting was low. The carpet helped muffle my footsteps, giving me cover.

Walking swiftly past the double doors leading to the dining room, I counted the doors to staff offices. Joseph's was second from the end.

It was locked.

All the center's interior doors had keypad locks. Each resident had a coded lock that staff had access to. Of course, most seniors shared their codes with each other. However, staff offices all had the same code. Although they treated me like staff, and I used a vacant office from time to time, if I were caught, I'd have a lot of explaining to do. It didn't take a rocket scientist to figure that they hid the code somewhere near the receptionist's desk. During my last visit with Lily, I ventured into the main office. Within five minutes, I found the code on a Post-it under the computer mouse pad. I memorized the number.

Now I quickly punched it in and waited for the red light to turn green. Before I could turn the knob, the door jerked open. I was face to face with Joseph.

His scowl covered his face and didn't hide the fury in his eyes. "What the hell are you doing breaking into my office?"

My brain went blank, so my tongue came up with an idea. "Oh, this is your office? I thought this was Opal's office."

"Hollis, I was wondering where you went to. I have those papers for you. Thank you for coming by so late. " Marla was dressed in a housecoat and carried her purse. She appeared as only an angel would. "Hello, Joseph."

He gave her a brief nod but said nothing.

My heart was beating so rapidly that I wanted to faint. "Yes, I'm on my way."

"I thought you said you were looking for Opal's office."

Before I could respond, Marla said, "That's because I told her Opal was holding my papers and would leave them in an envelope for her when she came by." Marla walked up to me and grabbed my arm, steering me back down the hallway. "Anyway, sweetie, I got things backward. Opal's office is across the hall. This is Joseph's office. I got things mixed up. Doesn't matter. Come along."

"How did you get the code?" he said.

"I—"

Marla held me tighter. "I gave it to her. We all know where to find the code. Besides, there's software you can buy and put on a USB device that can open any key lock." She moved past him. "You were right, Hollis. The customer service rep was so nice to explain everything to me."

Joseph was likely assessing his options. I didn't doubt his eyes were boring into my back.

"How did you know I was here?" I whispered.

Marla glanced behind her. "I went to get a catalog I left behind in the community room, looked out the window and saw you pull into the lot next door. I had no idea you'd come tonight, sweetie. I could have told you Joseph traded nights. I just came by to make sure you were okay."

"That's why I didn't tell you. I don't want you to get involved." It never occurred to me to ask Marla and save myself the potential embarrassment at being caught red-handed. "Do you really have the code?"

"No," she smiled broadly. "I thought I sounded convincing."

I gave her arm a squeeze. I looked back at Joseph, who was still standing where we had left him. From the grim set of his jaw, I could tell he hadn't bought any of it.

CHAPTER SEVENTEEN

THE SNOW MUSEUM was an Oakland landmark. A former Victorian-style mansion turned museum, it stood in quiet watch over Lake Merritt. In contrast to its stately turn-of-the-century presence, rows of expensive contemporary condominiums rose in the background.

Mark and I sat across from each other at one of the picnic tables that dotted the lawn facing the water. The smell of recently mown grass carried in the morning lull. It hadn't taken much to get him here; I think he hoped this was his chance to ingratiate himself with me.

"No one's here," Mark said.

"She isn't due for another fifteen minutes. I wanted us to talk before she arrives."

He handed Rena's Inquiry First printout back. "It's not too bad. That's good. I knew you had another reason for accessing Inquiry First. You could have been upfront with me."

"Sorry. I didn't want to involve you if I didn't have to."

"I'm not sure I can help your friend."

"I think Rena's a victim of circumstance, like me. At first, I was put off by her but now … I don't know, she seems okay."

"What do you think I can do?"

"Listen to her. I'm too close to all of this. I want you to hear her story in her words. The fact that she received a threat makes me think she might have seen or heard something. I know in my gut Abby was killed because she knew something about Rory's murderer. The police have backed off the suicide theory. That means there have been two murders likely committed by the same person in our diminishing book club membership."

"How many of you are left?"

"Five, including me."

"Don't you think it's nuts that one of your club members would be demented enough to commit murders that would only lead back to a club member?"

"Nuts and scary. Sadly, no one else has our book list. The other thing is—"

"Hi." Rena approached.

"Rena, good morning. You look great." I barely recognized her. She looked like a model. Dark sunglasses complemented the sophistication of her hair pulled back into a loose bun. She wore black slacks, a billowy white top and red pumps. Her well-toned arms sported a bright assortment of silver and red bracelets.

I motioned for her to sit next to me. "This is Mark Haddan. I told you I work with Mark, but I also consider him a friend."

She gave him a nod. "Hollis doesn't give me the impression she acquires friends lightly."

Mark gave a small laugh. "It's the first time I've heard her call me that. I tread very carefully." He held out his hand. "It's good to meet you."

Rena hesitated a moment then shook it.

My lack of social graces took over and my impatience grew. "I know you don't have much time. Show Mark what you showed me."

Rena's whole demeanor changed. Her smile faded and her

expression became one of apprehension. She pulled out the note.

He took it. "What is *The Long Pause*?"

"It's the name of the next book on our club's reading list."

Mark's gaze flicked first to me, then to Rena. "Okay, Rena, why don't you tell me how you got this."

She recounted what she told me. "Why me? I don't know anything. I just joined the group."

Mark said, "Did the others get any kind of warning?"

Rena shrugged.

"Not that I know of," I said.

"What did the police say?"

Rena looked out toward the lake. "I haven't told them about it."

He lifted a single eyebrow. "Why not?"

"Because ... because I don't like the police and ... and they might think I was trying to point fingers away from me because I'm guilty. I'm not, but they might think I am."

Mark gave Rena back her note. "This is a threat. You've got to take it to them. Of course, any fingerprints are covered with ours by now, but they might be able to find something. Take the note to them. It will look better for you." His voice softened. "Don't get caught up in second-guessing the police. They want to find the killer. You know you're not guilty, and there is a real killer out there."

I spoke up in case Rena still resisted. "Mark's right."

She gave me a woeful look. "Will you come with me?"

"Me? No. I think I'd do more harm than good, since they consider me a suspect." I put my hands in my lap. "Ah, Mark, could you go with her?"

Rena turned to Mark. "I know we just met, but will you come?"

Mark appeared taken aback. "Ah, I'm not a criminal attorney. I wouldn't be your best advocate."

"I don't want you to represent me. I just don't want to go alone."

Mark looked at me, and I shrugged.

"I guess I could accompany you. You should go as soon as possible. When can you make it?"

I listened vaguely to their arrangements to meet in the afternoon. I felt a growing disquiet rising in my chest. Rena said her thank yous and goodbyes, and Mark stood to leave.

I leaned over the table. "What if others got a note as well and I was the only one who didn't?"

He thought a moment then spoke the words I wouldn't utter. "That could mean someone is trying to frame you."

"Isn't it too obvious? No one would believe I'm that stupid."

"Maybe Rena doesn't realize she knows something."

"That's what I thought about Abby. Maybe she could identify the killer. Maybe one of the guys really is a serial killer."

Mark shook his head. "Enough. We're not going to get anywhere speculating. I'll encourage Rena to give her story, and then tomorrow or the next day I'll talk to the detectives assigned to the case." He brushed off his slacks. "I've got to run some errands before I meet her. I'm not sure who's around at the police station. There's a chance the detectives won't be there, but I'll let you know what happens."

I smiled. "Thank you. I appreciate you talking with Rena and…and talking sense to me."

"No problem." He hesitated as I got up. "Hollis, er…I have this one lingering case I need to get off my desk. One of the temps started to help me before she went on maternity leave. I'm running out of time getting the Riddick filings in shape for Avery. I could use your help."

I didn't bother to hide my distaste.

He sighed with acceptance and walked back to his car. I wanted to kick myself. Mark had shown me kindness and I had reverted back to the old me. I called out, but he had pulled away from the curb.

THE REST OF the weekend, while I waited to hear what had happened with the police, I caught up on laundry and housework. Rena never called and I didn't have Mark's phone number.

On Monday morning, with one eye on Mark's door, I sent him an email with information about the background on the Southern California cousins and a time he could drop off his case file so I could help him. I included a line of question marks, hoping he'd get the message to call. Later I was passing through the lobby when I saw a note on the office "Out" board. He was in court covering for one of the attorneys who was sick.

Keeping my frustration in check, I worked on locating cases related to breaking wills. Triple D had a great law library, as well as online access to a comprehensive software collection of case law. As a paralegal, I knew how to undertake case research better than most attorneys. It was more time-effective to do as much research as I could online before I tackled our law library. I still preferred having a book in my hand to scanning pages on the computer, though. I looked at probate cases appealed in the last year and then worked my way back until I found several "on point" cases. By lunchtime, I had a list of about fifteen potential precedents that warranted pulling their volumes off the shelf.

An hour later, after I made my way through the library stacks, I headed back to my office with a cart full of appellate volumes.

"Hollis," Mark said, standing in my doorway. "Can you make my travel arrangements to Los Angeles?"

"No." I stopped myself when I saw his teasing smile. "No, wait. Yes, I'll get one of the administrative staff to play travel agent for you." I gave him a humble smile.

"Thanks."

"Ah, do you have a moment?"

"Sure." He sat down.

I pushed some file folders to one side of my desk, clearing a space for him.

"I need another favor. Close the door. But first, what happened with Rena?"

"It was straightforward. A weekend duty officer took her statement and bagged the note."

"So Faber and Lincoln weren't there?"

He hesitated. "No, the duty officer said the detectives assigned to the case would be in touch with her. I thought I would talk with them today, but I had to show up in court."

"Don't worry. They'll contact her, I'm sure of that. What I need, Mark, is ..."

He leaned forward eagerly.

"Full access to Inquiry First."

He pushed away from the desk. "Ah, so that's what this is all about. Are you crazy? I can't order the software on my own. Not only is it expensive, I'd be interfering in an ongoing criminal investigation. Use the beta test version."

"I did, but I need more information."

"It won't work." He drummed his fingers on the desk pad. "You've been helping me out, and I'm really grateful, but—"

"I understand. It's just that I'm running out of options and time. Even so, I don't want to put you in a tough spot."

He tried to hide it, but I saw his long exhale of relief. "All right, if you're sure." His voice picked up energy. "Can you tell me what you're looking for or, I guess, who you're looking for?"

"Okay. Work with me on this. First, Rory was a known blackmailer. Second, due to the nature of having blackmailable information, his killer is more than likely a member of the club. My guess is that Rory blackmailed his murderer. Third, his murderer had to kill Abby because she could identify him."

"Inquiry First would help you how?"

"Inquiry First would give me detailed information about everyone's background. I'd cross-check each one with Rory and find out why he or she might be a victim, or maybe a murderer."

"I have to believe the police have access to Inquiry First or something even better. Why are you so determined?"

"Because I know them; I know how they think. I've been in their sights. I don't have time … I don't have time to let justice take its winding, often detoured, course."

"Were you blackmailed?"

"No. That's another issue. I think the police consider me a suspect because I can't prove I wasn't being blackmailed."

Mark took up a pen and doodled on a pad. "Okay. I follow your thinking but not your conclusion."

I threw up my hands. "What part don't you understand?"

"What difference does knowing everyone's background make? Your penal convictions make all of you easy targets in the mind of a blackmailer."

"But—"

"Let's just make that assumption. One of your club members, whose sanity I seriously question, is copying murders on your booklist. That said, don't you think the police already know this?"

I held my head in my hands and thought about what he said. "You're probably right. There aren't many of us left—Gene, Miller, Rena, Richard and me. I guess I'm burning out. I need some downtime from all of this."

"Good idea." He stood. "What are you going to do now?"

"Go home and think about something else. I've been looking at this from only one angle. I need to step back."

Mark seemed to buy my false bluster. After he left, I didn't even want to put into words the growing dread that my clock was running out on securing a pardon. Either I had to find the killer quickly or make sure I was no longer a suspect. The murderer was killing more than club members. He—or she—was also killing my chance to get my life back.

CHAPTER EIGHTEEN

I WAS IN a somber mood when I got home. It had been scary but also a relief to confide in Mark. If nothing else, I heard how my thoughts sounded outside of my head.

I peered into the refrigerator, looking for potential dinner candidates.

The doorbell rang.

One reason why I bought a condo off the beaten path was so that no one who came to the door could say they were passing by. I tried looking through the peephole, but the man had his back to me.

"Who is it?"

"It's me, Becky, I mean Hollis." Bill. He turned around and into my line of sight.

My heart pumped rapid-fire as a rush of adrenaline shot through my veins. Even so, fight or flight didn't seem to be an option. Thankfully, I still had my work clothes on. I hated that I cared what I looked like, but I wanted him to see what he had walked away from.

I ran my fingers through my hair, stalling. "How'd you find me? What do you want?"

"The reverse phone directory. I want to talk to you face to face and not through a door." He paused. "I'm leaving in the morning. I promise I won't bother or contact you again."

"You're going to have to leave without seeing me. We've already talked." I kept my breathing steady, hoping to calm down.

"I guess I don't blame you. I just wanted to see you one last time and to set some things right. I'm worried you don't know what you're facing."

"Said and done." However, I didn't move away from the door.

"Becky, I mean Hollis, I'm sorry I haven't got used to your new name. But you have to talk to me. I—"

"I don't *have* to do anything. I can't believe you even have the nerve to come here."

"I have no excuses. I never expected your forgiveness. What I did has haunted me ever since." He sighed and looked regretful. "I will never attempt to speak to you again and I won't contact your family. I've changed. I just want you to know about Rory, to see you, to tell you I'm sorry."

I started to feel foolish talking through the door. I opened it.

When he walked in, he immediately sucked all the energy out of the room, or at least out of me. He always had a way of filling a room and consuming all the air.

Bill wore my favorite cologne. He wore it when we were married. I wondered if he did it now on purpose. He was smart enough not to smile. I didn't know if the remorse in his eyes was real or not.

"You have fifteen minutes."

"I'll take it." He came straight in and sat down on the living room sofa. "You look good, Becky. Real good."

So did he. He was still handsome in a past tense sort of way. He hadn't changed a bit. I wanted to believe he'd started to gray or go bald, but his thick chestnut hair was photo-ready.

"Cut the crap, Bill. You have fourteen minutes."

"I want to explain why I … why I let things go the way they did."

In prison, I had imagined the conversation I'd have with Bill. It would take place in a hospital where he was dying from a debilitating disease that would take years to play out. During my visit, I'd hold the life support switch in my hand, but I wouldn't pull it. I'd let him live to regret another day.

Except that now, here I stood, struggling to remember the words I'd practiced for the past five years, in the same room with the man who I'd let redefine my world.

"It's too late for explanations. Your actions explained everything. You have twelve minutes."

He walked over to the glass cabinet and patted the frame. "Hey, you kept your grandmother's frog collection. I remember how much you hated it." He held it steady and started to open the glass door, then caught the look in my eyes. He pushed it closed. "You used to be kind. I guess I did this to you. I deserve it."

Trying to swallow the lump in my throat, I sat down. "Oh, no," I choked. "You didn't *do* anything to me. I did it to myself. But I'm free of you now, Bill."

Tears streamed down my face. I looked around blindly for a tissue. He grabbed a box off the mantel and sat next to me. I was furious with myself; I hadn't let myself cry over my marriage for years.

"Tell … tell me why." I hated my words even as I spoke them, but I couldn't stop them or the sobs.

He put his arm around my shoulders. I pulled away.

"I'm a loser, Becky. As hard as it is for me to say, you're lucky to be rid of me. I've never done a smart thing in my life … except maybe when I married you. Given an opportunity to do something selfless, I'll walk away every time." He started to pace.

"Then why are you warning me?"

"I think my lucky streak is running out. I've overstayed my

welcome in too many states. I'm going to leave the country. Listen, you're in trouble. I think I might have put you there."

"What's new?"

He gave me a sad smile. "I took a job for a friend, okay Michael—Rory—to provide insurance for some dummy real estate transactions. I didn't know it at the time, but he knew you. It's a long story. I know, I only have—" he looked down at his watch, "—nine minutes. Let's just say jerks attract jerks and I knew eventually I wouldn't be able to keep him away from you. However, it seems somebody took care of him for me. He won't be bothering anybody else anymore."

He was alarming me. I sat up. "You make murder sound like an inconvenience. Who are you talking about? Do you know who killed Rory? Was he blackmailing you, too?"

He shook his head. "I have a couple of ideas, but they're still only guesses." He leaned forward on the sofa. "The thing is, there are still people out there—a guy named Newton for one—who may try to get to me through you. Things are starting to move too fast. I need you to keep quiet. Don't tell them anything."

He was coming at me too fast. "I don't know anything."

"Right, that's exactly what you tell them. You've got to take this seriously. I need you to give me cover in case they get in contact with you."

Sometimes I can be really naive. This conversation was a flashback that hit me between the eyes and cleared my thinking. It was the same old Bill, except this time it wasn't the same old me.

Uncomfortable under my stare, he looked down at his watch again.

I stood. "I want to thank you, Bill. Your coming by helped me answer a lot of questions."

He stood, too. "Ah, sure, Beck, you know I—"

"I always wanted to know why you left me in that courtroom and afterward, how you could live with yourself knowing your wife was in prison because of you." It was my turn to smile. I moved toward him. He backed away. He was right to be fearful.

"I hated to do it." He spoke a little too fast. "I knew I could save you by cutting our ties. Without a record, we figured you wouldn't have to serve a full sentence. I didn't know they'd switch judges on us. I didn't know I'd only get county time. I told—"

"Yet you were the one to get released early." I moved to the door. "It's time for you to go."

He started to lean down as if to kiss me. He must have seen my *Kill Bill* expression and straightened up. He handed me a piece of paper. "Well, then, goodbye. You don't have to worry. I won't come by again. Here's my cellphone number in case you want to reach me."

I opened the front door. He walked down the front path to the walkway. Then he paused and turned. "Oh, and you can throw out those old pictures you told me about. The statute of limitations was up on my crime four months ago."

I slammed the door as hard as I could and stood at the front window as he drove away. My neighbor had a visitor who sat in his car and must have heard the door. Beneath bushy eyebrows and an equally thick mustache, he gave me a small smile. I pulled the curtain closed.

Tears poured from my eyes as I leaned against the window. Tears I swore I'd never shed again, hot angry tears. He could still set me off.

I grabbed a dish of leftover lasagna from the freezer and slammed it into the microwave. Minutes later, my hand shook as I brought a fork to my mouth. The pasta was flavored by the salt of my tears.

CHAPTER NINETEEN

PROBATE COURT WAS thankfully predictable. The court clerk stamped in the client documents and, when our file number came up, I stood next to the clerk and took receipt of approved copies. It was the routine that kept my sanity.

At about ten-thirty I returned to the firm and dropped several sets of filing papers to go out in FedEx. I went back to my office to clear my desk of pending case matters.

Without thinking, I caught myself picking up the phone to call Abby to share a salad. As I slowly put the phone back in its cradle, I missed her more than I thought I could. I wondered what the police were doing with Rena's information. In this case, no news wasn't necessarily good news.

I couldn't stop my thoughts from drifting to Lily as I sat at my desk and tried to come up with a strategy to prove or disprove Marla's fears.

Lisa, one of the two other paralegals in the firm, stood in my doorway with a pleading look on her face.

"Since Cathy's gone, I need a place where I can assemble the discovery on a complicated environmental case. My office is too small and people keep coming in and out."

I knew where this was going.

"You have more seniority than I do," she went on. "You have first shot at a new office. Would you mind if I used it for the next few weeks?"

A light came on in my head. Lisa's words hit me like a rock. I told her the office was hers for as long as she needed it.

That was it. Joseph was using Marjorie's old office. No one would think to look in there until they hired a new nurse.

I debated whether to make my next visit to the center when I knew Joseph would be there. Very likely he thought I knew about his nefarious dealings and would pick a day when he was away. If I visited when he was there, he might think I hadn't caught on yet and could continue with his sideline.

Going to the center after work was becoming a welcome habit. For a few moments it took my mind off the murders. This time I stopped and picked up sugar-free oatmeal cookies. I didn't want to trigger an outbreak of diabetes in the senior population with an overload of doughnuts. I passed through the lobby.

One of the new male residents whose name I couldn't remember approached me with his walker. "Hollis, I'm so glad you're here. Can you go to the library? Marla could use some help with Lily."

If Marla was already helping, I doubted I'd do any better. "Here, er…" I thrust out the bakery's box of cookies.

"Phil."

"Of course, Phil. Can you put these in the community room for me?"

He took the box and trudged slowly back toward his fellow residents.

I dashed down the hallway.

Lily was weeping.

Marla held her close and rocked her slowly back and forth. She had her hand over Lily's brow and murmured words of comfort. Marla saw me first and shook her head slightly in concern.

She murmured, "Lily, I want you to take some breaths and blink your eyes a few times." She kept her voice slow and steady. "I want you to remember we have to go through the garden catalog to order bulbs for the gardener. We told him we would."

Lily said nothing, but her crying lessened. I motioned to Marla that I would go get a nurse, but her eyes gave me a strong no.

"Now, that's better. You just had a spell. Breathe deeply." Marla patted her head and slowly straightened Lily in the chair. "Look who's here? It's Hollis. You need to pull yourself together if you want to ask her about your house."

Lily looked up. Her eyes and cheeks were red; her lips trembled. She righted herself and took a handkerchief out of her housecoat pocket to blow her nose.

"I used to be a museum curator. I know the value of my things."

Her statement caught me by surprise. "I didn't know that. I thought you told me you used to own a business."

"That's because you don't listen."

Marla smiled at me. Lily was back to normal.

She motioned for me to stay put while she walked Lily to her room. In less than ten minutes, she was back.

"Marla, I think Lily may need to see the nurse. She's getting worse. It may not be wrong medication. She may have an … an illness."

She sat down next to me. "Nonsense." She lowered her voice. "Hollis, if we get the staff involved, they'll take Lily away. They'll put her in a ward and probe her and stick her and scare her to … death."

"I know she's your friend, and I know you're worried about her, but I think you have to consider all the possibilities. She might need true medical help."

Marla grabbed my arm. "Just help me make sure it's not her medication. If I knew she wasn't being harmed, I'd be at peace with things. By the way, why are you here this evening? Did you come to search?"

I pulled away gently until her arm dropped to her lap. "I told you I wasn't going to speak about what I'm doing. I came to see if I left a folder in the community room. Tell you what. We'll make a deal. If I can't prove it's Lily medication that has changed her by the start of the week, we'll both go to see the director and tell her about Lily's behavior."

"Make it two weeks. I know you're trying to get ready for your hearing."

"No. One week. Next Monday. I'll either figure this out by then or there's nothing to figure out."

I don't think she realized how much I counted on having nothing to figure out. I needed a win. I was also burning out on trying to figure out who the guilty Fallen Angel was.

Maybe Gene was right about Miller being just another club member and not a killer. On the other hand, Miller brought the books. He knew the plots before any of us. Abby's murder was described in the book we'd just discussed. Miller would have had plenty of time to read the book and set up the crime scene. He could have left the note on Rena's windshield. Miller could easily be the one. I had to discover his secret. And I had to discover it before he figured out I was on to him.

When three thirty rolled around, I stopped shuffling papers. I just couldn't focus on work. I walked over to Mark's office and told him I was going to get the last signature from the Riddick heir.

"You want me to come with you?"

"I'll be all right." I preferred going alone but appreciated the offer.

"Have you had a chance to look over the Riddick will?" he asked.

"Yes. It's pretty basic. Why?"

"It looks like Imelda's nieces and nephews were fairly middle-class. It was the Riddicks that had the money." He leaned over his desk. "I just wondered why a twenty-something Imelda would even have a will. Her family didn't own any property. Why would she name Triple D as her executor?"

I was with him on this.

"We have a team meeting with Avery coming up," I said. "Let's ask him. We'll have all the signatures by then. I still have to complete the case research, even though it looks like we're going to get all our signatures. I've got plenty of citations."

I pulled out a large volume of court cases.

Mark seemed distracted. "Hollis, er ... your friend, Rena. Is she married?"

"What?"

He appeared fascinated with a button on his shirt. "If she's available, I'd like to get to know her."

"Rena, married? I don't think so." I smiled. "She must have made a big impression. You only just met her."

I smiled to see Mark blush as he said, "Maybe you could ask her if you could give me her number." He faked ducking as if I'd hit him.

"Very funny. You'd better duck. Do I look like a matchmaker?"

"No. You look like anything but that." Mark laughed. "Hollis, I really would like to get to know her."

The disappearance of his smile told me he was serious.

"I'm not making promises. I don't expect to see her very soon. We'll see."

I guess I'm still a sucker for romance. By the time I left work, I knew I'd call Rena. I was only mildly surprised at how willing Rena was for me to give her phone number to Mark. She also seemed to realize I drew the line at girl chatter and wouldn't engage in any speculative conversation about his eligibility as a bachelor.

My next call wasn't as easy.

"Homicide, Faber."

"Detective Faber, this is Hollis Morgan. I was wondering if I could talk to you about Bill Lynley. He contacted me."

He didn't answer right away. "Sure, do you want me to come there?"

I shook my head, thankful he couldn't see the look of distaste on my face. "No. Remember, I don't work too far from the station. I can come to you. What time is best?"

"How about after you leave work today? I'll stay until you get here."

I WENT THROUGH the security checkpoint. Minutes later I faced an obviously tense Detective Faber in what I knew to be an interview room.

"I'm going to tape this. Hopefully you won't mind?"

My throat went dry. I knew it wouldn't make a difference if I did. "Bill Lynley came to see me."

Faber's head shot up. "At your home? When?"

"Last night."

Faber's lips formed a thin line.

"I know. I guess I should have called you this morning."

"You guessed right. What did he want?"

"He told me I was in danger. That he and Rory worked on some kind of scheme with a third person."

"Who's the third person?"

"I don't know. He didn't say. He did say Rory started blackmailing some guy he and Bill did this scheme with. Only Rory dealt with him. He never let Bill see the guy." I realized how stupid I sounded. "Anyway, he thinks that's the guy who killed Rory."

"Did he actually say 'guy'? Or is that your word?"

I replayed the conversation with Bill in my mind. "I'm not sure."

"Did he say what the scheme was?"

"No."

"So why did he think you were in danger if you don't know the scheme?"

That was a question I had as well. "I don't know. I didn't give him a chance to tell me. I … I really wasn't interested in talking to him. I told him to go away. He lies."

Detective Faber tilted his head back. "You don't think he's lying now?"

"I don't know."

"Did he tell you where he's staying?"

"No, but I had called Rory's mother earlier to … to give my condolences, and Bill answered."

Detective Faber reached for his phone, punched in a few numbers and asked to speak to Lincoln. From the frown on his face, he must not have been around.

"Okay, Mrs. Lyn— … Ms. Morgan, we appreciate you giving us this information. We're still working out the details of the relationship between your husband and Rollins, er … Norris.

"Ex-husband and yeah, I … I just want all this to end as soon as possible." I stood to leave. "Am I still on your suspect list?"

I thought I saw a hint of a smile, but if it was there, it was too faint and vanished too quickly for me to be sure.

"Everyone—"

"Yeah, I know. Everyone's a suspect, but … but am I high on your suspect list?"

"It's undisputed that two murders were committed which involve your book club. We have eliminated no one from our suspect list." He came around the table and stood next to me. "Ms. Morgan, you were right to come in. However, I caution you that withholding information in a criminal investigation is a crime. We want to see this wrapped up quickly as well."

"I don't know anything else." It was the truth. I was tired of lying.

He walked over to the door. "Then I want to thank you for taking the time to come in. Next time, err on the side of being conservative and get in contact with us as soon as you think you have any information affecting this case. Not days later. Not hours later. Let us decide if it's meaningful. Thank you again."

I was dismissed.

OPAL MURRAY STOOD in the lobby of the senior center. I got the distinct impression she was waiting for me to arrive.

"Hollis, good to see you. There's something I want to show you. Can you come to my office?"

"Of course."

My curiosity was in overdrive. Since our last conversation, I didn't think Ms. Murray cared for my interfering in her turf. I followed.

"I wanted to follow up with you about Lily's medication. I asked her doctor to double-check our records and to give her a blood test to make sure mistakes weren't being made."

I was impressed. I hadn't thought of blood tests.

"And?"

"He found nothing to indicate things weren't as they should be." Opal folded her hands on the desk.

"Did he examine her? Did he talk with her? Lily's acting strangely and getting worse each day."

"Lily's getting old. I made a special effort to talk with her and interact with her during community time. Her behavior isn't out of the ordinary for someone her age." She picked up a cup and took a drink. "I know you care about her but this type of thing is inevitable."

"I'm not naïve. I know she could be a victim of dementia, but I don't—"

"You know I can't discuss Lily's health with you. I just wanted you to know I took your concerns seriously and followed up with the doctor."

I nodded. "Just tell me one thing. Have you seen a change in her? She's fine in the morning, but in the afternoon she drifts and becomes almost incoherent."

Opal frowned. "Yes, I know. It can be explained. Her doctor says her condition is to be expected. Dementia can come on suddenly."

Her words rolled off me. I believed that she believed the explanation. But I knew Lily and I knew I'd have to take things into my own hands.

AT HOME I finished putting together my recommendation packages for Rita and Avery to complete. I fixed myself a cup of tea. If I was right, this whole thing with Lily would be wrapped up quickly. I made another cup. When I looked at the clock again, it was almost midnight. I wasn't sleepy and I still smelled Bill's cologne. Why had he made such a big deal out of seeing me? He didn't say anything he couldn't say on the phone. I had a suspicion that, like any dog, he thought that territory once marked could always be reclaimed.

Well, he thought wrong.

CHAPTER TWENTY

TOO MANY RESTLESS nights and not enough sleep were starting to take their toll. Stifling a yawn, I snuck a look at my watch and hoped Avery wasn't planning on an extended team meeting.

"Okay, where are we with the Riddick matter?" Avery slapped several thick pale-green legal files between us, forming a low barrier. For the past twenty minutes, he hadn't looked up, and he was rambling through a description of the case status, repeatedly losing his train of thought.

I exchanged looks with Mark.

"Well, Hollis and I contacted all the heirs. Each of them signed the declaration and release."

"Spouses as well?" Avery asked.

"Spouses, too." Mark looked at me with an acknowledging nod.

"Good." Avery pulled a pad out and started writing. "Hollis, contact this appraiser and have him go out to the Riddick house as soon as possible. Try for next week. No later than the week after." He passed the paper to me.

I looked at the information. "I know another appraiser who

has worked for the firm in the past. He is fast, professional and a lot cheaper. I could give him a call."

"No, use Putnam. The firm will get a break on his fee because I've given him other properties as a package deal." Avery put the Riddick file in front of Mark. "I'd like you to prepare the court petition, declarations and order. I don't want this to drag out, so let me see drafts by the end of next week."

Mark nodded.

"All right. Anything else before we move on to the Gleason matter?"

Mark straightened up. "Yes. Isn't it kind of strange that Imelda Riddick would have a will made up when she was only twenty-three? I did some preliminary research. Imelda's relatives came from lower-to-middle class families. They didn't have any assets, didn't even own their own homes. Why would a young woman like that make out a will?"

Avery's jaw stiffened and his eyes narrowed. Not a good sign.

"What's your point?" His voice would have frozen lava.

I struggled with jumping in to save Mark, but he clearly was on a suicide mission and appeared to be oblivious to the mounting tension in the room.

"Shouldn't we check more into her husband's background? Maybe there are more assets or heirs on his side. There could even be a later will that—"

"Stop right there. Interesting, but irrelevant. I hope you didn't bill the client's estate for any of your wandering research. I'm the supervising attorney and you check with me before you go off on your own fantasy assignments." He picked up the next file. "Now, have you closed your old cases?"

Mark looked as if he'd been socked in the nose. I didn't give my sympathy often but he had it.

"I ... I'm fairly close to finishing. I just have some client letters to dictate. The Riddick heirs took up a lot of my time and—"

Avery held up his hand. "This is embarrassing. At least it is for me. You have time to go off on a tangent about a simple estate matter but not the time to do your job. You're on thin ice here, Mark. Don't risk losing it all."

I realized my hands were twisting in my lap. I was mesmerized. Avery was acting uncharacteristically mean. He wasn't usually the type to reprimand an attorney in front of staff or anyone else.

Something was wrong.

"Avery," I said, "I'm partly responsible for holding Mark back. I'm drafting the final client letters and haven't been able to dedicate the time needed to get them done. You'll have them on your desk Monday morning."

Avery jerked his head over to me as if he'd forgotten I was in the room. "Is that right?" His tone was disbelieving. He gave me a touché nod. I hadn't fooled him. "I'm a patient man. I can wait forever to make something happen. You both are wasting time by getting distracted."

Mark looked over at me in surprise. "You can work that fast?"

He had to be a lousy poker player.

"Not a problem."

Avery regained his composure, but the rest of the meeting wasn't over soon enough for any of us.

Mark and I had our own after-team meeting in the lunch room. Accompanied by the background hum of the vending machines, I slowly drank my tea. Mark showed his agitation by pacing the room.

"Thank you for in there."

I ran my fingers through my hair and said, "Couldn't you tell he doesn't like surprises? Or playing guessing games, particularly with clients' funds? You can't plead a case if you don't look up to see a client's reaction."

"I wanted him to know I had an inquisitive mind and could think outside the box."

"You better tread carefully. Get through your probationary

period first. Don't make any waves. Don't try to impress anybody. Just do your assignments."

"Yeah. I got it." He looked at me. "You'll actually do those client letters for me?"

I'd already started to berate myself for volunteering. "Don't push it."

Back in my office, I was amazed by how quickly Mark moved to bring me his files. In fact, I didn't mind helping this once. The letters were pretty straightforward and they kept me busy. My modus operandi was to finish my work and complete my hours ahead of schedule, sometimes days ahead. That way I'd be seen as a superstar, but on my own terms. Mark's letters were done by the end of the day. I'd hold them a while longer before I handed them in to Avery. I wanted to ask Mark about Rena, but we couldn't find time to talk. He stayed in his office behind closed doors.

I headed for the center.

Fortunately, I knew where Marjorie's office was located. After giving Marla an awkward hug goodnight, I pretended to head for the break room. The hallways were empty and the residents were in for the night. I tried the door to the vacant office. Not surprisingly, it was locked. It took only a few minutes for me to make my way back to the lobby. I prayed Joseph hadn't figured out how I got the code.

He hadn't. It was still there.

I memorized the numbers and headed back down the hall. In less than a minute, the keypad beeped and I was inside. The office was dark except for glare from the streetlights that crept between the blinds. A desk with a lamp and chair waited for an occupant, but other than that, the room was empty. A door leading to what appeared to be a closet was half open. I opened it. It was a closet, but with a second door, it also served as a small pass-through to an adjacent room. This larger room was equally dark, but a tall table with a stool, a small brown box, a weighing scale and a small machine were evident.

A pill sorting machine.

I didn't turn on the light out of fear that someone would notice. Instead, I walked around the table and over to a waist-high shelf that held pharmaceutical supplies. Nothing appeared sinister or out of place. There was a stack of papers in an inbox on one of the lower shelves. I took a couple of the top sheets and walked over to the window to see if I could make out the words. They were notices from various manufacturers touting one medicine or advertising recent breakthroughs in the market.

Hearing voices in the hallway, I put my ear against the door. Two women. A male voice joined in. I quickly placed the pages back on the shelf and slipped into the pass-through. Cracking the door to see out, the keypad beeped. The door opened. Joseph entered and turned on the light. I slid back into the shadows. He didn't look my way but went over to the table and put the small box under his arm. He went to the door, glanced around and turned off the light. I didn't realize I'd been holding my breath until I finally exhaled.

That was too close.

UNDER MY DOORMAT I saw the edge of an envelope sticking out and recognized Bill's effusive handwriting. Putting aside the fact that he had come back after promising he wouldn't, I sat on the sofa and opened the letter.

> Dearest Becky,
>
> I know you want to be called Hollis, but you will always be Becky to me. I guess I never wrote you a letter. Too bad it can't be under happier circumstances. I did a poor job of trying to talk to you last time. You know I'm not good at that kind of thing. I don't think on my feet as fast as you do and I'm too impatient.
>
> Anyway, I stopped expecting you to call my cell so I'm having it disconnected. I don't think you'd give it to the

police, but I thought it best to remove that temptation.

Rory dealt with some very unsavory characters. He didn't take my advice and blackmailed one of his partners. Like I told you before, he got greedy. All I know is that Rory couldn't control him. Whoever killed him might know about me. It won't be long before he figures out I have something he wants. I put it in a safe place, with someone I trust.

I'm using another name, which I won't share with you. I know you'll try to solve all this, but for your own sake, I hope you don't. Just be careful. There's a man who has a grudge against me. He has the situation all wrong, but he won't listen. He may come after you. Don't try to reason with him. Call the police.

I hope you can forgive me one day. That's it. Have a happy life. That's all I wanted to say. Except, I wish things could have been different for us.

Love,
Bill

Bill had always been one for drama, but something told me that this time I wouldn't hear from him again. I folded the letter, putting it in the envelope and then into my purse. I knew I'd have to turn it in to the police. The letter answered a few questions, but it raised others. I had a lot of chores I needed to do. Instead, I sat and watched the last filaments of the sun fade.

THE FORMATION OF the Fallen Angels had been based on trust, but now trust was out of the question. Our bond was broken. There was still one member for me to check out.

I had, unconsciously or not, saved investigating Miller to the end. While I wasn't ready to completely write off the others, I could almost check off all the boxes for Miller as the likely killer. Richard was desperate to keep his past from his wife, but he also seemed to have been willing to pay Rory for his silence, at least for a while. Gene's gay relationship with a minister gave him a strong motive, but I didn't believe he could have killed Abby. Rena had an alibi.

Then there was Miller.

I had brought Miller's Inquiry First printout home. It contained much of what Gene told me—which wasn't a lot. Even though our club selections were made by voting, Miller limited the books we had to choose from. He could select the books based on the murder scene he favored. Otherwise, the murderer would have had to read the club books after we voted. It took some planning to mimic the mode of each killing. I munched thoughtfully on a slice of pear. Finally, the murderer had to be a man. Whoever killed Rory and Abby had to be strong.

There was no time like the present. I punched in his number.

"Hollis, what's wrong? Why'd you call?"

"I want to talk about Rory's murder. I have an idea who murdered him."

There was silence. Miller cleared his throat. "Who?"

I wanted to hang up the phone and run in the other direction. "Not over the phone. Would lunch tomorrow work for you?" Being around other people seemed like a good idea.

"I've got a better idea. I've got a three-thirty flight to L.A., day after tomorrow. How about meeting me at the airport for lunch?"

Airports have a lot of people.

"Fine. I'll meet you at Gino's on the upper level at noon."

I slept fitfully. The cast in my dreams included a large turtle that had Abby's blue eyes. He wore an oversized alarm clock and told me I was running out of time. He ran away but his clock clanged.

It was six o'clock in the morning. I shut off the alarm and got up.

On my break, I went back to the bank. I was on a slippery

slope and didn't know how much time I had to find firm ground. Fortunately, this time the young woman I'd bumped heads with a few days ago was busy tormenting another customer. I approached a young man who appeared to be hiding behind his computer monitor.

"I'd like access to my safe deposit box."

His face filled with relief, as if he were glad I'd asked for something he knew how to do. Alone, I took out the contents: five pictures, divorce papers, prison release papers, my acceptance to Hastings and a small box. The police still had the chest I kept at home. I fanned through the photos. Four of them were of rooms in homes so Bill could provide his "fence" with a snapshot of coming attractions. I slipped them into a large envelope I had brought with me.

The last photo was of my family. *My family*. Rita's words about my family's view of me came back and my eyes glistened as if hearing them for the first time. *Breathe*. The safety deposit box held all my personal possessions. I had put them there when I knew I was going to prison. After I got out, keeping a safe deposit box seemed like a smart precaution. No one could go through my things. It was silly, but I didn't want to lose my papers. The sparse collection of memories made me feel human. I didn't bother to open the small box that held my wedding ring. No, I dumped it all into the envelope and got up to leave. I had to believe I'd get through this.

It was time to move on.

The young bank assistant tapped away on his keyboard. After signing the forms to close out my box, I headed back to my office.

I wasn't planning on going away anymore.

CHAPTER TWENTY-ONE

I SLIPPED THROUGH the Triple D lobby, grateful that Emily was preoccupied on the reception phone. I hoped to talk to Mark, except he was busy on a conference call. Avery looked up as I walked by, but he hastily turned back to the work in front of him. Back in my office, he'd put Lily's trust documents in my basket for processing. She'd be pleased with Avery's work, but likely not with me. Avery was right. Next time I'd think twice about which candidates qualified for pro bono services.

"Hey, how's it going?" Mark asked moments later. "You wanted to see me?"

"Where have you been? I keep missing you."

A hint of red crept up his neck. Could Rena have anything to do with it?

"I've been around. Why were you looking for me?"

"Are you ready for Avery? I think we should give him all our Riddick documents at the same time. It should be done today."

"Today? You said we had more time. I guess I can pull everything together if I have to."

"Good, then let's do it. We can make some brownie points with the boss."

He sat and began playing with the paperweight on my desk. "Hollis, I think Rena is real nice."

"Oh?"

"Yeah, we've gone out to dinner and took in a concert at the amphitheater." He put the paperweight down and started playing with the stapler. "You don't think she's involved in any of the book club mess, do you?"

"You mean, is she a suspect like me? No, I don't think so. She hasn't been a member long enough."

"Good. Good and there's no conflict because I'm not a criminal attorney."

"Yes, I know."

His nervousness was amusing. It was all I could do to keep from laughing.

"Okay, then. I've got to get back to work." He got up, but not before he knocked over my phone.

I waved away his apologies. "Go. It's okay. I'll let Avery know we'll be ready for him."

Luckily for Mark, the meeting with Avery went uneventfully. If Avery was impressed by our work performance, he didn't show it. The meeting conversation drifted and when the talk turned to fourth round draft picks, I departed for home.

THERE WAS A light tap at the front door. Often the kids behind my unit needed to go through my condo to my back patio to retrieve a ball. They always knocked, as if that would bother me less than if they used the doorbell.

I looked through the peephole. It wasn't neighbor kids. It was the police. I fought down alarm.

A uniformed female officer looked grim.

"Mrs. Lynley? My name is Officer Winton. I'm with the San Lucian Police Department; I'd like you to come with me to the Alameda County Sherriff's office."

Weariness and wariness slipped over me. "My last name is Morgan. I took back my maiden name. Why do I need to go to downtown? What's this about? Am I being arrested?"

"No. Nothing like that. Sorry for frightening you. We need your help with an identification. One of our detectives thinks you can help." The young woman turned halfway from me. Another uniformed officer stood at the curb in front of a marked police car. I knew for sure I'd be the topic of the next homeowner's association meeting.

"Who do you want me to identify?"

"Sorry, ma'am. I can't tell you because I don't know. My captain just sent us here to give you a ride to the station."

"Since when does San Lucian PD offer carpooling?" I willed the comment back, but it was out there. It didn't seem to matter.

"I'll wait for you to get your things."

Was I doomed to live a life on the speed dial of law enforcement? Sitting in the backseat, I was grateful they couldn't hear my thoughts. It only took a few minutes to arrive at the back entrance of a low white building located in the block next to the one that held Detective Faber's office.

Not surprisingly, it was Faber who stood in the lobby area talking to Lincoln.

"Ms. Morgan, thank you for helping us out."

"Did I have a choice?"

His eyes met mine. "I ... we didn't mean it to be that way. We're working with Oakland PD on a case. Early this morning a body was discovered in an apartment in an unincorporated area near Kensington. We think you might know him."

"A body I might know. Who?" My voice faltered.

"We ran the fingerprints. It's William Lynley. We'd like you to confirm it is, in fact, your ex-husband."

I don't know who else I expected to identify, but I still found it hard to hear it was Bill. I nodded in shock and turned away from Detective Faber's questioning eyes. Detective Lincoln was ready for me and offered a box of tissue from a nearby desk.

I shook my head. I wouldn't show these men my tears. "My god, how did it happen?"

"He was shot." Detective Faber sat on the edge of a desk. "The place had been wiped clean of fingerprints. Someone took great pains to ensure we wouldn't be able to identify the killer without going to some trouble."

"Did one of your books have a shooting, too?" Detective Lincoln didn't hide his sarcasm.

"No." Even if one had, I doubted I'd have had the strength to admit it.

Detective Lincoln ran his hand through his hair. "Well, finally that run is done."

Detective Faber looked at his watch. "There was nothing in his apartment when we found him, except for an empty wallet and a phony driver's license. We think he was leaving town when he was confronted by his killer. Ms. Morgan, you'd be doing us a service if you'd identify the body. Will that be a problem?"

"No. No problem." I closed my eyes for a moment. "I've never seen a dead body before, though."

"Like I said, you'll be doing us a service."

Nervousness gripped me as I walked into the cold metal-furnished chambers of the county morgue. Television came close, but nothing compared to the reality of a room filled with death. I looked down at Bill's ashen face and knew whatever spirit had made him Bill was gone. This man had ruined my life, but I let him. I said my goodbye to the Bill I once loved, not the Bill I saw now.

I nodded to Detective Lincoln, who lowered the sheet over his face and pushed the gurney to the side.

Gratefully, I allowed Detective Faber to lead me back to the hallway. We walked toward an interview room.

He stared at me. "When was the last time you saw your ex-husband, Ms. Morgan?"

It was his tone of voice that caught my attention. "The last time I came here to talk to you. I haven't seen him since."

Lincoln stopped inside the doorway. "No kidding? Yet, you're the last person he dialed on his cellphone."

"Well, I don't know about that. He told me he had his phone disconnected." I walked in front of Detective Lincoln and sat down. I fought the rising nausea.

"Interesting. When did he tell you this? You didn't mention it at our last meeting."

"He didn't tell me. He wrote me a letter. I forgot about it until just now." I had to pull myself together before something very bad happened. "I told him I didn't want to ever see him again so he wrote me a letter."

"Where's the letter?" Detective Lincoln asked.

"In my purse."

Detective Faber held out his hand. "We'd like a look at it."

My hand shook as I pulled out the paper. Detective Faber quickly read through it and handed it to Detective Lincoln.

Detective Faber spoke. "Ms. Morgan, we'd like to keep this letter. Do you have any idea about the third person Lynley referred to?"

"None. I told you I didn't want anything else to do with Bill. I don't know what he was involved in."

"Do you have time to continue talking for a moment? You may be able to help us with the link between your husband and Rory Norris."

"Truly, I can't. I don't know any more about Bill's connection to Rory than what you already know." It took an effort to keep my foot from tapping madly on the floor. I used my hand to stop my knee from shaking. "Despite this letter, Bill and I didn't keep in contact."

Detective Faber opened a file in front of him. "I believe you. The fact of the matter is that the only common denominator we can find between Rory Norris, Abigail Caldwell and now Bill Lynley is … you."

"Don't you think I'm aware of that?" I had to keep my frustration from turning into anger. "Except I don't know what it all means."

Detective Lincoln put a bottle of water in my hands. They still shook. "Ms. Morgan, what did Lynley mean, 'someone I trust'? That's kind of an odd thing to say to you. It's like he's telling you who might have the information, don't you think?"

It was odd, but I hadn't taken the time to think about what Bill meant. "I honestly don't know. I have no idea who Bill trusts, but I doubt it's me. I don't know what the bad guys might want."

"If he's warning you off, he's making an effort to tell you there's something to be on the lookout for." Detective Faber tapped the file with his pen. "I think it's a coded message. What do you think?"

"I … I—"

"I think he was trying to tell you something. He knew you might keep trying to find your friend's killer. He wanted to give you help without giving you an answer that could lead to more trouble for you."

Detective Lincoln sat next to me. "Ms. Morgan, where were you last night around ten?"

His question almost caught me off guard. "At home. I was home in bed. And no, there's no one who can give me an alibi. You don't really think I killed Bill, do you?"

"I know your ex was a jerk. He let you spend time in state prison. Time he should have spent. You lost one and a half years of your life. I know I'd be very angry, maybe even furious with my spouse." Detective Lincoln folded his hands. "Maybe, with all those months in prison, you had time to think about how you'd kill him, exercising some long-delayed justice."

I looked at him in amazement. He'd come so close to the truth. However, my dream scenario of punishing Bill to the fullest extent was merely bravado. "You must be crazy. I'd never put the rest of my life in jeopardy. Go look somewhere else for your killer, Detective. It isn't me."

Faber looked down at a paper in the file. "You know the odds are against you getting a judge to issue a pardon order to clear your record. With these murders hanging over you, it's a long shot."

It was as if he'd hit me in the stomach. "What?" I whispered. "How did you find out about my application?"

"Your name was cross-referenced with recent court filings. We get a daily list of public actions on anyone who's of interest in our investigations."

I couldn't speak.

Detective Faber said, "I'm trying to believe you, Ms. Morgan. I *want* to believe you. You're a very bright woman. I think you're still hiding something and I have to at least consider you had a motive for Bill Lynley's killing. What better cover than the shadow of the club's murders?"

"I didn't even know where he lived." There was desperation in my voice. "You've got to believe me, I'm not lying."

"So you say. I want you to go home and think about those books of yours, particularly the ones from the club. Maybe there's a book plot that ties back to your ex-husband's murder." Detective Faber spoke slowly. "Who would your ex-husband trust? You have as much an interest as we do in getting these murders solved. You've got a lot at stake. Think back. Help us."

Detective Faber motioned to Detective Lincoln, who stood and opened the door.

"Ms. Morgan, you look beat. I'll have you taken home."

IN MY KITCHEN, I laid out all the books the club had read over the past six months. If I found any clues, I might have to go back further, but taking things in six-month chunks seemed a good start. The two club murders were modeled after books read in that timeframe.

September's book had been historical fiction. In October
it was a spy thriller and in November we read a self-help
book that turned everyone off, especially the guys, which is
why we went back to drama. December was a memoir set in
England. January was *World at Midnight*. I lifted up the stack
of books. It was missing. The February selection had been
Storm Crossing—the source for Abby's murder—and March's
had been *The Long Pause*.

I thought back to our May selection. When the police came
to my home after Rory died, I didn't have the book to show
them, but it wasn't at the office, either. I got up and did a quick
search of the house. When I didn't find it, I got my keys and
went out to my car. The book was face down on the floor of my
backseat. With relief, I brought it into the house. I didn't recall
putting it there, but my memory had let me down a couple
of times in the past days. I had spent fifteen minutes looking
for my car keys the day before because I couldn't remember
putting them in a place where I wouldn't forget to find them.

I put Post-its on the pages of each book with the actual
murder descriptions. There were no similarities. Both authors
had their own style of mayhem. I checked for common victim
types but found none. The victims were as varied as the real life
copycats. The motives in the book murders were also different
and had nothing in common with either Rory or Abby—at
least as far as I knew.

I shoved everything to the side and poured myself another
glass of wine. First, Rory. Then Abby. Now Bill. I pushed back
a mounting fear and took a deep swallow. My pardon seemed
further away than ever.

CHAPTER TWENTY-TWO

I WENT TO the airport to meet Miller on my way back from getting the signature from Imelda's last nephew. The other Riddick heirs overnighted their signed documents to the office so I could kill two birds with one stone. I made a mental note to never use that saying again.

Worried about being late, I tried not to show my annoyance when Avery stopped by to ask about Bill before I left the office.

"I know you were divorced, but if you need to take some time off it's not a problem."

I shook my head. "We were over in every sense of the word years ago."

"I just want you to know, I'd understand."

"You're very kind. I always felt I could count on you. Fortunately, Triple D was on the temp agency's reference list. This job saved me." I shrugged. "Unfortunately, Bill had some unsavory colleagues. I guess one got tired of him."

"So the police don't have a clue? They don't think you did it, do they?"

My flinch was automatic. "No. I don't know … maybe. I'm just taking things one day at a time."

He nodded and patted me on the shoulder. I faked a reassuring smile.

CONSTRUCTION OF A new airline waiting area in terminal two was underway at the Oakland airport. I parked in short-term parking and maneuvered my way through the barriers to the elevators. All my eggs were in the Miller basket. My intuition told me that, although the others had good motives, Miller also had means and opportunity. While my nerves were on edge, at the same time I felt calm and resigned.

"Hollis, over here." Miller waved from a table farthest away from the counter but next to a large window overlooking a landing strip. He pushed a mug of hot water toward me.

"Thanks for remembering." I reached for the selection of teas.

"No problem. Look, let's get to it. You said you thought you knew who killed Rory and Abby. Who?"

"I need to find out something first. Where do you work?"

"Why?"

I fingered the tea packet, avoiding his eyes. "How do you get our books for free? At first, we thought you worked for a newspaper and could get them through the book review section, but you don't."

"We? Who's we?"

I mentally kicked myself. *Stupid mistake.*

"There's no we. There's just me. So?"

Too late. I had raised his suspicions. He looked at me as if I wore a wire. I had to regain his trust.

"Look, Miller, I have a lot on the line. I need to have these murders solved as soon as possible. I can't afford to be a suspect. Please, help me." I hoped my Little Miss Vulnerable voice would get to him.

"All right. I guess there's no harm in telling you. They weren't for free. I bought them at a discount."

"What! Are you joking? Seven books every month for the

last three years. Why?"

"The first month, I did get them for free. It was a fire sale at the independent bookstore where I shop. We didn't vote that first month."

I nodded, remembering.

"I liked being with the club. It really helped me get over some adjustment humps. I didn't want having to come up with books to be a deal breaker for members. I wanted to make being a part of the book club easy. It was my contribution. You understand?"

Not really.

"I guess. You didn't answer my question. Where do you work?"

If there was a dark cloud in the sky, it came to rest over our table. Miller rose up in his chair, leaned over and spoke through clenched teeth. "That's none of your damn business."

A man with roll-on luggage sat at the next table but paid us no attention. Miller slouched in his seat.

"Don't mess with me, Hollis. I have a life and a lifestyle I'm not about to put at risk to satisfy your nosiness. If you think you have something on me, go to the police. If you come after me, if you mess up what I have, you better take me out, because I'll be coming after you."

I believed him.

"Miller, I—"

"I didn't kill Rory or Abby, so back off."

He was clearly trying to intimidate me and, to a large extent, he was succeeding. "You use an alias. Aren't you worried about your real name and … background coming out?"

He grabbed my wrist. "How did you find out about my real name?"

His grip was firm, but I wrenched my hand back. "You mean besides from the police? Look, Miller, I don't want to reveal any of your secrets. You say you didn't kill Rory or Abby. All right, that's all I wanted to know." I stood. Where was the exit?

"Sit down for a minute." His voice returned to normal.

There were still people nearby. I sat.

"My wife … my wife has her own small business. She won't allow for any scandals. My brother … had a drug habit. I tried to help him out. It almost ended our marriage when she found out I'd been in prison, but we got through it. She's been able to keep our names out of the paper as suspects, but if your prying about me gets out, I'll—"

"You don't have to threaten me. I get it."

This time I stood and walked away without looking back.

DRIVING BACK TO the office, I mentally went over the scene. I don't know what I expected to find out, but if I were to have any credibility with the police, I'd have to figure out what I'd learned. Bill's letter pointed to someone who would kill to save themselves and Miller was the Fallen Angels' book link. He got us the books, and he could point us to the plots he needed. He wasn't stupid, though. Why would he copy the murders from books he provided? Why would he risk bringing attention to himself? It was clear he could ditch his mild manner when he wanted. If he needed to frame me, why make it so complicated? Rory must have been blackmailing him, too. I punched numbers into my cellphone.

Time wasn't on my side. I had to see Detective Faber before Miller got away. If I were the killer, I'd be planning to clear out.

"DO YOU WORK here now?" the guard at the metal detector asked.

I gave him a tight smile. "No, but I can understand how you might think that." I wrote down my visitor information and got the requisite badge.

The detectives stood up when I was escorted to the interview room.

Detective Faber extended his hand. "It was smart of you to get in touch, Ms. Morgan. You think you have something on

Marshall Sloane. Miller Thornton to you?"

This was not the time to tell him I already knew Miller's alias. I sat down in the chair he pulled out. My seat was still the suspect chair across from the two of them.

A recount of my book research from the night before didn't take long.

"So, only Miller knew the plots of the books to be voted on by the club."

Detective Lincoln shifted in his seat. His small frame up against the oversized table made him look even more like a kid. "How did he manipulate the book selection to reflect the plot he wanted?"

"He knew us well enough to predict what we would want. I can also remember him pushing us toward one book because he could get more copies. Besides, we didn't know he was really buying the books. We thought he was doing us a favor by getting them for free. Miller would bring us the books the next month after we voted. None of us went out and bought the book if we knew we were getting it for free."

Detective Faber said, "So, you do think it's Thornton?"

I bit back a response that I sure wouldn't be here if I thought it was me. "Yes. It has to be Miller."

"You don't sound absolutely sure."

I hesitated. "Miller's an avid reader. He actually enjoys discussing the characters and plot of a book. He comes across as hugely kind and generous. Today I saw a different man. He must protect his family and Rory could have blackmailed him. You probably know a lot more about Thornton's, or Sloane's, background."

"Anything else?"

I shook my head. "No. I went through all the books for the past six months. He was the only link I could find. Detectives, I think Miller did it. Besides, of all the remaining members, he's the most likely. Everything points to him. I admit I'm a little surprised. I can't see him killing Abby. Maybe Rory, but if he were desperate enough, who knows?"

"Well, you know what I can't see?" Detective Lincoln said. "I can't see a bunch of ex-felons forming a book club in the first place."

He was getting on my last nerve.

"The book club idea took a little getting used to. Jeffrey Wallace is not only a great parole officer, he's a good person. He saw the best in all of us. I don't think we wanted to disappoint him." I spoke the truth. "Clearly, Miller and Rory weren't as motivated."

"Interesting. I thought your book club was based on confidentiality. Members wouldn't have their pasts or their current lives questioned. How did you find out all this stuff out about Miller Thornton?" Detective Faber asked.

"Listen," I pretended not to hear his question. "You have to hurry. I spooked him; he's going to run. He was getting on a plane. Miller could have killed Rory because Rory knew he hadn't given up his old ways. Also, Miller brought in the books. He knew how to set us all up."

"You didn't answer my question."

"I found out Miller's alias, the one in Marin County, and called the phone number. I confirmed Miller lived there." I tried to keep my irritation in check. It was important Detective Faber believed me.

"You happened to find out his alias?" His voice held more than a little disbelief.

"That's why I called you. He may think he's been found out." I paused. "Look, I have to get these murders solved, or at least have my name taken off the suspect list. My expungement petition is in jeopardy. You said so yourself."

"Do you know of any connection between Miller and your ex?"

I rubbed my forehead. "No."

"Can you hold that thought? I'll just be a moment." Faber motioned to Lincoln and they left the room. After only a few minutes, Detective Faber returned by himself.

This wasn't turning out as I pictured.

"I … I guess I can't prove anything. Miller has a solid motive for killing Rory, Abby, too."

"Frankly, Ms. Morgan, we've already thought of that." Detective Faber's chair creaked as he sat back. "While we don't have a lot of results, we have more than you do. I want you to know we appreciate your efforts, but we want you to stop playing detective and leave the investigation to the police."

"But he threatened me and—"

"You were prowling through his personal background."

I bit my lip. "Right. Okay, then. Did Rena Gabriel tell you about the slip of paper she found in her windshield wiper right before Abby died?"

"Yes, she did."

"Did she tell you no one in our group had discussed the book, *The Long Pause*? Miller had just introduced it."

"You had a copy, didn't you?"

"I always like a sneak peek, but I hadn't read it yet."

"I see."

He just sat there looking at me. Detective Lincoln came back into the room and passed Detective Faber a note.

"Well, I guess that's all I wanted you to know. I won't bother you anymore."

Detective Faber stood and so did I. He walked me toward the door.

"Like I said, if you want to help us, Ms. Morgan, the best way is to let us do our job. You could be putting yourself and the investigation at risk. We'll continue to talk with Mr. Sloane, your Miller Thornton." He held the door open. "Oh, by the way, we don't have to tell you this, but since you seem determined to meddle, Thornton has a verified alibi for the time period linked to Abby Caldwell's death. He's also been cleared of Rory's death."

Miller had been cleared, but not me. Great.

"Yep, you caught him, all right. He's a librarian. His wife is self-employed in some mucky-muck finance company. They have three kids. You confronted him red-handed on his way to give a speech in L.A. He's been nominated as a finalist for librarian of the year." Detective Lincoln didn't even try to hide his amusement.

"I didn't know." The pit in my stomach seemed bottomless. "I'm sorry for wasting your time. He was the only one left."

CHAPTER TWENTY-THREE

EXHAUSTED AND HARRIED from a weekend of reliving over and over my conversation with the police, I went into the office early Monday. Mark was waiting for me when I got in.

"Morning." I put my purse under the desk and booted up my computer. "Excuse me if I'm a little grumpy," I said. "I've had a rough few days. I don't think I've ever seen you here this early, except for that time when you victimized the copy room."

"I know. I wanted to get a jump start so we could go over the Riddick matter before our next meeting with Avery."

I took a second look at him, trying to put the events at police headquarters out of my mind. He was dressed very GQ in a dark suit and light blue shirt with the same shade tie.

"Do you have a court appearance today?"

Mark grinned. "No, I just want to impress Avery with my professional look."

"Well, you definitely look professional. Don't worry; I think he's always hard on associates. They've never fired anyone. You passed your screening when you were hired."

He shrugged. "I hope so."

After getting coffee for Mark and tea for me, we took the files into the conference room. Our meeting with Avery wasn't for another hour, but clearly Mark needed this dress rehearsal to calm down.

He did a great job providing more than adequate answers to my mock questions. We were ready.

I leaned back in the chair. "So, tell me, how are things with Rena?"

He glanced up as if trying to place the question with what we were doing then smiled. "Good. Actually, really good. I like her."

"Just think; I may be responsible for bringing a happy couple together. I hope it works out."

"You hope what works out?" Avery entered the room and shut the door.

Mark and I both straightened in our seats.

"Good morning, Avery. Mark was just telling me about a young woman he's dating."

"Really? Well, I hope things work out, too." He put on his reading glasses. "You two ready? Let's get started."

If Mark was nervous, he didn't show it. He restated the directions we were given and how we approached the research. For the next thirty minutes, he discussed the applicable case law and appeals. By the time he presented our findings, I was impressed. He finished with a flourish by laying out all the signed documents in front of Avery.

Avery remained attentive throughout the presentation. Then he nodded and flipped through the documents. "Looks like you've done a lot of hard work. What about Glen Riddick?"

I frowned. "Who?"

Mark looked puzzled. "Who's Glen Riddick?"

Avery shook his head. "Glen Riddick is Imelda's husband's grandchild as a result of a relationship prior to his marriage to Imelda."

I sat up. "Avery, you never mentioned a grandchild. In fact, you said all the relations were on her side. How were we to know?"

Mark held up a file. "I have your notes here. There's nothing about a grandchild."

Avery shook his head. "I said from the very beginning we were trying to substantiate Imelda's right to have the estate determined based on her early, but still valid, will. I would think one of the first things you would have done was look at Charles Riddick's background to verify any possible claims from his side of the family."

"Why would we?" I said. "You told us she only had nieces and nephews." I was getting irritated. "Why didn't you bring this up at our last team meeting?"

Avery just looked at me. "It's called complete work." He turned to Mark. "I don't hold you responsible, Hollis, but, Mark, I'm surprised at you. Well, maybe not surprised, but I was hoping for more."

Mark snorted. "Was I being tested? This is load of crap. All this time you said nothing."

Mark's eyes were unreadable but, judging from the tension rising off his shoulders and the red flush creeping above his shirt collar, he wasn't happy.

Avery seemed unfazed. "Not *tested* in the sense you mean. I did want to see if you would take my word for it or take the initiative and question every premise. You failed. Isn't that what you told me last time—that you wanted to show initiative? That's the difference between a good attorney and a merely adequate one. Follow through." He stacked the file folders. "So, where do we go from here? I've decided that, in the essence of time, I'll contact Glen Riddick and obtain his signature."

I felt more than a growing annoyance with Avery and increasing sympathy for Mark. "Avery, I should have caught this, too. I've done dozens of estate claims. I should have checked both sides."

"As much as you'd like to be, Hollis, you're not an attorney.

He is." He pointedly put the cap back on his pen. "Mark, I got your memo regarding the value of the Riddick estate and your ideas for exploring other accounts. I'm not going to say this again. Drop this. If you'd done your job and reviewed all potential estate claims, instead of speculating on some hypothetical supposition, you wouldn't be sitting here with another assignment falling short. Triple D may have to rethink your contribution to the firm."

Mark started to interrupt.

"No. Enough said." Avery placed our work on top of legal file folders. "The administrative work that was done was done well. Unfortunately, not all work was completed. I'll take it from here. Both of you wrap up your Riddick files and submit your hours. We'll get together tomorrow and see where we are with our other cases."

Mark passed me in the lobby and headed for his office. The slam of his door could be heard around the corner. I quickly went through my Riddick files and completed the summary billable hours sheet. I ignored the hushed murmurs of staff, who had clearly picked up on the loud voices. After an hour or so, I went by Mark's office. He was gone. Needing to focus on routine work, I made up files and records for two new clients. After a while, one of the administrative clerks came to my office and asked in a whispered voice, "What's going on?"

"If anyone asks, tell them you don't know."

CHAPTER TWENTY-FOUR

WHEN I LEFT for the day, Avery was behind closed doors in a management committee meeting. I was more than ready to go home and have a soothing cup of tea.

There was one message on the answering machine. It was Clay.

"Hollis, good work on your personal statement. We're all ready for the hearing." My lawyer paused. "Uh…have the murders been resolved? Give me a call when you get this message."

Without any real news, I was glad I hadn't been there to take his call. I'd wait a while before contacting him.

I needed something mindless to do. I reorganized my kitchen cabinets. I approached my task as if it was the only one left to do on earth. With Spanish guitar music in the background, I tried not to think about my plight. I finished too soon.

I didn't have Mark's home or cell numbers. Rena had given me hers, but it probably wasn't a good time to test my hunch she and Mark would be together. I fixed myself another cup of white tea and sat outside on my patio. The sun had set, and the sky was a steely gray-blue. My neighbor had planted a fragrant clematis vine that had wrapped itself over the fence that separated our units. I inhaled the subtle fragrance, trying to fight off the self-pity. I had bet the rest of my life on getting a pardon. The thought of it slipping away gave birth to an ache I could only locate in my heart.

The police assumed the killer had to be someone from the club. I agreed with them. Except, what if the killer had nothing to do with the club? On the other hand, who else besides club members would know which books we'd selected? There was the off chance spouses or friends could follow our reading habits, but I put that thought aside. I had to start somewhere. I didn't have any answers except the circular one—suppose the killer was from the club. I went back into the kitchen, emptied my mug and poured myself a glass of wine. In my bedroom, I tried to read a novel that wasn't from the club, but I couldn't concentrate. Something told me there was something I was missing, something that didn't make sense. Maybe I was too close to see the pieces that didn't fit.

Maybe it was time to let the killer find me.

THE NEXT MORNING there was a note on my office door telling me to see Avery at nine. Since I'd turned in my Riddick files, I was curious about the reason for the meeting. With an hour to go, I took advantage of the spare time and read over my court statement; it put me in a calmer mood. A few minutes before nine, I went to see Mark but he was checked out.

Avery waved me into his office. "Come on in. Shut the door. I don't want us to be disturbed."

I sat down with pad and pen in hand. "Ready."

Avery folded his hands on his desk. "The firm has let Mark go." He paused. "With our billable hours down, we can't afford to carry any dead weight."

I frowned. "That's not fair. He's a good attorney. I know his ideas about the Riddick matter bugged you, but at least he took initiative and thought on his own."

"He forgot to employ the most basic of legal premises—validating the information you're given. Make no assumptions. Erroneous thinking is lazy thinking. It can be costly thinking."

"It was you, his supervisor, who gave him those assumptions."

Avery shook his head. "I wanted to see how he'd perform. He didn't. I'm not going to argue the point with you. Besides, he hasn't brought in any new clients."

"Have any of the other new associates? Our team's billable hours are doing fine, especially with the new clients you signed up this month." I knew I was pushing my luck, but I was puzzled by Avery's attitude. "I'd like to see the comparative hours report."

Avery stiffened. "This is a personnel matter. The committee has made its decision. Since when did you become a Mark fan, anyway? It's not like you to defend an associate."

I had to think about that a moment. "Mark's okay. He helped a friend of mine. I just hate to see anybody get a bum deal."

"I appreciate that." Avery flashed one of his winning smiles. "I always knew you weren't as tough as you pretend to be."

I didn't smile back. I looked at his expensive haircut and how well his Brooks Brothers suit fit his broad shoulders. He'd be Item Number One on any single girl's wish list. Not mine.

I shook my head. "Oh, but I am."

THE REST OF the day went downhill from there. I asked the receptionist to let me know if Mark came into the office, but he didn't. I hated to resort to illegal invasion of privacy, but these were extenuating circumstances. The personnel office emptied during lunch and it was easy to lift the emergency contact list kept in a folder on top of a file shelf labeled: "Confidential Emergency Numbers." Our manager must be a believer in hiding in plain sight.

I called Mark twice but got no answer. He could be reading the caller ID and not answering since the call was from the office. I'd left my cellphone at home and didn't feel like using the public phone in the building lobby.

Finally, mid-afternoon, I tried to reach him twice more. No answer. I walked over to a public phone next to Kinko's and punched in Rena's number.

I got her machine.

"Rena, this is Hollis. I'm just checking in to see how you're doing. Let me know if you're interested in going out for a drink on Friday." I left my number and hung up.

I didn't know how much, if anything, Mark would confide in Rena, and I certainly didn't want to be the one to cloud their couple bliss with questions. I felt sure she'd tell Mark and he'd know I was looking for him. In the meantime, while I waited to hear, I wanted to find out answers to a couple of questions that bothered me.

I waited until I heard the last partner turn off the main lights and leave the building. Security would be coming around in a couple of hours to check on our offices. My heart thumped in my chest as I walked briskly down the darkened hallway to the other side of the building. It was as if I were on a spy mission. I was.

I knew Avery's office as well as I knew my own. I turned the light on. Like many lawyers, he was disorderly but disorderly in an organized fashion. The stacks of client files that tilted unsteadily on his desk and side credenzas were still in alphabetical order. I ignored them and went to his deposition briefcase sitting on the floor behind a box of files destined for storage. The briefcase held no discoveries.

Avery's work habits included keeping the most current matters closest to his phone. There was a good-sized stack of files to the left of his computer monitor. I went through them hurriedly but couldn't find what I was looking for. A corner of a piece of paper stuck out from under his calendar desk pad. I lifted the pad. Several papers were scattered about. Two were receipts from his car dealer for service on his Jaguar. I glanced at the amounts. They rivaled my condo payment.

A billing report from Accounting for the previous month had several red check marks next to the amounts. The remaining pages contained a listing of Internet searches for boat sales. I looked back at the billing report. Only the management committee got to see how well the partners did. Support staff got an annual bonus and a great lunch, but the partners got the real payoff. According to the report, Avery was doing quite well. His clients brought in more money than any of the other attorneys.

I glanced down the list. My eyes went to the retainers and fees paid. Unlike some clients, probate client fees were a percentage of the estate. I took pride in noticing Mark and I were working on a couple of the most profitable matters in the firm. I looked for one name, Riddick.

Imelda Riddick's estate was valued at five million dollars with twenty percent of the gross estate plus direct costs coming to Triple D. I breathed a sigh of relief. I'd filed the appraiser's numbers with the court and was glad to see the estate value listed matched the average of the value amount in the appraiser's report. Everything was as it should be. Even so, I was unwilling to face my doubts, or even think about the implications. Avery had never given me any reason to question his integrity before, but lately he hadn't been acting like himself. I was more than glad to see I had hit a dead end. I put everything back the way I found it, closed the door behind me and went home.

THE NEXT DAY, I hadn't been in my office long when my cellphone vibrated.

"Hollis, I got your message." Rena's voice sounded tentative.

I held the phone to my ear as I closed my office door. "I'm looking for Mark. Do you know where he is?"

She paused. "He's right here. Hold on."

There was an even longer pause.

"Hollis, don't worry about me. I'm okay."

I reacted to his use of the word "worry," and then I realized

I had been. "Good. Just taking off like that wasn't very professional."

"Don't go there." Mark's voice turned cold.

"Okay I won't. So, what are you going to do?"

"I'm going on an interview tomorrow morning."

I couldn't hide my surprise. "Tomorrow? How did you get an appointment so fast?"

"In fact I have three interviews. One tomorrow and two next week." He paused again. "Maybe I'm not the loser Avery thinks I am."

"Mark—"

"Like I said, let's not go there. Well, I've got to get going. I'll stay in touch."

"Promise?"

He hesitated. "Yeah, I promise. Wish me luck."

"You don't need luck. You'll do fine."

We said our goodbyes. I wanted to sound encouraging, but I had my doubts. I wondered if he counted on Triple D to give him a reference.

THE ADMINISTRATIVE CLERKS took no time in packing up Mark's office. I was going to offer to do it, but Avery had finished the final touches on Lily's trust documents and wanted me to proof them. Writing off my hours so he could work on paying clients made more sense. Avery also asked that I go over the documents with Lily so when she met with him, her questions would be relevant and not take up so much of his time. As I put all the papers into my carrying case, I questioned why Avery chose probate law as his specialty. His brilliant legal mind was made for litigation. The empathy needed to deal with families who are coping after a death was not his forte.

I left the office right after lunch to visit the senior center. Lily was tired and cranky. She used a hearing aid, and I knew that if she'd had a bad day, she deliberately pretended deafness. After an hour of my repeated explanations, we hadn't made much progress.

"Lily, you don't have to list of all your belongings in your will. Your estate isn't that big."

"What? What did you say? My estate isn't big?" She fiddled with the papers. "I have a beautiful house and priceless furnishings. Your fancy law firm—"

"Lily, you're not paying for any of this. Our work is pro bono. It's free. Your house is your biggest asset. Your furnishings and housewares will be itemized and appraised. I'm only saying that things like your souvenir spoon collection and the back issues of *Life* Magazine will be distributed by your niece. We don't have to go into that level of detail."

"Who will she give them to?" Lily's hand shook. "My niece … my niece, who hasn't come to see me in a year. She doesn't know what I want. I have to put everything in writing. I'm not stupid. If it's not in writing, anything can happen. No one cares about old people like me. My—"

Marla put her hand on Lily's shoulder. I hadn't noticed she'd come into the room.

"Lily, you're working yourself up." Marla sat down next to her. "I've met your niece, Gloria. She's a nice young lady. Now, sweetie, you know she was just here a couple of months ago. She truly reminds me a lot of you."

"It seems like a year." Lily's hand patted Marla's. "You're right. She is like me." She laid her head on Marla's shoulder. "I just hate being treated like I'm old."

Marla nodded. "Let Hollis do her job and finish. I want to take you out to the garden. We've got a new gardener. He'll be here in a short while to bring us new cuttings. Now, Hollis, what is it you need Lily to do?"

I took a breath and gave Marla an appreciative smile. "Lily, why don't you tell me all those items you want to go to someone special and I'll make a new list. It'll take a little longer but I think you'll be happier. I'm going out to your house to take the inventory. We'll just amend your will to show the additional items." I knew I'd be the one drawing up a new will. If I returned with these documents one more time, Avery would send me out right after Mark.

Lily gave Marla a smug look. "Let's see. Did I mention my souvenir spoon collection?"

Marla's wisdom wasn't lost on me. When I let Lily speak her piece, there wasn't much to put on a new list. After a little more than an hour, we were finished. I promised Lily I'd return with the new papers for her final signature.

Marla walked beside me to the front door. "Thank you for being patient with her."

"Your intervention helped. Thank you for reminding me about why I come here."

"How's the other thing going? I mailed my letter like I said I would. I made sure it said what you needed."

Not quite knowing how to respond, I looked away and then back. "Too bad you can't fix everything."

THE THIRD TIME had to be the charm. If I was going to do this thing, I wanted to know one way or another if Lily was in danger. I needed unequivocal proof Joseph or someone else was deliberately trying to harm her. I knew from my previous visits that center work schedules were posted in the staff break room. I knew, too, that Joseph was scheduled to work a night shift tonight. If I were going to play pharmacist, I'd do it when the least amount of staff was present and the residents were asleep.

Dinner was still being served when I gave a nod to the receptionist, who was on the phone, and walked down the hall. I turned to see if she was paying any attention to me. She wasn't. I quickly tapped numbers onto the keypad and got a beep. Marjorie's office was as I left it. The sun had started to set and the soft orange glow made the room appear ethereal.

In the pass-through closet, I slid down the wall and sat on the floor to wait. I closed the closet door on Marjorie's side.

I checked the time on my cellphone. Dinner had to be over and Joseph, as one of the two nurses on duty, would soon be finishing rounds.

The keypad beeped and the lab door opened. Someone entered and turned on the lights. Joseph had a white paper bag with him. I cursed inwardly because by sitting on the floor I'd lost my sight advantage. I edged my way up. I wanted to see what was in the bag. I wasn't disappointed. He reached in, pulled out several prescription bottles, and arranged them in a straight row. Then he went to a side cabinet and brought out three large bottles of pills. He dumped pills from one bottle into the pill sorting machine. It whirred for five seconds, filling three of the little tube-like containers. He poured them into three of the brown prescription bottles.

I cracked open the door a couple of inches. Joseph didn't seem to notice. He was intent on hurriedly redistributing pills to three sets of four bottles.

I slipped out my cellphone and took a photo, making sure the flash was off.

From the larger bottle he counted out another set of pills and, without hesitation, put them in a plastic bag that went into his inside pocket.

I caught him in living color. I didn't think I'd made any noise but for some reason he froze and looked around. I backed away from the door frame.

He took a couple of steps out of my vision range. The door clicked open; then it closed again.

I moved back to see through the closet doorway. Checking his watch, he went back to the table to finish. I didn't want to push my luck by taking any more pictures. I prayed the two would suffice. I breathed in and out as silently as I could, but it was several more minutes before he started to pack things up. He picked up the bag, looked around and put it back down. He looked as if he was missing something. He paused for a long moment, opened the door and left.

I licked my lips. I quickly took another picture of the table setup. I thought of venturing closer, but it was too risky. Standing, I leaned against the closet wall, keeping to the shadows. I knew Joseph would come back to pick up the bag.

I almost toppled over when the door to the pass-through on Marjorie's office side pulled open.

I screamed in surprise.

"This time you're not going to talk your way out." Joseph towered over me, his fists balled tightly.

"What are you doing?" Going on the offensive was my best bet.

Joseph didn't answer. Instead, he put one hand over my mouth and the other gripped me by the elbow. He all but shoved me into the lab room. I twisted against the foul smell on his hand. He didn't release his hold.

"I assume you saw everything you shouldn't have. Now you leave me very few options."

I winced and tried to pull away. I could only manage to muffle, "It's over, Joseph. Whatever your game is, it's over."

"Not if I take you with me. I've disappeared before. I can disappear again. I just need a little time, and a little luck." He pulled me over to the cabinet. Apparently he couldn't find what he was looking for.

I willed myself to become dead weight but he dragged me back to the pass-through. My breathing became labored as his hairy hands covered my face.

The keypad to Marjorie's office beeped.

We both froze for a quick moment. I squirmed under the pressure of his arms around my neck.

"What's going on here?" Marla stood in the doorway. She must have quickly assessed the situation because she immediately turned and headed back down the hall.

"Come back here, ol' woman," Joseph snarled, still dragging

me. Marla moved out of sight.

"Hell." He looked at me in disgust and shoved me roughly into a corner.

I fell to the floor as he dashed out of the office. I could hear the facility's rear door slam. I rubbed my mouth and neck and slowly got to my feet. There was light coming into the room from the doorway and I made my way gingerly toward the source.

Someone screamed.

CHAPTER TWENTY-FIVE

I PULLED MYSELF together and stumbled as fast as I could into the hallway. Marla lay on her back, her hands across her chest. Opal leaned over her. I half-ran to them.

"Oh my god, what happened to you?" Opal covered her mouth.

I tasted blood from my cut lip and looked down at my dust-covered clothes. "I'll be fine. What happened to Marla?"

Opal straightened. "I don't know. I found her like this. I think it's a heart attack. She's barely breathing. I called nine-one-one on my cell."

I knelt next to my old friend and held her limp hand in mine. Her chest rose only slightly with each breath.

Please don't die.

THE NURSE HUSTLED in the hospital room and took Marla's vitals. I wasn't the cause of her heart attack, but no one could convince me my delay in catching Joseph hadn't contributed.

I felt the beginning of a tear as I watched Marla sleeping. She looked so frail, all and more of her seventy-nine years. Her cheeks were hollow and her skin seemed thin as gauze. I leaned over and brushed back a curl that had drifted into her eyes. She stirred and looked at me, this time with recognition.

"Well, I must be alive if you're here." She winced as she turned her head. "What happened, sweetie?"

"You had a heart attack. The doctor was just here and said she'd be back to look in on you this evening. Don't you remember talking to her?"

Marla frowned. "I'm not sure. It seems like a dream. How do I know this isn't a dream?"

I smiled. "I'm here to tell you that you're alive and well. I'm so very happy to see you."

A small smile creased her face. Then she looked alarmed. "Hollis, is Lily okay? Did you follow Joseph? Was he arrested?" She licked her parched lips and pointed to the plastic pitcher. "Can I have some water, please?"

"There's probably a reason why the pitcher is empty and I'm not getting into trouble for you again. Dr. Francis will be here shortly." I sat down on the bed. "Lily is fine. She sends her best wishes. She misses you."

"Coward." She licked her lips again. "That's good about Lily. What about Joseph?"

"Joseph is gone. He got away." Marla's heart attack was all the distraction he needed to slip away before the police came. "By the way, Opal has been here every day to visit. When I came yesterday she told me his escape was a perfect solution because it saved the center from going through the bad publicity and legal harangue."

A few beads of sweat appeared on her brow.

"So he's free to hurt others, again."

"Oh, I don't know. I think he's running out of rocks to slide under." I bent over and dabbed her forehead with a tissue. "The police have his prints, and it turns out he and Dr. Walker were working together. Walker was arrested and ratted out … I mean he gave information about Joseph. He felt no loyalty to his partner. Both of them will be going to prison for a very long time. It wasn't just Lily they were hurting, but two other residents, the ones who were bedridden, were also getting the wrong medication." I straightened her covers. "I'm sorry it took so long to nail Joseph. You were right about everything."

"Stop it right now," Marla snapped with some force. "You put yourself out there for us."

"But I—"

"No, there's nothing to forgive." Her head sank back into the pillow. "So, now, sweetie you can forgive yourself." Closing her eyes, she fell asleep.

LILY MOTIONED ME to come over to the table where she sat. Tiny discreetly left us alone.

"You're looking a lot better than you were the last time I was here." I sat down. "How are you feeling?"

"I feel much better." She picked at the armrest on her wheelchair. "Marla told me you saved my life."

"I think that's an exaggeration. Marla saved your life."

"Don't argue with me, Hollis. It isn't attractive."

Lily patted my arm, gently took my chin and turned me to face her. "I've decided to have a conversation with Avery Mitchell. He doesn't understand me the way you do. I want you to handle my trust. You can be my representative. You'll do just fine." She kissed me on my forehead. "Yes, you'll do just fine."

I couldn't speak. My words were blocked in my throat.

I CONFIRMED LILY'S house appraisal with Putnum for the end of the week. I'd go in the day before and inventory all of the items she wanted designated as bequests.

Rena called the office and left a message to contact her only if I couldn't meet at Caron Bistro for dinner. I looked forward to an evening of talking about something other than what was going on with my life. Since Mark had left, I had even less reason to be social with my fellow workers, and I was hungry.

Caron's was designed for intimacy. It was divided up into

large cubicle-sized rooms with two or three tables each. For those who liked to eat outdoors, its veranda offered large round tables sheltered by dark green umbrellas to protect from the sun. Tall standing heaters were for colder days.

Rena gave me a hug. Mark, too. We chose the veranda.

We exchanged social amenities and ordered glasses of wine. Mark was visibly relaxed and seemingly back to his old self. "Do you miss me?"

"It's only been a few days." I took a sip. "How are you getting along?"

"Not bad. Fortunately, there's always a place in a successful firm for an ambitious associate attorney. This time I'm being picky. I want to make sure I take the opportunity to interview the firm."

Rena smiled. "Mark was asked to come back for a second interview with McCloud's."

I nodded in acknowledgment. Headquartered in San Francisco, McCloud's was the biggest law firm in the country, maybe even the world. "Do you think you'll like working for a legal machine that portions out the law?"

Mark leaned forward. "I told them to give me a niche where I could excel. It didn't matter how small." He sat back. "Anyway, we're just talking. We'll see if the second interview goes as well as the first."

I hoped my skepticism didn't show on my face. The legal community was an active rumor mill that could make or break reputations. The waitress brought our food.

I turned to Rena. "How about you? Read any good books lately?"

She gave me a horrified look. "Hollis, how can you ask that? I'm scared to death. The police don't seem to know any more about that note than I do."

I wanted to kick myself for being so tacky. "Sorry. I've been obsessing over the whole thing. Maybe the note was planted on you to throw us off. I think the killer is finished and just wants us to think there's more to come."

Mark wrinkled his brow. "Huh? I don't get it."

"Suppose the killer only wanted to kill Rory. Then he murdered Abby because she might be able to identify him." I took a breath. "Bill is part of this, too. He was Rory's partner. He had to die because he knew too much, or maybe because he got too greedy."

"Who's Bill?" Rena asked.

"Her ex-husband," Mark said. "Okay, let's take this further. Why would a book club member make the murders so obvious?"

So much for getting together with friends and talking about something other than my problems. I ran my hands through my hair. "Maybe the book murders were a decoy. Whoever did the killings wants to implicate all of us. It all goes back to Rory and—and a threat to someone who can't afford to take a risk."

I pondered that. "What I can't put my brain around is the killer must have been blackmailed by Rory and read our books. He deliberately chose specific books so he could copy the murder."

"What do you mean?" Mark asked.

"I went through our selections for the past six months. Rory was killed like our last selection, but Abby was killed like the spy thriller we read three months before that. I'm still trying to figure out if the killer read the book and then set up the murder or if he located the book that had the murder he wanted." As I thought out loud, some of the pieces started to fall into place. "The books in between were memoirs and self-help manuals. They were too complicated for a murderer to mimic. The killer knows our selections and has known them for some time."

"It has to be a club member," Rena said.

I took a deep sigh. "Maybe, but I'm having a hard time getting a handle on my lead suspect. I'm sure of one thing, or as sure as I can be. The killer was a victim of Rory's blackmail."

"Bill wasn't killed like in a club book," Mark said.

"No. He was shot." The memory of the figure in the morgue sent a chill through me. "He knew Rory and he might have been a blackmail victim, but he doesn't fit the pattern."

The waiter came with our meals and refilled our water glasses. Food helped to dilute the impact of the wine and veer the subject back toward the mundane.

I waited until they both had food in their mouths because I didn't want to hear their first response. "On another matter altogether, I had this crazy idea. It didn't turn out to be anything, though."

Mark looked at me. "What was it?"

"Remember the Riddick matter? It bugged you that she wrote a will when she was so young."

He nodded.

"Well, it kind of got to me, too. I couldn't shrug off your questions. What if the will was a fake? Maybe the estate would have gone to his side of the family. Or maybe something wasn't up front with the valuation."

"Yeah, that's what I thought. That's why Avery fired me. He thought I'd wasted too much time … thinking."

On this point I agreed with Avery but didn't want to say so. "So I retrieved the old file from storage. It shows the date Triple D filed Imelda's will sixty-five years ago. As odd as it may seem, young Imelda Nelson did make out a will."

Mark shrugged. "So much for that. I'm glad, though. Her family seemed like they could use the money. Riddick was middle class but a smart investor. The proceeds from the house alone should keep them financially secure for a good long time."

"I didn't know the breakdown of the estate."

"Yeah, the house was the main asset. He also had stocks and mutual funds, and I think some type of retirement bonds. I don't remember how much it all came to, but it was in the millions. Over the years, she spent a lot of it to live on and I guess some went to charities, but it was still sizable."

I nodded. "I got the same feeling from the family members I spoke with. They'll be happy to get anything."

Through the dessert course, we went back to chatting about world affairs and the state of the economy.

Waiting for the check, Mark opened his mouth as if to speak then closed it again. I looked at him, but it was Rena who spoke. "What? What do you want to say?"

Mark looked at me. "I didn't mention this to Avery, but I ordered another appraisal."

"You did what?" I said in amazement.

He frowned. "I knew the court would need more than one appraisal to verify the value of the estate. So I went ahead and ordered one."

"Mark, Avery said he'd take care of the appraisals. He'd already ordered two." Estate appraisals were expensive. Although Triple D had appraisers on retainer to lower the cost, the reviews still ran in the thousands of dollars.

"I know. I know, but I figured appraisals can take a while and if the two appraisals differed greatly, then we'd need a third to validate the one that gave the best assessment. I figured Avery would be pleased when I showed up with a third appraisal. Think of the time he would save—and my initiative."

I shook my head. "You did an awful lot of figuring."

"Yeah, well, obviously taking initiative isn't big in Avery's book."

I had to concur with him on that one. "So where is the appraisal?"

Mark rubbed his forehead. "It hasn't come in yet. I had it done by Bethel. They promised me it'd only take a week, but their server crashed and they fell behind with their formal reports. I hoped that—that maybe you could intercept it."

Rena said, "Why bother? You don't work for Dodson, Dodson and Doyle anymore. You're going to have a new job."

I looked at her and then back at Mark with more understanding. "He needs a recommendation from Avery or someone from Triple D management."

He nodded. "It should come to the office under my name, but you know those guys. Sometimes they send it to the name of the estate and it sits in the unknown mail bin." Mark leaned in. "Just intercept it and toss it. It doesn't matter what it says. Avery is satisfied that the estate is valued appropriately. You saw the calculations from the two appraisers. It's overkill."

"What if Avery finds out?" I couldn't help but ask.

"Then I'm screwed."

I finished off my glass of wine and chased it with a big sip of water. "Wouldn't it be easier if you just called Bethel and asked when and where they sent the report?"

"I did. They said they finally sent it to the office a few days ago. I checked every day up until I left, but it never came. I think it must be lost in the mail room."

The building's mail room was not called the "black hole" for nothing. Most of us at Triple D sent things overnight. Mark had experienced firsthand what happened when urgency met incompetence.

"I'll be on the lookout for it, and I'll give you a call when I retrieve it. It'll still be a problem when the bill comes, through."

"Yeah, but that's thirty days from now. I'll deal with it then, if I have to."

Rena started to fidget. I was ready for bed.

I picked up my purse. "Enough. I'm out of here. Thank you very much for the dinner." I smiled at Mark. "Let me know how the interviews go."

We said our goodbyes outside. It was a beautiful evening. The kind I dreamed about seeing again when I was in prison. I wanted to enjoy it but I was drawn back to my world, where my future hung by a thin thread.

At home, Clay's voice greeted me on my message machine: "Hollis, give me a call tomorrow. I'll be in the office early. The court clerk assigned our hearing to the court calendar. I need to know how the investigation is moving forward."

Ah, yes, the investigation.

THE NEXT DAY Clay agreed to meet me during my lunch hour. His receptionist was gone and he ushered me down the hallway into his office.

"We got a confirmation that your hearing has been moved up two weeks. I received the last of your references yesterday. I'll file them with the court tomorrow." He tapped a file folder on his desk.

My heart immediately went into overdrive. "Two weeks ... so we got Judge Pine?"

Clay hesitated. "No, that's what I wanted to tell you. Pine had a heart attack last weekend. We've got Mathis."

I couldn't believe it. Wasn't anything going to go my way? "Clay, from what you told me, I don't have a chance in hell to get a pardon from Mathis."

"It's rotten luck. If I didn't believe your petition has merit, I wouldn't bother with any judge. Mathis can be difficult, but he's fair. We're going to make sure your petition is one he can't refuse."

I tried not to give into stress and or let discouragement take control, but I was tired of fighting. The pardon was the only thing that kept me going.

"So, tell me, are you still a suspect?"

"The police still don't know who the killer is." I sighed. "They haven't said so, but I get the feeling I'm not their prime suspect. To be honest, it could just be my wishful thinking."

"What makes you think they're still considering you?"

"The police searched my house and found nothing. There's been another murder. They found my ex-husband's body in an apartment downtown."

Clay ran his hand down his face. "Bill Lynley! Good grief, what is happening? They don't think you did it, do they?"

He looked like he was on the verge of a heart attack.

"No, no. I have an alibi and they have nothing to link me to his death."

"Well, we'll just have to proceed as if all this will be worked out. Hollis, I'm not going to mislead you. If you're a suspect, Mathis will throw your petition out. I'm going to be out of the office the rest of the week. So on the following Monday I want you back here for a prep session." He made a note on his legal pad.

We talked for a few minutes more about what I knew of Bill's death. I tried to downplay any concern the police might have regarding my involvement. I wasn't sure if Clay bought it all.

BACK AT WORK, I rushed to finish working on my in box of case matters. I wanted to make a call before I left for home.

"Ri, hi, it's Rebecca."

There was a pause.

"Rebecca, is everything okay? Are you in tr—"

"No, I'm not in trouble." I spoke through clenched teeth. It was going to take time before my family would see me as I was now. "I called for a couple of reasons."

Another pause, this one a little longer.

"Yes, go ahead."

"How is Kirk? What did the test results say?"

My brother-in-law had always treated me with kindness, more so than my family members. At least he seemed to give me the benefit of the doubt.

Rita cleared her throat. I could almost see her pinching the bridge of her nose, her habit when trying to compose herself.

"The results were good. The cancer was caught early. He has six more treatments and then they'll keep him under close watch."

I smiled. "That's real good news. I know you must be relieved."

"What else, Rebecca?"

What was it about my family that always put me on the

defensive? My sister's coolness made me feel about eight years old.

"I want to thank you for your reference letter. My attorney says it struck just the right note."

"Good, I'm glad," she said. "I hope … I hope you'll have another chance to prove yourself. You deserve it."

"I intend on taking advantage of that chance, Ri. I'm much wiser now."

"Good, is there anything …?" She almost didn't let me finish my sentence. I knew she was struggling with conflicting emotions and judgments, and wanted to get off the phone.

"Bill is dead. He was murdered."

Her sharp intake of breath reassured me that she wasn't as robotic as she'd sounded since the beginning of the call.

"Oh, my god, they don't think—?"

"No, they don't think I did it." I wasn't able to hold back a sigh. "Well, that's all I wanted to tell you."

There was a moment's silence.

"Here's a thought, why don't you plan on coming home for the fourth of July?" she said. "Yes, I think that would be a good idea. Kirk will be finished with his treatments."

Her offer was a shock and now it was my turn to pause.

"Ri, what about Mom and Dad?"

She laughed. "I'll start talking to them now. They'll have a couple of months to get used to the idea."

At that we both laughed then grew silent, knowing that a couple of months might not be enough.

I murmured, "Even if it doesn't happen, thanks for the suggestion."

Rita spoke quietly, "I miss your laugh, Becca."

"I miss you, too, Ri."

THAT NIGHT, MY happy thoughts about Rita were interspersed with thoughts of Bill. His face kept slipping into my alpha levels. Sometime around three a.m. I awoke, my eyes wide open. The full reality of Detective Faber's comment hit me. The only thing that linked all three murders … was me.

CHAPTER TWENTY-SIX

I WAITED UNTIL the firm's lobby was empty and walked nonchalantly over to our receptionist.

"Emily, did you go down to the mail room, today?"

"No, I haven't had a chance. I've been stuck here on the phones. The clerks are having a staff meeting, and I won't be able to pick up the mail until after lunch."

"I'll go. I need a change of scenery."

"You will?" Emily looked at me with more than a little surprise. "Hollis, do you even know where the mail room is?"

"Of course I do. It's been a while, but I've been there. It's in the basement, right?" I grinned at her. "Just send somebody for me if I'm not back within the hour."

She smiled with hesitancy. "Right."

I found the mailroom in record time, considering I only missed one turn. Two young men, more than likely interns, busily pulled letters and packages out of a large canvas bin. The constant drone of the air-conditioning unit forced me to speak up to be heard

"Excuse me. Where is the pickup for Dodson, Dodson and Doyle?" I called out.

A youth with enough tattoos on his arms to resemble a Persian rug pointed to a far corner next to the only window in the room. Avoiding boxes and bins, I made my way to our area. I had a new appreciation for receiving any mail at all.

A large white plastic container with the firm's logo was almost full to the brim. I had a suspicion Emily had either missed the morning pickup, or Triple D was doing even better than I thought. I took the bin over to a long side table that was relatively clear. I shoved everything down to one end and started to sort the mail. First, I separated the letters from the large mailing envelopes, which left me with a much smaller stack. I scanned through the oversized envelopes, searching the return addresses for Bethel's logo. In a matter of minutes I held a large tan envelope with a three-day-old note attached saying it had been delivered to a wrong address. I didn't care. I dumped everything back into the bin and called out goodbye to the young men, who didn't even look up.

Emily was on the phone. She waved at me to put the mail on the far side of her cubicle. Clutching the Bethel envelope, I was ready to retreat when she held out the date stamp for me to properly log in the mail. It was easier if I just went along. I returned to my office, shutting the door.

Bethel was considered one of the best appraisal firms in the area, but they were a small company. Triple D used them when a value was likely to be contested. However, Avery rarely used them because a year ago he'd had a falling out with one of the owners. Male ego. If Avery knew Mark had spent money and, even innocently, hired a firm he was at odds with, he'd give Mark the reference from hell.

In the nineties, California cracked down on appraisers who either weren't qualified or couldn't justify their assessment. Since then, appraisals followed a standard format. An introductory letter described the assignment, followed by a regional, then area, then site description of the property. Some were twenty pages and others were one hundred and twenty. There was a value comparison of like properties. The evaluation closed with the value computation for the subject property. Finally, at the very end, the appraiser provided a résumé or qualification narrative.

The Riddick report was thick. I turned to the end to read the comparables and the valuation summary. Bethel had listed ten recent sales within two miles of the Riddick property, all similarly built, and all within the last six months. The two appraisals Avery received showed the Riddick property value ranging from four to five million.

Bethel's evaluation came in at two million.

I blinked to make sure my vision wasn't blurred. Then, as a sanity check, I confirmed I was reading about the Riddick property. The difference of three million on the high end was glaring. I needed to compare the other two reports to Bethel's. They were in Avery's office.

I walked past his office. The door was closed. I looked over at the "Out" board. One of Ed's favorite topics in management meetings was to harangue us about signing out on the "Out" board. Signing out let everyone know where we were and when we expected to return—an inexpensive tracking tool. Our team was always held up as an example of staff doing things right. When I saw the line after Avery's name was blank, I knew he was behind that closed door. I had to wait.

I was tempted to call Mark, but he'd told me he had job interviews today and I didn't think a cellphone going off in his pocket during an interview would be helpful. I went back to my office to read the full Bethel report.

It was clear Bethel hadn't embellished the valuation by using the listing prices for comparable properties, but had only included closed escrows. This made the findings more defensible. Sometimes appraisers inflated a value by basing it on a seller's asking price, not the price it eventually sold for. The real estate market was still reeling from the sub-prime market debacle. Conservative appraisers were erring on the side of only including done deals.

If Imelda's estate was worth not five million but two million, it would have major ramifications for estate taxes and how much her heirs would benefit. As executors, Triple D was responsible for liquidating the assets and distributing the proceeds. We got a percentage of the valuation, in this case an inflated valuation.

I got up and fetched a bottle of water from the lunch room. My agitation made me hyper and I avoided Emily, who was probably beginning to question my trips back and forth through the lobby. Avery's door was still closed. I stopped at Emily's desk and glanced down to see if his phone line was lit. It was.

"Do you want me to give you a call when his line is free? It will save you a few steps."

"Thanks." I walked back to my office and closed my door.

Mark's instincts had been right, but I wasn't sure what it all meant. We had three appraisals, but one was totally out of the ballpark. When Avery got the Bethel invoice, he wouldn't be happy.

My phone rang a few minutes later. "Hollis, he's off his phone."

I rushed out and knocked on Avery's door. "Can I interrupt you for a few minutes?"

"Sure, you're just the person I wanted to see. Have a seat." He pushed aside some paperwork to make a six-inch space on the top of his desk for my notebook.

"Your friend Lily is driving me crazy. She's got this notion her property is worth millions. I've spoken with her niece. She seems intelligent and understands what needs to be done. This pro bono matter is taking many more hours than you led me to believe it would."

I felt chastised. "Sorry. I thought I had everything ready to go for her to sign."

"You did. She changed her mind. A friend at the center told her she should have a detailed inventory to back up the appraisal. I told her a detailed inventory is expensive and is only needed for large estates. Your summary listing of items would be more than adequate."

"She didn't buy it?"

Avery pursed his lips. "No, she didn't buy it."

"Let me do a detailed inventory. My hours are the least costly."

He paused.

"Okay, that could work. Try to get it done by the end of the week. I've driven by the house. It's nice, but it's not the Getty estate." He reached into his top drawer. "Here are the keys."

"I'll take care of it as soon as I can."

"Fine. Now, what did you want to see me about?"

I swallowed, debating whether I should go for broke and totally piss him off or cut my losses and leave.

"Ah, I just wanted to see the appraisals for the Riddick matter. I didn't get a chance to read the full reports."

Avery stared at me. "It's not necessary. The matter is on its way to being closed. No thanks to Mark, we were able to wrap everything up quickly. I got your note that we're getting an expedited hearing. As always, your work is top grade. Have I told you how much I appreciate you?"

The compliment seemed a bit overdone, but I smiled. "Why, thank you for the kind words. I try hard."

"It shows." He lowered his voice. "Now, if you work your magic with Lily, I have a new client I'm tempted to let you work alone. I'd like to see you stretch your talents and manage a case. Think you might be interested?"

"Of course I'd be interested."

"Good. I'm off to San Diego for a couple of days. Let's wrap this thing up with Lily and we'll be able to move on to better opportunities." He looked down at his watch. "I'm meeting with Ed and Phil in a few minutes. Leave a message on my phone if you get into a bind. I can always get one of the associates to help you."

In the hallway, I shot my fist into the air as a silent cheer. *Yes!* Handling a client's case by myself, even with Avery's oversight, was a treasured perk and would give me solid experience.

But I was a little disappointed to think he believed I could be so easily distracted that I didn't notice he'd waved me off the Riddick appraisals. I might be wasting my time, and even risking my job, but I had to satisfy my curiosity.

I hadn't started out intending to search Avery's office, but by the end of the day, I decided I would.

I WENT HOME to have dinner and returned to the firm at eight-thirty. Even so, one of the associates was still in her office. She was typing away on the computer and didn't even raise her head when I passed by. I closed Avery's door behind me. My heart beat like it was coming out of my chest. My mouth was dry, but I plunged ahead.

From the rows of stacked case files, it was clear that Avery had started to organize his papers. Usually twice a year, when he was no longer able to stand the clutter, he cleared his desk. This was not a good sign. There was a chance he'd removed the Riddick file. After a few minutes, I found the court papers Mark and I had prepared—along with the tax documents, bank records, and to my relief, the appraisal reports. I stooped to lower the bulky material onto the floor.

"What are you doing here, Hollis?" Avery's voice held none of the warmth it had earlier. In fact its coldness chilled me.

Thinking fast was one of my strongest skills, but I was pretty sure that this time Avery wouldn't find it an asset. I straightened up, letting my discomfort show.

"Hi, boss. I know what you're thinking, but you know me. I got something in my head and can't let it go. I just wanted to go over the Riddick appraisals. There was—"

"What did you think you were going to find?" He moved toward me but stopped to look at the top of his desk.

I tried to take the offensive. "Uh, I wanted to comp—, I

mean, *review* the two appraisals. This is a crazy market and I wanted to see what they used for market determination."

"Why?" His green eyes bored into mine.

I frowned. "One of the Internet sites showed a much lower value. I usually don't give online values any credence, but it was so much … lower." The lie fell easily from my lips. This was not the time to practice telling the truth.

Avery just stood there, looking at me. Then, from his bookcase, he picked up the folder he must have come back for.

"Get out of my office."

I moved away from the box and picked up my purse. "I was wrong. I'm sorry."

"I'm sorry, too."

CHAPTER TWENTY-SEVEN

I N THE MORNING, I tried to reach Mark. He wasn't picking up his phone. We had talked about meeting at Lily's house so we could go to lunch after I finished with the inventory. I went into the office, grabbed a couple of pens, and signed out. I didn't want to run into Avery. I needed time to think about the implications of the appraisals on the Riddick estate and what I was going to do about it.

Inside the stuffy old house, my blouse was already sticking to my back as the day started to heat up. It was hard to believe that just a couple of weeks ago I had been freezing in my overcoat. Weather was never boring in the Bay Area.

For the fifth time in five minutes, I looked at my cellphone for the correct time. Where was Mark? I counted on him checking his messages. We needed to talk about the Bethel appraisal, which lay in the trunk of my car.

The house was dark and quiet. I felt too much like an intruder. I pulled back the living room drapes. The light burst in. The room was lovely. I couldn't quite imagine the cantankerous Lily I knew living in such a serene abode.

The bright colors of the Spanish tiles encircling the fireplace shone even in the half light and the overhead chandelier was a graceful, open-framed sphere with six globes of clear glass that seemed to float from the tray ceiling. Lily must have hated having to leave it all behind for the starkness of the senior center. No wonder she was so grumpy.

I tiptoed across the thick carpet to the adjacent dining area. A massive rectangular table with eight chairs was covered with ghostly white sheets, but I could make out the heavy ornate mahogany legs underneath. At the rear of the room, I was drawn to the floor-to-ceiling stained glass windows. Pictured in the Craftsman-era style windows were rolling hills that gently sheltered a valley flowing with a wide pathway of what appeared to be vibrant yellow daffodils. A young woman stood off to the side in the foreground and pointed to the real side yard that bordered the house with lush green hosta plants. These were the windows Lily wanted to preserve.

"Peaceful, isn't it?" Avery said from the entry.

He startled me, but I didn't turn around. "Very."

"I looked on the board and saw that you were signed out to come here." He walked over to stand next to me, looking at the windows.

He wore a cotton sports jacket and a T-shirt over jeans. Our eyes met. Under other circumstances, one of us might have suggested we check out the master bedroom. I had the feeling we'd never know what we could have been.

"I thought you were going to San Diego. Avery, I'm sorry about last—"

"Not important." He held up his hand. "My meeting was rescheduled until tomorrow. I'll leave later tonight." He reached into the small plastic grocery bag he carried. "I brought you some cold water. It's warm outside and real stuffy in here."

Just holding the chilled bottle was relief to my sweating hands.

"Thanks. You always think of everything." The coolness was heaven as it went down.

He opened a bottle and took a long chug. "Do you know why I came all the way out here?"

I took a breath. "I guess you didn't trust me to itemize Lily's belongings."

"No, that's not true. You're a professional. Better than some of our associates." He walked around the room and opened one of the many cabinet doors that encircled the dining area. "I just thought that, considering Mrs. Wilson's propensity for paranoia, it'd be better if two of us did this."

It was a lie and I was anxious to know why.

He turned on the light, and the rest of the dark corners disappeared.

I thought about that a moment. "Lily can be a real handful. She's gotten more distrustful over the years, always thinking people are stealing from her. Still, even paranoids have enemies."

He smiled and took a small notebook from his inside pocket. "Okay, let's get started. I need to be able to verify the condition of the furniture and the personal contents. Have you been upstairs yet?"

I shook my head. The heat was really starting to get to me. I felt a little lightheaded. For now, I hoped Mark would see Avery's car outside and keep going. I fingered the cellphone in my pocket and turned off the ringer.

Avery stepped back and motioned for me to go in front of him into the butler's pantry. Floor to ceiling glass cabinets lined the walls of the small room. He started counting the crystal wineglasses on one side as I worked on the other.

"Hollis, you know I think a lot of you."

I stopped and looked over at him. He was going through the lower cabinet and handling the figurines. "What do you mean?"

"I mean, there has always been this thing—a tension— between us. You can't tell me you haven't felt it."

"It's one of the reasons I never wanted to be alone with you."

"We're alone now."

I sighed. "Yes, we are. I've tried hard not to get in a situation like we're in." We wrote down the tallies on our inventory sheets and moved into the main dining room.

"You should have tried harder." His voice had an edge.

I took a quick look at him, but his back was to me as he counted serving dishes. I couldn't see his eyes.

"Hey, have you read *The Long Pause*?"

"What?" His question caught me off guard. I took another swallow of water to hide my growing wariness.

"The book, *The Long Pause*. Have you read it yet?"

"Yes ... well, no … it's a … or at least it *was* the next book for my book club. I only started to get into it." I don't know why I lied. I'd finished the book just before Rory was killed. "I … I didn't know you liked fiction." I took slow, deep breaths.

Avery opened a corner hutch and started counting vases. "I guess I was reminded of *The Long Pause* because it takes place in a house like this."

"I thought it took place in Austria."

"I wasn't referring to the location. I meant the house was empty." He smiled and put his bottle to his lips.

I gave a nervous laugh. "When do you have time to read?"

He stopped to open the buffet cabinet door but didn't look up. "Actually, I was inspired by you. I've sort of followed what your group was reading."

I hoped the shock his words sent through me didn't register on my face. The phrase "bells went off in my head" was never more true. I opened the china cabinet's massive glass doors and, without looking at him, pretended to concentrate on counting plates. "Really? Why didn't you tell me? Did you ever borrow books out of my office?"

"Why, yes. I tried to return them quickly so you wouldn't miss them."

"You did well. I didn't know they were gone except for …" I couldn't say the title. I couldn't say anything; the pieces were falling too quickly into place.

Avery stared at me. "Were you going to say, except for the plot copied by Rory Norris' murderer?"

"I was going to say *World at Midnight*." I feigned a puzzled look. "Did you know Rory Norris?"

He looked away. Then he chuckled. I tried to take another deep breath but I only succeeded in shallow gulps. I was feeling faint from the heat. I steadied my hand by gripping my clipboard.

He motioned for me to follow him into the kitchen. "How long do you think we can keep this tap dance going?"

"Avery, you're starting to creep me out. I don't know what you're talking about. Speak English." I struggled to keep my voice light. The cabinets I opened revealed a modest assortment of pots, pans and serving dishes. I checked the number on my list.

Avery opened a small door that apparently led to the laundry area.

"Isn't it beautiful?" He blocked my view.

I walked over and barely leaned into the narrow passageway. "What?"

"The woodwork. Look at this." He pointed toward some unseen object.

"Oh, yeah, it's nice." I edged backward and turned to go. The vibrator went off on my phone. Automatically, I slapped at my pocket. It seemed like minutes before the last quiet rumble died off.

I thought Avery paused, and for a moment, I was sure he must have heard the noise. He didn't turn around. He began looking through what appeared to be the silverware drawer. I exhaled.

"Well, I'm going to start going through the upstairs rooms. I promised Lily I'd look for her hand mirror and brush." As nonchalantly as I could, I eased back into the main hallway. I tried not to glance toward the front door.

He followed. "You know, don't you?" He came around me and blocked the stairs. We weren't close enough to touch, but the look in his eyes was enough to hold me in place.

I would have to talk my way out of here. Avery was no fool, and I was pretty sure he'd already killed three people. Sliding my hand into my pocket, I felt the metal of my cellphone. I couldn't remember if I'd dialed directory information or Mark last. I prayed it was Mark as I carefully flipped open the phone.

"No, really, I really don't know." Then I shook my head. I'd had enough with pretending. Lying now would not help me stay alive. I leaned against the stairway post. "What happened to you?"

Avery turned away from me and then he looked back with resolve. A little moisture gathered in his deep green eyes. "What happened? Life happened. One day I was preparing the estate papers for a wealthy, elderly widower in Half Moon Bay. His wife had died and left a sizable sum of money and real estate. I noticed the appraiser's inventory had a couple of value errors. Also, the insurance binder had special sections that didn't seem to mesh with the items I knew."

I was afraid to say anything. He wasn't looking at me anymore. His eyes were searching out the past. Still, he blocked any run I might make for the front door. I tried to clear my head to think, but the heat was unbearable. Avery looked cool as an ice cube.

He held out his arms as if pleading for understanding. "I called the appraiser on it immediately. He wasn't our usual contractor, but he had good references. At first he said I had it wrong, that the market value was volatile. Then he let me know the percentage margin was small, even though the dollar difference was substantial."

"I don't understand."

Avery looked down at Lily's inventory list. "Let's say the personal and real property is worth one million dollars, but it gets appraised for five million. The insurance carrier would be informed to verify the assets and make sure they were protected. The firm gets five to ten percent of the appraised value to cover our costs to close out the estate, or to establish the estate's worth."

"Not the firm—you."

Avery slowly turned his head to look at me. He gave me a nod. "True. Triple D's partners have a generous arrangement regarding trusts, wills and estate planning. It's not as lucrative as litigation, but I keep a bulk of the percentage."

I edged toward one of the lower steps and sat down. I couldn't stand any longer. Sadness weighed on my chest. "You started signing off on inflated appraisals." I sighed. "Was it for the money?"

He ran a hand behind his neck. "It's always for the money."

"Rory was the appraiser, wasn't he?" Through my haze, I was able to put the final pieces together. "You killed him because he blackmailed you. You faced the loss of your lifestyle and career. Was the third person, the insurance link … was it Bill Lynley?"

"Your one and only." Avery looked down at his watch.

I had to distract him. Slowly standing, I reached for the notebook pad and pretended interest in the inventory listing. "Why did you give me a job? You knew I had a prison record."

"Bill asked me. He didn't want you to know he was behind it."

"He got me the job at Triple D?"

Avery raised his eyebrow and gave me a look I couldn't read. "Call it insurance. At first, Rory didn't know about you and Bill. Somewhere along the way, he and your ex talked about parole officers, and Jeffrey Wallace's name came up. Rory put two and two together. He figured out your relationship with Lynley. He just held off adding you to his to-do list of people to torment."

"Oh, no." It was all I could do to keep from sitting back down on the stairs.

"Rory needed Bill's help. Bill wanted out, but Rory told

Bill he knew about you and used you to keep Bill in line. In exchange, Bill agreed to continue to phony up insurance policies we needed for our … transactions. Rory had to agree not to expose or blackmail you."

At that, I gave up and sat back down. "Bill actually protected me?"

Beads of sweat dotted my forehead. My brain felt like oatmeal.

Avery handed me another bottle of water from his pack and took one for himself. "Don't make him an angel. Your ex was a crook, Hollis. He made good money out of this."

I took a deep swallow of water. "And you, didn't it bother you at all?"

"You mean you and me?" He appeared to be going to sit down next to me and then didn't. "Yeah, but it was too late. I'd gone too far. I know you. You wouldn't let me get away with it."

"No, you're right. I wouldn't." My head stared to ache.

Just then, through my jacket pocket, my cellphone vibrated like a bee convention.

Avery held out his hand. "I'll take that."

"Are you … are you going to kill me, too?" The boldness in my voice surprised me as I handed over my last link with the outside world.

He slid the phone closed. "I don't want to, but I really don't want to go to jail." He put it on the dining room table.

I shook my head. "I've been the victim before. I never thought … I never thought I'd be one again."

"I need you to do one more thing before this is over." Avery's voice was firm. He handed me a pad and pen. "Write, 'I did it. I'm sorry.' "

I looked around the entry and tried to stand. I sat back down unsteadily. "You … you … you can't m-make me." A ringing began in my ears and short flashes of light passed in front of my eyes. "Wait …wait, they'll know it's … it's you."

"How? You just figured out it was me."

I shook my head. The movement made me dizzy. "I … I think I knew something was wrong all … all along. I just did … didn't want to believe it."

He looked down at his watch. "I gave you a strong narcotic and muscle immobilizer that will put you to sleep in about fifteen minutes." He leaned toward my face. "You're going to have to die anyway, but I thought you might still have a soft spot for Mark. Sign the note. If you don't, he's going to take the fall for Bill's death."

I blinked my eyes to keep them focused. It was becoming harder to keep my words in order. "How? Why … why Mark?"

"Because he likes you. He followed you and found out about the club. I won't bother you with the story details. Suffice it to say, I've got enough evidence to make him an easy suspect."

He pulled out a large manila envelope and emptied the contents on the coffee table. "You're going to commit suicide because you can't face going back to prison." He looked over at me. "Rory was blackmailing you. You were going to lose your court appeal. You thought Bill was going to testify against you. You wanted Bill dead. You killed him."

Oh, dear god, how to keep him occupied.

My tongue took on a cotton feel and my lips were increasingly losing feeling. "How'd … do I d-die?"

"With this." He lifted a bottle.

"Th-they will know it was mur-murder. Narcotics and p-poison leave tr-traces."

He crossed his arms and leaned against the doorjamb to the hallway. "I don't think so. This poison disappears over a relatively short period of time. Water actually does a great job of diluting and carrying it out of your system—through your sweat." He lifted up a vial of clear liquid. "It's a derivative of choline. One of my more nefarious clients got it for me."

"Th-the water?"

"Yep. The water. The poison is potent and gets into your bloodstream fast. It will paralyze your limbs then your lungs."

Even my muddled mind caught the implications. "The—The *Long Pause*. It's not the same p-poison but this is l-like the bo-book sui-suicide."

"Yeah." Avery again glanced at his watch. "Look, I've got to go and I need you to get upstairs, so let's move."

I was determined not to rise from my seat, but Avery took less than a minute to drape me over his shoulders and carry me upstairs. The ornate pattern of the wallpaper became a blur of color. My dizziness increased. He put me down on the bed in one of the guest rooms.

Twisting my shoulder, I did the best I could to shift my weight against him, but I was only successful in bringing us both down on top of the bed. Avery rolled off me and perched himself on his elbow.

"You're so tempting, but I'm going to have to pass." He rolled up to sit next to me. "I didn't want to hurt you, Hollis. Things just got out of control. If only you weren't so damn nosy." His voice seemed almost robotic. "I made sure you'd go under easy. It won't hurt or anything."

"Av-Avery don't d-do th-this, pl-please." It was becoming more difficult for me to make the right words come. "Y-you'll be found out."

He walked around the room. "I don't think so. I've been very patient setting things up so that the focus won't fall on me." He looked back at me. "I don't make mistakes."

I shook my head. "Wha-what about Ab-Abby? She was a mistake."

"She was a necessity. I killed her to protect my identity."

My head seemed to weigh a ton. "I … I can't mo-move."

He ignored me. After looking once more at his watch, he peeled off the plastic gloves I hadn't seen him put on. "I've got to go now. I'll be back later this afternoon. It will all be over."

We looked at each other a long moment. I wanted to tell him I'd speak up for him with the police if he let me go, but I thought of Abby. Even if I died before the sun set, Avery Mitchell must be punished. I wouldn't try to make things easier for him. For a moment I thought he could hear my thoughts. He turned back to look at me. Then he was gone.

I lay back on the pillows and closed my eyes. What felt like cement made a slow syrup-like path through my veins. Bending my arm was akin to moving lead. I laboriously scooted next to the edge of the bed. There was an old clock on the dresser. It was almost one. I twisted my body and, with what little force I could muster, I rolled and hit the carpet with a muffled thud.

The area rug was thick and, as a tickle crept up my nostrils, dusty. I almost laughed as a loud sneeze erupted, but what caught my attention was, for the moment, my brain cleared. The harsh sneeze must have opened some neural passage.

My brain might have cleared, but my limbs were like bags of bricks. No one knew where I was. Avery said he noticed I was signed out of the office. I had no doubt he erased my destination or changed it to show me going home. No one would look for me. Mark might try to call, but Avery had my phone. I lifted my head a few inches off the floor. The room was dark, with heavy drapes covering the windows. Other than the bed and dresser, there was no other furniture. I had to catch the attention of a passerby.

I twisted myself again and heaved myself into another roll. I sneezed again. The fringe of an idea faded in and out of my mind. My legs edged over, maybe another foot. The windows seemed miles away. I did this two more times until, with no small degree of satisfaction, I was at the end of the carpet and next to the shiny hardwood floors. My arm reached out and my hand tugged on a drape as hard as it could. It didn't budge. I looked up at the clock. Two. I must have dozed. A tear slipped down my cheek.

My mind started to drift toward sleep again. I pushed my nose against the coating of dust on the floor. A sneeze didn't come this time. With increasing difficulty, I raised my arm until my hand touched the coolness of the floor and, after what seemed like hours, I moved my fingers in the dust. I dozed off.

My eyes fluttered open. The clock said two thirty. Maybe the drug wasn't working. I was groggy and my brain was barely alert, but I was awake. I twisted my body again and started to roll back to the other side, only to wake up what felt like moments later to wonder where I was and what I was trying to do. This time, I didn't have the benefit of a clear head and I fought to keep my eyes open. I couldn't tell if I made progress. My breathing was even shallower. I couldn't hold things together anymore. A heaviness settled into my chest.

I let my eyes close.

CHAPTER TWENTY-EIGHT

IT WAS COLD. The air conditioner must be on full blast. The dampness on my forehead was both welcome and irritating. I raised my arm to wipe it dry. I couldn't.

"Hollis, Hollis, wake up. I'm here with the paramedics."

The voice was familiar and strange at the same time. The words echoed in my ears.

I slowly turned my head. Two paramedics busily strapped me to a stretcher.

"What's going on? Is this a suicide attempt? What did she take? What's her name?" A young man in uniform came into view. I couldn't answer.

Mark stood aside. "Her name is Hollis Morgan. She didn't commit suicide."

"You saved her life. Hollis, can you hear me? What did you take? Was it pills?"

"C-cold." My voice came out as a whisper.

"You're cold? Here's a blanket. What did he give you?"

I squinted, but my eyes failed me. "M-Mark?"

"Hollis, I'm sorry it took so long to find you, but I didn't know where you were. For a while I could hear you and Avery talking, but no one at the firm knew you were here."

I felt painful pressure on my forearms. The pain helped me to gather my wits. I must have groaned.

"Sorry. Sorry. They told me to keep the tubing up. Finally, I called nine-one-one and they triangulated the signal from your cellphone. Hollis? Stay with me, Hollis."

It took all the focus I could gather. "C-cold. Not … cide."

"She's delirious and we're going to give her something to knock her out. She's slipping back into shock."

I looked up pleadingly at Mark. "Av-ry. Not su-cide. C-choline." I winced in pain as I was lifted into the ambulance.

"I understand. You didn't try to kill yourself." Mark looked at me with a worried expression. "Hollis, it's going to be okay. Don't worry. I saw the letter 'A' you wrote in the dust. He won't get away. We'll find Avery."

CHAPTER TWENTY-NINE

SOUND WAS MUFFLED as if I were under a blanket. I turned my head toward the only source of light. It came from under a door. I tried to speak but my lips were parched. I had no saliva to wet them. Squinting, I tried to make out where I was. A hospital. The back of my hand ached with the long tubing running into a large plastic bag of clear liquid. My chest was connected to another tube of pale yellow fluid and I couldn't tell if it was running in or out. I shifted slightly and the pain that shot from my lungs immediately brought tears to my eyes.

The door opened. A young woman entered.

"Hello, there. I'm Nurse Kelly." She deftly checked the screen on a black box at the side of my bed. "Glad to see you're finally awake."

"Wh—?"

"You're in St. Matthews Hospital. You've had a tough time. Luckily, the poison didn't reach your lungs. Even so, you had enough everywhere else that we went ahead and pumped you clean."

She carefully changed the fluid bags, but the slight shifting of the tubes made me cry out.

"I'm so sorry. I know you're in pain. As soon as the doctor gets here, she'll prescribe something for you."

"Wata."

"Water?" She looked down at the chart at the foot of my bed. "I think we should wait until the doctor comes. She should be here any minute. How about I wet a towel and dampen your lips?"

I closed my eyes. The moisture from the towel was welcome but sorely inadequate. Mercifully, the doctor came in just as Nurse Kelly finished organizing the blankets.

"I'm Doctor Garson."

I squinted again. Although the voice was deep and gravelly, it belonged to a petite blonde who looked to be in her fifties.

I licked my lips and tried to speak.

"No, don't bother. I know you're uncomfortable. We're going to fix that right now." She gave directions to the nurse for pain medication and to remove my IV. "We'll also give you some water. Not a lot at first, but four ounces at intervals to start. Then, by this evening, you'll be feeling better and can go on a bland diet." She poured water into a paper cup and brought it to my mouth.

It wasn't cold, but it was wet. I slowly sipped and swallowed.

"Thank you." I laid my head, which felt like a bowling ball, back down on the pillow. "What's wrong with me?"

Dr. Garson read my chart. "I have good news, and promising news."

"Promising news, first." My words still came out scratchy and slow, but at least they came.

She grinned. "Ah, a pessimist at heart? We won't know for several days exactly how much damage was done to your respiratory system, but the fact that you and I are talking is a very good sign."

"What happened?"

She sat on edge of my bed. "You were in pretty bad shape.

The drug you took was what we call a cocktail mixture. The razor cuts on your wrists were deep, but I've seen a lot worse."

My gaze went to the tubing into my arm.

She followed my eyes. "We'll remove that soon."

"I didn't take it on my own. There was—"

She patted my arm. "We know. You were given an exotic poison that strikes the nervous system but hides out in your circulatory system until it's too late, because all medical eyes are on your brain waves. You were lucky you got in here when you did with the information we needed to find the antidote."

I frowned, trying to remember how I got there. Only vague images appeared in my memory bank. No single one emerged as a winner.

"How did I get here?"

"The paramedics got a call from a man." She looked down at my chart. "A Mark Haddan. He's been here every day. Haddan usually shows up right after lunch. In fact, I think he was coming out of the elevator when I came to see you."

"Every day? How long have I been here?"

She put her hand on my shoulder. "You came in on Thursday. Today is Sunday."

"Sunday."

"I know it's scary to lose track of time. Be glad you weren't conscious. You wouldn't have been very comfortable." Doctor Garson hesitated. "Ms. Morgan, the police have been here, too. I was told to call them once you regained consciousness."

The word "police" acted as an instant haze remover. A light came on in my head like a curtain lifting. I remembered everything up until my arrival at the hospital. "How long do I have to stay here?"

"Oh, you're past the worst of it. I think one, maybe two more days of monitoring your vitals should be enough. Is there someone at home who can be with you?"

"No, I live alone."

"Then it will be at least two days for sure." Garson patted

me one more time and, after promising to see me the next
afternoon, left me in the reliable hands of Nurse Kelly.

I FELL IN and out of sleep. The hospital nurses' comings
and goings kept me in a mild world of wooziness. The next
morning, after breakfast, my nurse checked my temperature.

"Are you ready for visitors? They've been waiting."

"Yes, who—"

Marla pushed past the nurse with Lily holding on tight to
the rail of her walker.

"Hi, sweetie, we couldn't wait to see you. Lily and I have a
taxi waiting so we can't stay long. He's Opal's nephew's friend;
she got him to bring us here. I don't want to abuse his patience."

Lily came along the other side of the bed and squeezed my
hand. Her eyes were teary.

There had never been two faces I was more pleased to see.

"Thank you both for coming to visit me. I'll be back to see
you soon." I returned the squeeze of Lily's hand.

Lily licked her lips. "I'm holding all my mail for you to open."

I nodded with understanding.

"Let's go, Lily." Marla patted me on the shoulder. She couldn't
hide the tears brimming in her eyes. She swiped at her cheeks
with the back of her hand and gave me a forced smile. "Oh, and
don't forget the doughnuts."

I laughed. "I won't."

They walked out, leaning on each other.

I picked up a book I'd left lying open on my tray.

Mark entered with a rush of air, followed by Rena carrying a
coleus plant in a colorful ceramic pot.

"How are you? Are you going to be okay?" He started
to give me a kiss on the forehead and then backed off, as if
remembering we didn't have that kind of relationship.

"It's all right, Mark. Actually, I could use a friendly kiss
about now." I smiled. He leaned over awkwardly and gave me a

modest peck. "Rena, it was so considerate of you to come and see me. Thank you for the plant."

Rena nodded sheepishly and went about moving things around to make space on the little tray table by the bed. "Mark and I have been really worried about you. What does your doctor say?"

I recounted the doctor's evaluation.

"A drug," Mark said. "Is that like any of your books?"

I looked at him appreciatively. "It was a novel we were getting ready to read. We hadn't read about any murders by drugs lately. He just wanted me incapacitated so he could do my wrists. Besides, I don't think Avery had much time to plan. He made it up as he went along."

Mark shook his head. "Avery. I just can't believe it."

I closed my eyes then opened them.

Mark gave me a penetrating look.

Could he see my other pain ... the pain of being betrayed by Avery?

I shifted to find a more comfortable position, but I only succeeded in pulling on the needle that ran to the back of my hand. I winced. "I'm starting to get tired. I think I need to catch a little sleep." I smiled. "Thank you both for visiting. I won't forget it."

"Of course you're tired," Rena said. "This is your first full day awake. We'll check on you later."

"Mark, wait," I called.

Rena waved and walked out. Mark stood next to my bed. "Yes?"

I took his hand. "Thank you for saving my life." I ignored his obvious discomfort. "I don't remember much, but I do remember you finding me. Thank you."

"You're very welcome." His eyes took on an impish glint. "When you're back on your feet, maybe you could help me with a research project my new firm gave me."

"Forget about it." I smiled. "No, I'm teasing. Congratulations."

We both laughed until I started to cough. He gave me a tentative hug and a wave goodbye.

I didn't say anything about the tears I felt, or the tears I saw.

I relished the silence. I needed some time alone to rewire my psyche. Avery was gone and I was alive. It was over. I'd be able to go on with my life. The only surprise was how much I had cared for my intended killer. He was, after all, the one who had given me my second chance.

I didn't realize I had dozed off again until Nurse Kelly came in to take my temperature. "How are you feeling? You hardly ate anything earlier."

"Not real hungry yet, but I think I'm going to live."

"Of course you are. Are you up to a visit from the police? They're outside."

"Do I have a choice?"

She just smiled. I looked down at my gown to make sure all would not be revealed. I was no longer attached to the metal guardian holding my tubes off to the side of my bed.

"Ms. Morgan, that was a close call." Detective Faber strode in with Detective Lincoln not far behind. Their combined bulk filled my little visiting space.

"Detectives. A bit too close, but they tell me I'll soon be good as new."

Lincoln sat under the TV mounted on the wall. "We have an APB out on Mitchell. We searched his home and found evidence pointing to another condo he has in the Maldives. We're pretty sure he's on his way there. The State Department is on the lookout for him."

I shifted in the bed to try and sit up. "It's a townhome. It's somewhere near the capital."

Detective Faber nodded. "We know."

"What's the capital of the Maldives?" Detective Lincoln took notes.

"Malé. Before you ask, no, I've never been there. Once, I heard him making reservations at one of the resorts."

Detective Faber gave me a worried smile.

"They should have no trouble finding him. It's a small island."

"The trouble won't be in finding him. The sticky point is the U.S. and the Maldives don't have an automatic extradition agreement. It may take some time to get him back."

Avery would have counted on that.

"Ms. Morgan, can you tell us exactly what happened from the time you left your office until you woke up here?"

And so I told them my story. It already seemed like I was speaking about an event that had happened weeks ago, rather than a few days. Both detectives took notes.

"I vaguely remember Mark talking to me, but I really didn't realize what had happened until I woke up yesterday morning."

"He saved your life."

Detective Lincoln walked over to the window. "Let me see if I have this straight. Avery Mitchell was being blackmailed by his partner in crime, Rory Norris. He got tired of paying and killed him. Mitchell thought Abby Caldwell could identify him, so he killed her, too. Finally, when he thought you'd put all the pieces together, he had to get rid of you."

I nodded. "Yes, that's what he said."

Detective Faber tapped his notepad against his chin. "So, how did the murders from your club's book selections play into everything?"

I pushed the button to crank my bed up to a full sitting position. "I've thought about this a lot. We were easy targets. Abby and Richard didn't know Rory was their blackmailer, but Avery knew Rory was blackmailing him. Avery hired Rory to fake appraisals on his cases. He then called Bill Lynley in to write up false insurance policies. Between the three of them, the den of thieves was complete."

Pausing, I reached for some water. Detective Faber met me halfway with a glass.

"Somehow, Avery found out I was in the same book club as Rory. Knowing Rory, he never could keep his mouth shut. Once

Rory knew about Bill and me, it balanced what Bill had on him about the blackmail. Rory's need for cash made him desperate enough to blackmail his fellow club members. He was going to leave the states." My voice started to quaver. "Abby didn't have to die. You were right. I was the only common variable between Rory, Abby and Bill. Avery was bright and creative. I read club books on my breaks at work and sometimes I left the book overnight. Avery 'borrowed' the book or went out and got his own copy. Copying the killings deflected suspicion from him and onto a bunch of ex-felons, a no-brainer. He killed Bill because he knew too much."

My throat choked up. I couldn't say anymore. "Please, I'm tired now."

Detective Lincoln crossed over to stand next to Faber at the foot of my bed. "That's some story. Everything pretty much checks out, except for one minor fact."

He really knew how to get on my last nerve. Realizing that he wouldn't leave until he made his point, I said, "That minor fact would be?"

"Avery Mitchell didn't kill Bill Lynley."

CHAPTER THIRTY

ONCE I GOT my head around the fact Avery hadn't killed Bill, I could see that he had a legitimate alibi; I tried to conjure up other possible murderers, without success. Still, no matter who had killed Bill, the Fallen Angel murders seemed to be over.

Avery, in his fervor to cover up his misdeeds, had left two loose ends. Rory's ledger was still missing and I was still alive. Even so, I also couldn't forget that, according to Bill, there might be someone out there who thought I had what they wanted.

After four days in the hospital and a week at home, it was time to rejoin the world. Clay had gotten a ten-day continuance for my hearing, which was practically a miracle. Fortunately, the court clerk had read of my near-death experience in the newspaper and, with Bill's murder, it didn't require much effort for Clay to plead extenuating circumstances. My hearing date was set for the following week.

Collecting my visitor's badge from the security guard at the entrance, I swore this would be the last time I went to see

Detective Faber. He probably wouldn't need to see me after this visit anyway.

"So, Ms. Morgan. It's good to see you up and about. Should you be out so soon?"

We were back to meeting in his office. I was pleased my innocence was no longer in question.

"I'm still taking it easy, but I had to see you about the ledger."

"What ledger?" Detective Faber didn't fool me.

"Yes, Detective Faber, the ledger. The ledger you're going to need to nail Avery to the wall, once you get your hands on him. The ledger that might lead you to Bill's killer."

"What do you know about a ledger?"

"Let's not go down that road. Not 'a' ledger. 'The' ledger. The ledger Rory used to keep the accounting of his blackmail activities. The ledger that could provide the motive for the three murders."

"Where did you hear about a ledger?"

"Richard Kleh, sucking on his tooth, alluded to one early on. Then I heard about it again from Bill. Rory was a compulsive record keeper. He had records for everything."

"In our searches, we've not uncovered a ledger or anything like one. Where do you think it is now?"

"I think Bill had it. Do you remember my telling you how Bill answered the phone when I called Rory's mother? I think he was looking for it then. He needed to get leverage over his other partners in crime. The ledger was critical."

Detective Faber picked up a sizable file from the side of his desk. "Unfortunately, other than a few clothes, a box of books we compared to the booklist you gave us, and some childhood mementos, we found nothing at Rollins' mother's home or in the apartment where your ex-husband was killed."

"Detective, you know more than you're telling me. Don't you think I've earned a bit of information?"

"What is it you want to know?"

"You know from Bill's letter he used another name. Have

you found out the name he was going to be using?"

"Yes. Lawrence Keller. We also tracked down, with the help of the FBI, a package of false identification documents he mailed to himself to start his new life. The ledger wasn't in that package."

"So, you did know about the ledger?"

"We figured there had to be something to keep track of payments. From Rollins' phone records, we've identified several of his contacts who've turned out to be victims. Don't worry, though. Mr. Mitchell will be making the trip back to the States within the week. Maldives is going to give him up. Conviction would be a slam dunk if we had that ledger. Even without it, Mr. Mitchell is in big trouble. He won't be pleading his way out of this one."

I became tired, which only fed my frustration. "You don't think he can get off?"

"It's not a sure thing. We've got him on your attempted murder, but to get him on the Rollins and Caldwell killings, well, I won't kid you, I'd feel a lot better if I could get my hands on that ledger."

My legal background agreed with him.

Detective Faber looked up at the clock. "Is there anything else?"

"Yes. Do you have any leads on who killed Bill?"

"The fact that we're not meeting in the interview room should tell you we don't think you did it." He opened up a file. "Mr. Lynley had a very unsavory partner, a guy named Keith Newton. Do you know him?"

I shook my head. "Bill mentioned a 'Newton' when he contacted me, but it was nothing more than a mention."

"Well, Mr. Newton left behind some forensic evidence we think ties him to the murder. We have an alert out for him. He's not going to get away."

I stood to leave. I was suffering from information overload.

Detective Faber stood as well. "I know this hasn't been an

easy time for you, Ms. Morgan. I appreciate all your efforts to keep us informed and allow us to do our job."

He held out his hand. I shook it firmly, having only a few qualms about getting ready to do just the opposite. Then I headed home.

I WENT TO the center to report to Lily that her house was going on the market and that her furnishings at the auction house had already attracted a fair amount of interest from potential buyers.

"I'm counting on you, Hollis, to tell me what's a good price. I trust you to tell me the truth."

I blinked rapidly at her words.

I took a deep breath. "Lily, I won't betray your trust. I know how much you need your money."

Lily smiled and patted her hand. "I never doubt your word."

Tiny came over to where we were sitting. "Hollis, I'm so glad you're feeling better. We've missed you … and the doughnuts."

I frowned. "Sorry. I forgot to pick some up."

She looked forlorn. "Cookies?"

"I'm teasing you, Tiny. There are doughnuts in the kitchen."

She gave me a wave as she headed toward the door. "I knew you wouldn't forget."

Lily leaned over to me. "Can you see Mr. Herbert before you leave? If you're not able, he said he'll understand. He needs help with his DMV application before his driver's license expires."

"Mr. Herbert still drives? He must be almost ninety years old."

"He's ninety-two. He keeps his license in case one of us needs to go somewhere and we can't get the senior van service to take us."

I guessed that the friend of Opal's nephew saved his vehicle for special occasions. I rubbed my forehead. "Still—"

"The doctor approves him every year. If he thought he was a danger, he wouldn't sign off."

"Okay, okay. I'll help him. Where is he?"

"He's in the library. His daughter dropped off these boxes a few months ago so her husband wouldn't get them." She picked a pair of glasses to put on her eyes. "They're getting a divorce. Now it's been settled, Mr. Herbert says she's coming to pick them up. She put some important paper in there and needs to go through everything."

I wanted to tell Tiny this was really more information than I needed to know, but then her words struck a chord.

I thought I knew where the ledger was.

AFTER MY LAST conversation with Detective Faber, it occurred to me that Bill could have left the ledger with Rory's mother. Maybe she was one he "trusted." Newton must have known about Rory's ledger and killed him to get it. I remembered Bill wanted to talk but I wouldn't let him. He knew I'd figure it out.

"Mrs. Rollins, I don't know if you remember me, but my name is Hollis Morgan. I was a friend of your son, Ror… Michael. We were in the same book club."

"Yeah, I remember you from before. That book club. I just can't imagine Michael as a bookworm. It still makes me want to laugh. How can I help you?"

"I'm actually calling about his friend, Bill Lynley. I was wondering if he asked you to hold any boxes. I know a senior center that would really appreciate having used books for its library."

"He sure did, honey. No problem. He brought these boxes here after Michael was killed and asked me to hold them for him. I guess he won't be coming to pick them up. Too bad. He was a nice young man. I was just getting ready to put his junk in the garbage, but it would be good if you could take it off my hands. Do the seniors need clothes? I've got some. They're old but still can be worn."

Clearly, Bill hadn't brought his boxes to her until after Rory was killed and the police had searched through his belongings. They didn't check Rory's home again after Bill was murdered.

My heart raced. "Mrs. Rollins, let me help you. I can come by tomorrow and take the clothes, too. Is it okay if I bring a friend to help me carry out the boxes?"

"I don't like having a bunch of strangers in my house, but I guess it's okay. Besides, the police got everything they wanted. You'll have to come before I leave for the chiropractor."

We agreed on a time in the morning.

JUST AS I hoped, Mark gave up his Saturday to come with me. My equilibrium was still off and I kept bumping into the boxes scattered over the floor in Mrs. Rollins' extra bedroom. My doctor said there would be residual evidence of poison in my system for weeks to come, but that eventually my balance would return to normal.

Other than two small boxes of clothes, Bill left fairly heavy cartons. One was full of books. The other contained bank statements, cancelled checks and tax forms. Mark walked in front of me. "I can make a temporary desk, and we can put the boxes on top where you can go through them easily."

"All right. There aren't that many. I'll know it when I see it."

He lifted a box, sat it a few inches from my reach and started taking books out one by one. I thought Rory might have inserted a ledger among the contents of the box, but after sifting through all the paperwork and assortment of books, I didn't find the ledger among them.

"What do we do now?" Mark started putting pages and books back.

"Wait." I picked up a book and fanned its pages. Nothing fell out. I picked up another.

Mark followed my lead.

"It's got to be here," I said.

"Maybe Newton got it," Mark said. "Or maybe Bill hid it before he died."

"Maybe, but I've got to be sure we're not overlooking it."

He started in on the last box.

I brushed my forehead with my arm. "Wait, look at this." I picked up a blue spiral notebook shoved between two thick hardbacks. The first two pages were blank, but the middle pages had been neatly ripped out, leaving a few blank pages at each end.

Mark looked it over and handed it back. "Do you think the blackmail records were in here?"

I nodded slowly. "Yes, I do. I know this sounds corny, but hold the page that was next to the torn pages up to the light. Can you see anything?"

Mark pulled a lamp sitting in the corner over to the makeshift table and plugged it in. He lifted the page. "There are writing impressions, but not enough to see anything."

I rummaged around in my purse. "I've got a pencil. Let's try rubbing it lightly over the page."

I was as surprised as Mark when after a little effort, a few words—it looked like two entries—appeared.

"We should take this to the police," Mark said. "They have equipment that can read this stuff." Mark examined the page more closely.

"Can you do it today? I want them to have it as soon as possible, but I'm really getting tired. I'm ready to go home."

Mark lowered his voice. "Hollis, don't worry. Avery will be convicted. This page will add to the stack of evidence against him."

"I have to do what I can to make sure he gets a full sentence. Then I can let it go. Avery tried to kill me. He killed my friend. He betrayed dozens of clients." I sighed, "I need to read between Bill's lines. I just need to figure it out."

We took the boxes of books and clothing and put them in Mark's SUV. Walking out to the parking lot, I bumped into the doorjamb and pretended not to notice Mark's concern.

The beaming sun playing against the pale blue sky belied my frustration.

He started the engine. "You know, Hollis, I think we work pretty well together."

I almost smiled. "We'll see." For a moment I couldn't describe what I thought. There was pain, this time from my heart. I knew I'd be missing a certain pair of green eyes I wouldn't be seeing again.

CHAPTER THIRTY-ONE

I STEADIED MYSELF and gave a slight wave to Mark as he pulled away from the curb. The night was quiet and the sound of kids playing next door didn't take away from the stillness.

Turning the key in the lock, I sensed movement to my right. A tall man stepped out from the bushy cypress shrub and grabbed my elbow. I screamed into his gloved right hand as he gripped my mouth. Shoving me into the house, he used his left hand to lock the door behind us before he growled in my ear.

"Mrs. Lynley, I don't think you know me, but I knew your late husband." He shook my head with his hand firmly squeezing my mouth. "If you stop screaming, I'll remove my hand. If you play games, I want you to know I will hurt you."

I nodded in understanding. He released me and smiled. I recognized his smile. He was the man in the car parked in front of my neighbor's when Bill had come by my condo. He had followed Bill.

I wiped my mouth with the back of my hand. My heart pounded and I couldn't seem to catch my breath. The man in front was about a foot taller than me. His bald head was fringed in dark brown hair, and he had a frazzled-looking mustache over large lips.

He kept a grip on my wrist as he closed the shutters.

I stood shaking beside him. "What do you want? Did Bill owe you money? I don't have much, but you can take what I have."

He looked at me with large, flat, brown shark eyes. "Your husband wasn't a very nice man. He took something from me that I need back." He smirked. "I think you know it wasn't money."

I licked my lips. "Bill never told me what he was doing. He was my ex-husband and …"

He moved around the room and started throwing books off the shelves. I tried to calm myself and clear my brain. I edged toward the kitchen doorway.

"He took a ledger that puts me in a very bad light." He finally turned to look at me.

I stopped moving.

"Well, I can tell you Bill didn't give me a ledger. I don't know who you are and I don't want any trouble. Please, please leave."

"I wish I could, but I've looked everywhere for those pages and Lynley didn't have them on him. So, I'm thinking he left them with the lady in this picture." He tugged at a slightly crumpled photo in his pocket. He held it out for me to see.

I stared at him.

"Look at it. It's you and him. He was holding onto it when he died."

Bill held onto our honeymoon picture.

Glancing down at the doomed couple, a tear escaped my eye. My intruder must be Keith Newton, Bill's killer. I had to get a grip on my thoughts.

"Yes, it's me, but like I said, we divorced years ago. I never saw Bill after that."

"You're lying, but that's okay." He stood in front of me and shoved me into the dining room. "Sit. This may take a while."

I sat. I did a quick calculation of his bulk versus mine, and it was no contest. All I could think was now would be a good time to beg. Otherwise, I'd have to make a run for it.

"Leave now. I don't have any papers. Bill was never here ..." I stopped. A gong went off in my head. Remembering Bill's visit, I hoped my realization wasn't obvious.

I had a pretty good idea where the papers were.

"I don't think you get what's going to happen." He loomed over me and his sour breath assailed my nostrils. "You've seen my face and you probably realize I killed your husband. I have to have the ledger. I'm going to have to kill you, but I'm willing to make it quick if you help me out with this little matter."

I couldn't speak if I wanted to. Fear combined with anger held me silent. I balled my hands into fists. I had to buy time.

He stood back and pulled a lengthy cord out of his pocket.

"What are you going to do?" I knew I didn't want to know the answer.

He only looked at me. "Lie down on your stomach."

That isn't going to happen.

"How do I know you won't kill me anyway?"

"We're not having a conversation. I said get on your stomach."

I quickly looked around. I stood slowly, stiffened my back and thrust my body against my grandmother's étagère. I hit it as hard as I could with my shoulder and felt it give under my weight. It only wobbled.

"What the—"

I didn't let him finish. Just as he made a grab to pull me to him, I shoved one more time. The étagère came crashing down on top of Newton. He fell with a thud, even as the breaking glass, splitting wood and frog figurines covered him.

My eyes immediately went to the thin envelope secured by a single piece of tape to the back of the cabinet.

Newton started to move.

Not looking up, I snatched the envelope.

I was out of there.

I WAS AMAZED I didn't have a trail of Highway Patrol cars behind me. Pulling into the police parking lot, I drew a deep breath. I was still deep breathing when Faber came into the conference room. I told him what happened.

"Rest here." He pointed to a couple of chairs and called out on his way out the door. "I've got to catch a murderer."

I must have nodded off because when I opened my eyes he was sitting across from me, reading.

He pulled out several tan sheets of paper from a file folder. "You found the ledger."

I looked across his desk to the neatly written columns of names and numbers. We studied them together.

"How many people were in your club?"

"Not that many, I assure you. Evidently, Rory wasn't as rehabilitated as the system would have hoped. Looks like he was branching out."

"The names are in code." He turned the pages toward me so I could read them. "Do you recognize any of these phone numbers?"

I looked at the dollar amounts entered, ranging from five hundred to eight thousand. It was clear EA1 and DR1 were different people. EA1 was making monthly payments of seven hundred dollars while DR1 was paying twenty-five hundred a month. Rory must have had a sliding payment plan based on ability to pay. What a guy.

"Yes, FA2 is Abby. That was her cellphone number." My throat was constricted and my eyes filled with tears.

"Do you see an entry that could be Avery?"

"I don't think the initials shown relate to real names. There's no 'A' or 'M' listed." I looked down the list. "Wait, here he is." I pointed to his Triple D cellphone number prefix.

"Avery Mitchell was JP1," Faber said.

I looked across the columns. "He's been paying twenty-five thousand a month. Wow, no wonder he was always chasing new clients. JP must stand for 'jackpot.' "

Faber reached over and touched me lightly on my shoulder. "Are you okay? You look funny. You want to sit down?"

"No, I'm going home. It's time for me to move on."

The Fairy Tale's Book Club 259

Esher nailed over and touched the platform my shoulder.
"Are you okay? You look faint. You want to sit down?"
"No. I'm going home. It's time for me to move on."

CHAPTER THIRTY-TWO

"ALL RISE IN the State of California Superior Court, County of Santa Clara," the court clerk announced with authority. "Judge Mathis presiding."

Clay Boone nudged me and smiled. He motioned for me to relax. In a few minutes my life would be decided, and my lack of control over the situation made me extremely nervous.

"Good morning." The judge was an elderly man. He wore a maroon bow tie and a crisp white shirt under his black robe. His wispy white hair curled around his ears. "Let's get started." He pulled a stack of papers from a brown legal file.

The court clerk stood and spoke from a small table to the right of the judicial bench. "Your Honor, the first matter this morning is a petition to the court for an order of Certification of Rehabilitation for Hollis Morgan, aka Rebecca Hollis Morgan Lynley."

"All right. Let's hear from … Mr. Boone."

I tried to remember the pep talk Clay had given me before court: "I've got to tell you ordinarily I wouldn't care as I do about the outcome of a petition. You made me care. You won me over with your intensity and determination." He put a hand on my shoulder. "You made me believe in you. So will the judge."

I certainly hope so.

Clay moved to the center of the room and gave me a brief reassuring smile. "Judge Mathis, eight years ago my client, Hollis Morgan, was a first year law student with honors. She was married and lived an uneventful life. She hadn't been in trouble with the law. She'd never even gotten a speeding ticket, but that was soon to change. Her then-husband was a dishonest, disloyal con man. He was real good at the con. He deceived my client into signing documents that would eventually lead to her incarceration for insurance fraud. And—"

"She couldn't have been too good of a law student if she didn't know he was asking her to commit a crime." The judge looked over his glasses at me. It took all I had in me to look him in the eye instead of holding my head down.

Clay had warned me to prepare for comments like this from Mathis. He had a reputation for interjecting his personal views. Even so, I swallowed hard.

"In fact, your honor, she knew what she was doing, but not why. Her ex-husband was defrauding his customers, just as he lied to Ms. Morgan."

"Okay, let's move on. I have a busy calendar this morning."

"My client served her time and was released eighteen months early for good behavior. Since that time, she has completed her parole per her sentencing. In fact, one of the letters of support I have here for Ms. Morgan is from her former parole officer, Jeffrey Wallace. Additionally, Ms. Morgan, for the past several years, has volunteered her time to assist seniors with their personal paperwork and legal issues." Clay walked back to stand next to the desk where I sat. "Another letter of support is from the director and one of the seniors at the center, indicating Ms. Morgan is not only knowledgeable, but kind and generous."

"What does she do now?"

Clay walked back to the judge's bench. "Ms. Morgan is a paralegal for Dodson, Dodson and Doyle here in Alameda County. She's worked there ever since achieving her paralegal certificate after her release. She has gotten superior performance evaluations and we have a support letter from the firm's managing partner, Edward Simmons."

"I know the firm, and I've known Ed for years." Mathis shuffled through the pages. "Yes, here's his letter."

"Yes, Your Honor, she has—"

"Enough, Mr. Boone. I'd like to hear from Ms. Morgan."

My heart beat so fast and hard, I was lightheaded. Standing, I walked with a slight limp to the raised bench where Clay stood.

"Good Morning, Your Honor." I couldn't stop the tremor in my voice.

"I'm going to be quite honest with you, Ms. Morgan. I don't like Certificates of Rehabilitation. I don't like the fact that criminals are allowed to have their pasts ignored while their victims still live with the consequences. You seem to be intelligent … and, according to your support letters, a saint. Clearly, you're more than what they say. You committed a crime that may not have physically hurt individuals, but it violated a trust. What has changed? Why are you different now? Why should I change my opinion of you?"

Could I make it to the door faster than it would take the guard to catch me? I looked at Clay. He'd told me I might have to make a statement, but my rehearsed speech was nowhere to be found in my memory bank.

Judge Mathis leaned over. "Ms. Morgan, surely as a paralegal you're sympathetic to a busy court docket. I'd appreciate it if you showed courtesy to the court by making a reply … today."

"I'm sorry, Your Honor." I wet my lips. "I'm trying to think of what I could say to reassure you I'm no longer the person who went to prison. Every day I try to not only live a good life but also live a life as far from prison as I can. Every morning when I wake up, and every evening when I go to sleep, I'm so happy to be free. I don't take anything for granted anymore. I don't want to miss any opportunity to live my life to the fullest. I haven't stopped learning, either. Recently, I lost a friend. She was killed. I really didn't know she was a friend until she was gone. I've learned friendship is one of the most valuable gifts life can offer." I paused.

"I love the law," I went on. "I want to finish law school. I want to be an attorney. I need this certificate, not for myself, but to prove to society I've learned my lesson. I'm not perfect, but I'm not stupid. I'm so sorry there are people out there who I've hurt. I'll never again do anything that would be considered a crime against another person, or against our society. I can't help those whom I've hurt, but I can and will continue to help others. I'm definitely rehabilitated."

Judge Mathis just looked at me. After a long minute of silence, the judge glanced over at the clock on the wall.

"Mr. Boone, you could take a few summation lessons from your client." Mathis began putting papers back into a file. Then he held up the last one. "I received a communication from the police department yesterday indicating you were recently considered a suspect in two murders."

My bouncing heart sank and my throat began to tighten.

Clay Boone jumped up from his seat. "Your Honor, my client was cleared of—"

The judge held up his hand. "Yes, I know, Mr. Boone. That's here, too. Please sit down." He looked over at me. "Ms. Morgan, along with the communication was a memo from Detective Michael Faber. He expressed some very strong opinions about your request for a Certificate of Rehabilitation."

"Oh." A tear edged out from under my lashes.

"I have heard many cases in my court that were worked on by Detective Faber. He's rarely wrong in his assessment. He's an excellent detective and a good man. He highly recommends your petition be awarded, and I'm inclined to do so." Judge

Mathis picked up his gavel and struck it on the small wood block. "Certificate of Rehabilitation is approved and awarded to the petitioner."

He took off his reading glasses.

"Good luck, Hollis Morgan."

R. Franklin James grew up in the San Francisco East Bay Area and graduated from the University of California at Berkeley. She and her husband currently live in northern California.

The Fallen Angels Book Club is her first novel and the first book in the Hollis Morgan Mystery series.

You can find R. Franklin on the Web at: www.rfranklinjames.com.

9 781603 819176